Silent Sister

Book 5 of the Masterson Files

By Andrew Allen Smith

Silent Sister

Edited by Jules Nelson

Edited by Dana Jean Smith

Covid edition Cover photo by Andrew Allen Smith

2024 Cover by Bilal, Photo by Andrew Allen Smith

ISBN: **978-1-7340960-1-9**

Version 1 2020

Version 2 2024

Dedication

I had a difficult time with the dedication of this book. I should dedicate it to the numerous readers whose continued prodding moved this to completion. I could also dedicate it to the editors who prodded away and pushed me a little further. With that in mind I do so to all of those people and so many more. I would be remiss if I did not include Diana Duell in that role as she found items editors and publishers did not.

I would also like to thank everyone in law enforcement who put their lives on the line consistently and often with considerable risk. Many people often overlook the silent sentinels who protect so many people and are only noticed in times of extreme good and extreme bad. Although the members of law enforcement in this book are fictitious there are real people who face the same perils daily without press or notation. Thank you for doing what you do.

Prologue

The jungle was thick. Thicker than most, if not all, in North America. The foliage was wet with the constant humidity and the dumping rain that never seemed to end under the cover of the endless trees. Alan Spears pushed through with careful precision, avoiding making sounds, leaving a track, or any trace.

Alan was dressed in black pants and a black t-shirt with a tactical vest overtop of it. His massive arms were covered with sweat, rain, and pieces of jungle. At about five feet to either side of him, two black and tan German Shepherds paced him. Both Shepherds were huge, at least 110 pounds each. They both also carried solid black tactical packs on their backs, and both were wet from the rain and dense forest.

Alan stopped and looked forward. The woods began to clear ahead, and he was not sure what to expect. He pointed to one of the dogs and pointed to the ground. The dog crouched without hesitation. Alan pointed forward, and the dog slowly began to crawl forward, belly to the ground. Creeping forward, Alan turned to the second dog and made a gesture. The dog knelt and stayed in that position as Alan followed the first.

The second dog stopped and lowered its head, watching in front and then looking side to side with ears pinned back. Alan crept forward beside the beautiful animal and looked before him. The clearing ahead opened and changed from dense jungle to solid rock followed by lush bluegrass. Alan pulled out a small ATN scope and surveyed the area.

Before him lay a house of extreme proportions. Alan guessed the house to be at least 10,000 square feet and made almost entirely of stone and marble. The open design was reminiscent of Spanish design with crisp angular lines and colorful accents. As Alan scanned the area, he could see cameras scanning as well. Alan took the time to watch their angle of view and was certain he was not in the view of the cameras at this point.

To the north and south of the house, he saw two guards walking methodically, but neither were carrying a visible weapon. They were, however, dressed in silk suits in oppressive heat, so Alan was sure they were armed. Alan felt underdressed in his tactical gear when he saw how crisp these men looked in their white silk blazers and white shirts. Both men wore hats that made their outfits complete.

The dog in front of him pushed down to the ground, and Alan saw that a third guard was walking the perimeter. Unlike the other two guards, he had an AK-74 and was sweeping with the weapon in front of him as he walked within fifteen feet of them. Alan froze and slowed his breathing as the man walked by with his finger on the trigger guard. Both Alan and the dog waited as the man walked further in the distance.

Alan considered his next move. The dog in front of him, Brahma, watched the area in front of them with far more intensity than any camera. The dog behind him, Mara, slowly scanned to the side and behind them as she waited. Alan had a job to do and there were inevitably more guards. Moving forward in the daytime would be to his disadvantage. He would wait. He began moving backward and slid away from the grounds. As he reached Mara, he made a noise with his mouth that sounded like a small bird, and Brahma scanned the area, turned, and crawled back to them.

Alan and the two dogs worked their way back about 100 yards and found a small enclave. It allowed the three to be relatively protected. From this point, they could see all the area around them. Alan sat Indian style and leaned back stretching. The position was comfortable and functional as he could stand rapidly just by pushing up. He reached into Mara's pack and brought out a sealed Ziplock bag. Inside was a significant amount of jerky. Taking out a piece he took a bite, then split the remaining and gave it to the two animals. Each took the jerky gently and then gobbled it down. Both looked at him, waiting for him to have another piece, which he did, then they took their pieces and gobbled them down.

Alan leaned back against the outcropping behind him and looked at his watch. It was a few hours from dusk, and then another several hours before everyone would be asleep. Alan was certain there would still be guards, but they should be able to move around more easily in the night. He knew the dogs would be able to with no issue. He was the weak link.

Alan napped while both Brahma and Mara kept a cautious eye on their surroundings. Waking to a snap sound, Alan got up and Mara trotted back to him, a snake in her mouth. She dropped the snake to the side of the enclave and sat back down, watching the jungle as if nothing had happened. Alan had seen dogs kill snakes before in many ways, but Mara had not experienced a snake before, and Alan was always fascinated with how an animal knew instinctively how to deal with a situation.

Sunset fell. The dense rainforest shielded them from much of the splendor, but Alan could still see the amazing colors that shattered the sky. Alan got up and stretched. Knowing the night jungle would have many predators, he would need to be awake and involved. Alan checked the harnesses on the dogs then took out a small folding bowl from Mara's pack. He filled it with water, and the dogs lapped it up with minimal sound. When they had their fill, Alan put the bowl away, checked the packs again making sure they were comfortable but tight. Alan then took some time and checked his packs as well. The straps were tight but comfortable. It was important that everything stay comfortable so he could move effectively.

The jungle was more than just dense, and it would be difficult to hear any sounds from the villa even though it was very close to them. Alan and the dogs worked their way back to the edge of the lawn clearing and the darkness was full upon the house. Lights blazed but very few exterior lights were on. Pulling out the ATN scope, Alan scanned the area and noted there were many motion sensor outdoor lights. These would go on and off as anything approached. Alan was sure they were set off by animals all the time. He decided to take advantage of human irritation.

Alan made a motion to the dogs and both sat in front of him at attention. He pulled out a small LASER pointer and tapped it then pointed it at a spot in the lawn a few yards away. Alan then made a gesture and Brahma ran to the point and came back. The lights stayed off. Alan moved the LASER point a few yards further. He made the gesture again and Brahma ran to the point. As he reached it, the lights came on, but Brahma was already returning and in just seconds was under cover of the deep foliage. Alan made a gesture and the dogs flattened to the ground while they waited.

A guard came out and walked the area. Alan watched as the guard swung the AK-74 from side to side and looked for the cause of the lights being activated. After just a few minutes, the guard went back to the house. Alan waited a full five minutes and repeated the same action, but because he knew where the sensor trigger was it was easier. Again, the light came on and again a guard came to investigate. This time the guard swept the area a little more thoroughly, and he walked with more vigor in his step. As the light went off Alan reached into his pack, pulled out a small stake with a holder on it, and placed a small box on it. The box contained a LASER that Alan aimed at the light fixture until he found the point that the light came on again. He pulled out a small remote, and the LASER turned off. Alan and the dogs moved back and waited.

The guard came out again and walked the area, this time he was walking it rather quickly and kicking the brush at the end of the lawn. After a full ten minutes he went back to the house. As the light went off Alan keyed the remote, and again the guard came out. He walked along the perimeter of the yard, then looked up at the light and looked around for anything. Stomping his foot, he walked back in the house.

On the fifth time, the light did not come on.

Alan had chosen this side because of a small patio a few feet up. After about thirty minutes of trying to get the light to come on, Alan and the dogs worked their way up to the patio. They were slow, making sure the light did not come on. Alan was reasonably sure there was no camera on this front. After a few minutes, he and the dogs made it to the patio. Alan scaled the patio wall and pulled himself up. The two dogs easily jumped the six-foot distance, balanced on the thick cement railing, and jumped down to the marble patio with a faint click as their nails hit the surface.

Alan checked the door. There was no visible alarm and the room beyond was decorated with a small bed, and a small dresser and little else. Pulling out a small meter, he swept the door and found a sensor on the lower side with minimal voltage. Alan found it and finally could see the wiring harness. He took out a glass cutter and scored the window. He tapped and nothing happened. Checking again, he cursed himself for not realizing it was not glass but instead Lexan. Alan put the glass cutter away and pulled out a small hole saw. The drill was small, and the hole saw would cause a little vibration. They had time so Alan went at a slow pace that did not cause any issues. Once a small hole was complete, he pulled out small pliers and disabled the alarm. Alan opened the door and no alarm sounded, nor did anyone show up in the room.

Alan motioned to the dogs, and they came in the house then lay flat on the floor. Alan closed the door and moved into the house. The dogs stayed fast. The lights in the house were on, but low. Alan remembered being told about the hallway and the rooms he needed to visit. He walked slowly down the hall until he came to a bend then walked into a door. Alan opened the door with caution.

Inside the room was a young girl of ten years old. Startled, she sat up in her bed but did not scream. Alan put his finger to his lips and the girl nodded.

"Your mother sent me to get you," Alan whispered.

The girl nodded.

"I have to get your sister."

The girl nodded but then whispered back. "I can get her."

Alan smiled. The girl's mother said the oldest would cooperate. She had told her mother how bad it was, and also told her that her father was not letting them come home. That had been two months earlier. Alan had been contracted to rescue the two girls when diplomatic possibilities were found to be unavailable. The DEA had keen interest in his gathering intel on the father and was willing to pay very well, but Alan took the rescue contract only.

Margarite was ten, her little sister Magda was five. The two girls were being held by their father to ensure their mother did not testify or do anything against him. He had no allowance for visitation and was on several wanted lists for smuggling and drug involvement. He and his men took the girls anyway while in the United States and smuggled them out of the country. Once back in Venezuela, their father simply decided to keep the girls. It was his right in his mind, they were his children.

Margarite put on a sweater and said, "I will be right back. Magda is asleep. I will need to get her up and bring her in here. I have some clothes for both of us. Mommy told me to get them ready a long time ago. What took you so long?"

Alan smiled at the young lady. "Sorry, traffic."

Margarite giggled and held her hand over her mouth. "Sorry. I will be back."

The little girl left the room and closed the door behind her. Alan wondered if he should be worried but considered for a moment and thought it best not to worry. Their mother had assured him Margarite would cooperate.

As Alan waited, fully on guard, he considered the types of jobs he now did. He had retired from his position in law enforcement and was now working full freelance. Freelance had a unique meaning for him as he often did jobs that no one else would take, and often for little compensation. He had agreed to do this job for expenses and enough money to put a new roof on his cabin in Kentucky. He was not surprised that so many others had turned down the job. The DEA perk would have given him money for some time, but he was not interested in working with them again.

The mother was estranged and had little money. She owned a small restaurant in Louisville, Kentucky and its funds had been exhausted as she tried to get her daughters back. Alan was introduced by a mutual friend from a time he worked in Frankfort, Kentucky with local investigators.

The door to his side clicked. Margarite walked in followed by a little girl in a white floral nightgown, rubbing her eyes.

"Who is this?" Magda asked in a loud voice.

"I'm going to get you to your mommy," Alan whispered.

"Is Daddy coming too?" Magda said in a normal voice again.

"Not this time, but we will get daddy next time," Alan said in a soft voice.

Magda started to tear up. "I want daddy and mommy too," she started to cry.

Margarite held her sister. "You need to be quiet now, for mommy."

Magda bit her lip and started sniffing, but she stopped crying. Alan and Margarite helped her get on a small outfit of pants, shirt, and a light jacket.

"We need to get to the end of the hall," Alan said. "The door there will let us out."

"The alarms are on at night," Margarite stated. "They will go off."

"I have fixed the alarms," Alan replied. "We will be fine."

Margarite peeked out the door and was acting very mature for her age. Alan guessed her situation had forced her to grow up faster than many in this day and age.

Margarite motioned, and Alan picked up Magda. She was lighter than he thought and that would work to their favor. The three of them worked their way down the hall to the back bedroom. As they entered, there was silence, but Margarite walked to the doors and jumped. The two dogs did not move.

"Don't worry," Alan said, "They are with me."

Margarite walked forward and laid a hand on Mara. She looked up at the girl but did not move.

Alan made a gesture, and the two dogs stood. He reached into his pack and pulled out two harnesses. He fitted one on Margarite, and one on Magda. Moving a few items on his vest he attached Magda to his front vest, and he attached Margarite to Brahma, almost like a saddle. At about 60 pounds Brahma would be able to carry Margarite for some time.

Margarite looked at him. "I can walk."

"I know, but we will get a little way away before we do that," Alan replied.

"Ok," the girl replied.

Alan pulled out the remote and hit the button. The LASER hit the sensor outside, but still no light came on. He opened the door, and they walked out together. Alan scaled the fence and jumped down. Brahma jumped to the top of the fence with Margarite and she held tight, looking a little worried, but the dog jumped down with some effort as silent as any cat.

They crossed the yard at a high speed. Margarite giggled as Brahma trotted with the girl on his back. Magda was a little more apprehensive as she rode against Alan's chest. They reached the edge in moments. Alan picked up the LASER he had left there and put it in his pocket.

"I wanna ride the puppy," Magda said.

Alan was patient, "In a little bit."

"I wanna ride, now," Magda repeated.

"Mara will give you a ride in a little bit," Alan said. "She is tired right now."

"OK," Magda said in a disappointed tone.

Alan was surprised but elated the white lie had worked. Mara could have easily carried the girl, but Alan was worried she might wiggle free or interfere and wanted to keep the situation under control.

They worked their way through the thick brush and were soon deep in the woods.

Behind them, Alan heard voices yelling and sounds of movement, but they slowly outpaced the sounds as they continued along. Maya was in front, Brahma followed with Margarite, and Alan ran behind, watching his step as he jumped over fallen trees and rough terrain.

As they neared the road where his jeep was hidden, a car sped past. He had wished they would not be noticed for a little longer, but it could not be helped. Alan heard more voices but ignored them until they reached the Jeep. It was a CJ5 and was fully capable of going off-road, but this jungle would make it near impossible as the slick undergrowth and thick trees would cause issues. He needed the road.

Alan helped Magda into a back seat where a car seat waited. Her mother had insisted even as Alan stated, "Car seats are not the optimal option in a chase situation." In the end, he agreed and brought one along with him. Putting Margarite in the front seat, he pointed, and the two dogs got in the back with Magda. Mara licked the little girl's face, and she giggled.

Alan waited for a few minutes. When no cars came, he started the engine, pulled on the road and headed towards Canaima. As he drove, he pulled a Glock Model 30s from his vest and put it on his lap. The road was empty, but he knew they were looking. They heard the gravel hit the bottom of the jeep as they continued. Ten minutes later, they approached the main road. Before them, a truck blocked the road. It idled with the door open and the lights on.

Alan looked over at Margarite and then to his pack. He reached in and pulled two pairs of muffs from the pack as he moved forward at idle speed, under 10 miles per hour.

"Put these on." He handed a pair of muffs to her. Looking in the back seat, Magda sat with a nondescript expression, facing forward. The two dogs looked ready to do anything. Dog people seem to know that a dog is willing to do almost anything to please a master, yet Alan treated his dogs like partners. They were even more committed than most. Mara and Brahma were focused on him, ready, waiting, and more than willing to do anything.

"Brahma," Alan said, "Voran!"

Alan opened the door just a little, and the dog jumped out of the car and disappeared into the woods.

Alan then put a pair of muffs on Magda, with some disagreement, before he looked forward at the truck in front of them. He waited for a full ten count and then sped up towards the truck.

Two men stepped out in front of the truck with flashlights. They waved the lights back and forth to signal Alan to slow down. He did not. As he continued his approach, the men raised their rifles, older AK-47s, and began yelling. A few shots were fired, but the men were obviously trying to scare, not hit the jeep.

As Alan began getting closer, the shots began to hit the vehicle. Apparently, they had their limits. Reaching over Alan pushed Margarite down but kept going. He looked up at odd intervals to avoid getting shot.

A moment later, the gunfire stopped. In front of them, Brahma had grabbed one man's gun and pulled it away before tackling the second man. The first man was trying to get his weapon. Alan drove the Jeep around the truck as Brahma raced after them. Alan slowed down and reached back, opening the back door and the dog dove in. Alan floored the Jeep and it responded with a jump. He looked at the two girls briefly before checking the mirror and saw the truck coming up on them fast.

As it approached Alan slowed down and heard the clang of gunfire. He reached out the door and fired all ten shots at the truck, aiming for the front tires. The slide locked back, and Alan put the weapon in his lap.

The truck kept coming.

Alan reached into his bag and pulled out another magazine, then paused, reached back in and pulled out a grenade. He had only brought one, but it seemed like a good time to use it. As they passed a tree he started counting and watched the mirror until the truck passed the tree as well. The count was a little short, but that was ok. Alan pulled the pin and let loose the spring assembly. He counted to one then dropped the grenade out the window far enough it would not get close to them. He counted and the resulting explosion blew off the front tire of the truck.

Alan drove hard and fast.

Fifteen minutes later, they were at the airport, pulling up to the King Air 250 that Alan had waiting for him. He got out of the Jeep and Margarite grabbed her bag. Alan holstered his weapon, put on his pack, and turned around. Magda was asleep and he didn't want to wake her. He took the car seat and unhooked it with careful precision to not wake her if possible. He nodded to the dogs which took off to the plane. In moments, they were waiting at the door, Margarite catching them in short order.

Alan fit the car seat in the first row and set up Margarite in the front seat next to him. The remaining seats had been removed for the dogs to sit, and for the extra fuel tanks in the cabin. Stowing everything, he noticed Magda was stirring and there were headlights coming in the distance.

Alan fired up the engines, checked the fuel levels, and prayed the rest was still good as he had no time for a normal checklist. He was not sure if the lights were closing on him, or if they were just there, but he knew he needed to be gone. The girls were locked in, the dogs were in the back and likely holding on to the rope handholds, and the plane was ready. Alan put his headset on and handed the second to Margarite. Soon the plane was moving towards the runway.

If there was any mystery on whether the headlights were coming for them, the flashes of gunfire eliminated that. Alan gunned the engine, rocketing up the runway. It was not a big airport and he did not have time to swing around. Throwing down the throttle, he pushed the aircraft to the limits and pulled up as he reached the end of the runway. Sliding into the air with grace and more than a little apprehension, the plane carried the girls away from their past.

Alan, Margarite, Magda, Mara, and Brahma were on their way to a small airport in Brazil where a friend and pilot, Jay, would be waiting with his plane, the Happy Scotsman, to take them home to America. All he had to do was fly straight and get there.

Below him, watching the plane disappear on the night horizon, a man fumed with anger. His anger fueled something else, vengeance.

Chapter 1

The axe swung deep and hit the log square, splitting it in two with minimal effort. Alan set another log on the top of his splitting area and swung again. Looking over to his side, he saw the two solid back German Shepherds watching him with focused interest. They watched the axe swing, then the pieces of the split log fall, then Alan pick up another log to split. The pile to the side was getting bigger.

The dogs, Shiva and Vishnu, were only a few years old. Alan had trained many animals and always kept two for himself that were the best of the best. Alan had virtually retired from his life in the service, law enforcement, and freelance consultation. Instead, he just wanted to relax. Swinging an axe was relaxing to him. Being with the dogs was always challenging and relaxing all at once.

The stack of split wood was about 40 logs. Alan stopped, grabbed a few scattered on the ground and walked over to an already started rick of split wood. He put his pieces on and looked over at the two dogs watching him attentively. He smiled. Snapping his fingers, the dogs ran to each grab a log and brought them to him. They dropped the wood at his feet, and tail wagging, ran back to get another piece. Alan began stacking the wood with excited haste as the dogs were very rapid at the ability to grab a piece, run it to him, drop it, and repeat the process. It was a furry black assembly line of split wood and wagging tails with Alan trying to keep up.

In less than five minutes, the split woodpile had been moved to the rick, and they were ready for another run of him splitting. The two dogs ran to Alan, and he hugged them as they pushed him over, licking and wagging their tails.

Alan and the dogs looked up as they heard clapping. They looked over to see Melody King walking out to them, her long brown hair flowing behind her. Melody was a vision of loveliness, and Alan had not been this happy in a long time, if ever. He had not expected this bond to grow between them. When he involved himself with an old issue in Washington DC concerning Michael Masterson, an assassin with similar goals of retirement, she had come into the fold. While Alan was a man that solved problems, Melody was a woman who figured them out. A skilled investigator with the Army, Melody had been pulled into an investigation by Alex Brown and his team to solve a mystery. She had done so and somewhere along the way Alan and Melody just clicked. Alan and Melody had driven cross country in his 96 Impala, and along the way, had fallen into something more than love. Since then, Melody had been involved with another issue then decided to retire and live with Alan. They had talked through it and it made sense. Not just for him, but for her as well.

Now they lived in his small home in Dubois, Wyoming, or wherever they wanted to be. It was Alan, Melody, and the dogs against the world. The four of them were enjoying all life could give them. Alan's property was over a square mile and was adjacent to property owned by Michael Masterson, which was even larger. This allowed Alan and Melody to live in as much isolation as they wanted but with the freedom to go anywhere. Unlike many dog owners, the property and the dogs unique training offered them the ability to leave and allow the dogs to roam, eating either at the house with a complex set of automatic feeders or catching game on their own.

"Wanna help?" Alan asked.

"Looks like you don't need my help," Melody replied as Shiva rubbed against her.

Alan was amazed that this woman, who he had met only a short time ago, had somehow gotten the dogs to trust her. They were, of course, tame and easy to get along with as they were well socialized, but the dogs were at ease with her. He often wondered who they would listen to if there were an event. After all, the dogs now followed her commands with the same tenacity and rigid stoicism as they followed his own.

Melody walked to Alan, enveloping her. Where Melody was tall for a woman at 5'10", Alan was mountainous for a man at 6'6" and as wide as any monster of legend. He held her tight, and they kissed slowly. The dogs walked back to the woodpile and lay on the ground.

"I think they are bored with us," Melody laughed.

"Maybe," Alan giggled back at her and lifted her off the ground with no effort. He held her close. She did not resist at all. After a long moment, he lowered her back to the ground.

"Want to help?" Alan asked. "We could be done in short order and then take a walk, ride, or anything you want to do."

"*Anything I want to do* sounds good," Melody replied with a wicked grin. "What would you like me to do?"

"Stack or split?" Alan asked.

"How bout I stack," Melody said.

"OK," Alan laughed, "This will be a workout for everyone involved."

Alan walked to the woodpile then called to the dogs. They ran to the side of the pile. He motioned to Melody and the dogs were excited, shivering with nervous energy.

Alan picked up the first log, split it, and the pieces fell to either side. Shiva and Vishnu grabbed the pieces and with rapid grace, took them to Melody, dropping them at her feet.

As the dogs returned to the splitting log, there were already four more pieces where Alan had split two logs. The dogs grabbed one each and ran back to Melody, this time faster. As the dogs returned to the pile, they grabbed another piece each and ran back to Melody, dropping the logs.

Melody was laughing and picking up the logs, stacking them in the rick. Her pile was getting bigger as the dogs were throwing dust, running faster and faster to cover the 20 feet from splitting log to rick.

It did not take long for the unsplit yet cut wood to be gone. After 20 minutes, Alan was covered with sweat and wood chips, the dogs were panting with enormous wet tongues hanging out of their mouths to the side, and Melody was nearly buried in at least 60 pieces of split wood.

"I think I lost," Melody laughed. "That was amazing." Melody laughed again and kept stacking a few pieces at a time. "I kept getting distracted watching how dedicated they were to beat you."

Alan pulled his shirt off and wiped his face with it. At 6'6", he was intimidating. Without his shirt, he showed rippling muscles, a tight six pack, and arms that would put a weightlifter to shame. The veins in his arms were distended from the high-speed workout splitting wood, and he was pink and sweat covered with the exertion.

"Hubba hubba," Melody said. "Trying to distract me some more?"

"Well, I was trying to cool off, but if I am distracting? Well, I will go with that," Alan laughed.

He walked to Melody and began helping her stack. "Isn't this cheating?" Melody asked.

"Maybe, but I am hoping to spend some time with you."

Melody stopped and put her hand on Alan's chest. "You have me all the time you want me."

"Woof," Alan said, and Melody laughed with him.

As they stacked the remaining wood, Melody asked, "Have you ever thought of teaching them to stack?"

"I tried that once," Alan replied.

"What happened?" Melody asked.

"Well, they got the idea pretty quick. Most Shepherds are like two-year old or three-year old children. You can teach them quite a bit, but they sometimes lose the concepts along the way. Anyway, I was splitting wood, and the dogs were running it to the stack. The stack was growing. They must have stacked a full rick, but they just kept going. I looked over and saw one of the dogs on top of the rick dropping another piece. It was at least 6 foot tall. As he jumped off, his momentum toppled the whole stack. Both dogs stopped, looked at the mess, and then looked at me as though they were bad. Ears back and all. I never had the heart to try again. They sulked for a few hours, then we went running and they forgot about it." Alan wiped his face with his shirt again, "I was actually quite impressed. If they had not jumped off the pile and knocked it over the stack was pretty straight."

Shiva and Vishnu looked at them, stacking the wood, and Shiva yawned.

Alan and Melody were finished with the stack in just a few minutes. They both used Alan's shirt to wipe the sweat from them. "Ewww," Melody said. "this thing is soaked."

"Swim or shower?" Alan asked.

"Hmmm, both are good choices," Melody replied.

The dogs perked up and looked towards the house. Alan also looked at the house and perhaps beyond.

"What is it?" Melody asked.

"Someone is here."

Chapter 2

Jonathon Michael Masterson watched as a small bulldozer moved pieces of tree and burnt house from a foundation. Weights and other items were uncovered as the bulldozer worked with great care over the house that Michael blew up some time ago. The house, in Ivel, Kentucky, had been a masterpiece of design. Michael had discarded the house, thinking the location had been compromised. His life as an assassin forced him to consider situations that would leave minimal evidence or trace when he moved on. A remote detonator had ensured that no one but the most tenacious investigation team would have any interest in the home.

It was a slow process. He had explained to the contractor that he wanted to leave as much intact as possible. The contractor, who had been referred by a nearby neighbor that Michael had helped once, was following Michael's direction and making sure nothing was upset unless he was told to upset it. Normally, that would not be a good deal for the contractor. In this case, Michael had offered him twice his normal pay and promised more work rebuilding the structure.

Michael was wearing jeans, a black t shirt and Under Armor tennis shoes. His well-defined arms were evident in the tight shirt. David, the contractor, saw the pistol nestled in the back of his t-shirt, but said nothing.

Michael was an ex-assassin by choice. Several years ago, he had made a decision not to kill his mark and instead had killed the man paying him. He did not do that for any other reason than a particular moral code. It was an interesting thought that an assassin would have a moral code, but Michael's moral code was well defined and rigid. If something did not fall within the code, he did not spend much time thinking about it.

As a child, Michael had learned he could divorce himself from emotion, becoming unaffected by situations. He also found that he was a naturally good shot with almost any weapon. He put that skill to work in college, working for the government and some private interests. Over time, he amassed a significant amount of money and found he had a talent for investment as well, making even more.

As his skills became more widely known, Michael was pursued by bigger and bigger clients. He improved his skills even more, making many deaths look like accidents. Still, he had a code to himself. He did not like killing for the wrong reason. He would do it, but it was not preferable. Instead he worked for the private sector, killing escaped criminals or criminals who found loopholes in the law. This was more fulfilling than working for the government where a no-questions-asked policy was usually in force.

As he went through college, he not only got his degree, but he also improved his ability to invest, built several homes, and learned a variety of hand to hand fighting techniques. Michael spent every day living and was almost never passive, his passion for life was at the forefront of who he was daily.

As Michael watched the bulldozer, Abby Tarkington walked to his side. Abby had started dating Michael in college, and they had become more than lovers. They were also the best of friends. Michael's life was more than complete because she was in it. Abby showed as much love for Michael as he showed for her.

There was a fire between them. They did so much together that it blended well. Michael's passion knew no boundaries when it came to Abby. Abby felt the same.

At 6'2", Michael was a formidable man. Abby was small compared to him, at only 5'2". With long blonde hair and crystal blue eyes, she didn't look like a threat, but she had proven over and over she was a force to be reckoned with. Abby was the daughter of General Samuel Tarkington, and her childhood had consisted of being an army brat tomboy who just wanted respect. By the time she had met Michael, she was an expert marksman and was well versed in many fighting techniques.

The bulldozer turned off. The contractor got off the machine, walking to Abby and Michael.

"Michael," David said, "I need to stop for a bit and maybe get some guys to come up here to help with the finer cleaning of this foundation. There is a door into the mountain that seems intact, but I bet you knew that."

"Yes," Michael confirmed. "Why don't you take the rest of the day. Come in tomorrow with a crew then we can continue and go over some plans for the rebuild."

"You know I appreciate the business, but this might go better if you got a bigger company to come in. My dozer is a bit older, and if you want big stuff done, I may not have the equipment," David explained.

"If we need anything, we will get it," Michael said. "I am sure you will do just fine. We will help each other out here."

"You're the boss," David said. "I'll see you in the morning."

Michael watched David climb the hills. Michael looked down and put his arm around Abby. "Got any plans for tonight?"

"Spending it with a tough guy," Abby said.

"Really?" Michael asked. "I don't know many tough guys. I think I want to meet him."

"I bet you do," Abby giggled.

"I would rather you spend it with me," Michael said as he put his arms around her.

"Well," Abby snuggled under his arm, "me too."

"We don't exactly have a house here, and the closest hotel is Prestonsburg," Michael started, "Sleeping in the DB9 is out. The tent is fine, but I would rather get a good meal and sleep in a bed tonight. How about you?"

"Sounds good," Abby said. "What about the Alpike down in Ivel?"

"Never stayed there," Michael said. "Worth a try."

Michael and Abby walked arm in arm to the top of the hill and the waiting DB9. As they looked out over the land that Michael owned, they heard a hawk screech.

"It is beautiful here," Abby said.

"It always has been," then Michael looked at her, "but you make it even better."

Abby smiled at Michael. "A little corny, but I love it."

Michael kissed her and opened her door on the passenger side of the DB9. "Flattery will always work," she said as she got in the car. Michael closed her door, walked to the driver's side of the car, and they were soon on the road.

Chapter 3

Alex Brown sat in the mess hall of the Blue Grass Army Depot, outside of Lexington, Kentucky. He was assigned there with a team of unique individuals that solved problems no one wanted to see or know about. Originally, Alex was brought in under the pretense of finding Jonathon Michael Masterson and killing him. This was later found to be a rogue agent's ruse to flush out Masterson, and eventually, to get revenge on him for an interpretation of events that happened a long time before. Now, the team unraveled problems uncovered by General Samuel Tarkington, and in the process, traveled the world to protect the United States of America's interests.

Alex was watching another interaction between two of his team, Rachel Brown and Jim Simpson. Rachel was a tall, muscular woman who had proved herself in combat many times, Jim was a reluctant team member, redrafted by Tarkington for his skills in martial arts and a variety of weapons. Usually, they were sparring in the gym, but today they decided to spar verbally. As always, they were drawing a crowd.

"I know you disagree, but maybe the 5.7x28 round is the wave of the future," Jim continued. "It has good penetration and is a small, easy to-carry round. With the pistol and rifle you could carry more and effectively handle more than a soldier carrying a 9mm and an M16."

"That round is just too small. You lose feet per second on the round by nature of the cartridge. Let NATO do what they want, but an M16 has good penetration and solid firepower. The 9mm is pretty much a universal round for pistols. Sure, I like the 45 better, but the M9 is a good weapon and fires about every time."

"Pbbt," Jim disagreed. "The M9 likes to be goofy sometimes, we all know it. Imagine having a pistol with as much range as a rifle. Hell, I don't know why you are resisting you have seen it in action."

"Yeah, so what," Rachel said, "One guy. And I have seen him use just about every weapon I know of. You said it yourself."

"Why do you think he carried the 5.7 round?" Jim countered.

Rachel sat quiet for a second.

"Well?" Jim asked.

"I'm thinking," Rachel snapped. "Give me a second."

"While you are thinking, someone get me a donut," Jim said to the group of people around them.

Ronnie Coomer came in and sat next to Jim. He had a tray full of food, including several donuts. Ronnie was the youngest person on the team. He was full of spirit, but a little shy. "I brought extra donuts and thought you could have a few, Jim," Ronnie said.

"Now here is the perfect man," Jim said. "Thank you, Ronnie, for the wonderful meal." Jim took two chocolate donuts from Ronnie's tray and set them before him. He took a bite, "Oh, this is heaven," he laughed.

Ronnie began to eat his eggs and bacon with one donut on the side.

Terry Drake and Barbara Stone both worked with the planes and were stationed in Lexington, though they did come down often. Although they were part of the team, they also flew others all over the world. Still, their primary role was with the team. If Alex asked, they would be there as soon as possible.

Jim finished the first document and licked his fingers. "Well?" he prompted again, just to needle at Rachel and get her to answer.

"I'll get there," Rachel said.

"What's the question?" Ronnie asked while he continued to eat.

"Why don't we use 5.7 weapons instead of our current issue?" Jim said.

"Easy," Ronnie replied. Rachel and Jim both swiveled to look at Ronnie as he ate. "If we were to use a 5.7 pistol or rifle, we would not get the ammo issued from supply. We would have to buy our own."

Rachel laughed, "The kid has a point."

Jim smiled. "Touché."

Rachel and Jim laughed as the crowd disbursed, not expecting quick resolution to the normal fireworks between Rachel and Jim. All three looked over to Alex, who sat a few seats down.

"What's up this week, boss?" Jim asked.

Alex Brown was designated leader of this team after losing friends and seeing through multiple lies in an ongoing case. General Samuel Tarkington had seen this ability, to question the norm, in all the members of the team. It was their rebelliousness that made them of value. At first, Alex did not pay attention to the team and instead read through a file.

"Ahem," Jim grumbled. "Too busy for the peons like us?"

Alex looked up, "Sorry, reading. This case file is a mess."

"Another Masterson mess up?" Jim chided. "He was actually the man on the grassy knoll or something like that?"

"Nothing that dramatic," Alex said in an easy voice, "but that would explain a few things. If only he was about 50 years older."

"Yeah, that's a problem," Jim said.

"I am reading a file on a drug lord that was never closed," Alex began. "Tarkington sent about 30 files for us to look through and see if we could tie up the loose ends. This was one of them. Carlos Juarez is his name."

"He has been operating out of Venezuela for obvious reasons. Most of the issues revolve around his integration with the country and the politics there, but there are references to ties here in the states. Multiple missions have been mounted against him, only to fail or be shut down for inexplicable reasons. The DEA has been after this guy for a long time, but he has been able to stave off any potential efforts for extradition, and to eliminate even the most random surveillance.

"What does this have to do with us?" Rachel asked. "We get to go stomp him?"

"I wish," Alex replied. "The reason it is on our desk is that one of the shutdown activities was to send Michael Masterson in to eliminate him. Michael, apparently, was on the runway and was told to stand down. His full fee still paid."

"Well, that's not fair," Rachel chided. "How can he get paid if he doesn't do the work?"

"Who shut it down?" Jim asked.

"It's not very clear, but it appears there was pressure from a house committee on law enforcement that somehow got wind of it all. They requested follow up and Tarkington pulled the plug before they could get close enough to uncover his operations. Not that he does anything wrong, just that he skirts the edge of acceptable practice in the House and Senate guidelines." Alex explained.

There was quiet for a moment. "Why would anyone want to look at him now?" Ronnie asked.

"The case was never closed. He has come up on the radar again as a political activist in Venezuela. The summation is that he is pulling strings to get someone new on the ballot that is even more under his control." Alex stated. "Marshals are also noting that his ex-wife and two children are being moved as a credible threat now exists on their lives."

"Kids are here?" Rachel asked.

"Yep," Alex said. "Why?"

"Well, if he is a good dad, get the kids. It will make him talk," Rachel replied.

Alex flipped through the file, "His children were liberated from him after he unlawfully took them from their mother and held them in Venezuela. The government was involved but not effect. It says here, they were returned home, but it does not say who was successful at getting them. Or how they did it."

Alex opened a leaf in the file. "Wow."

"What?" Jim asked.

"His place is a fortress," Alex relayed. "Whoever went in must have had a big team, and I bet it was intense. Look at the way this shows up on IR. The whole area is pocketed with motion sensors and cameras."

All three team members got up and walked behind Alex to look at the diagrams.

"Wow," Ronnie said. "That is bigger than my uncle's house."

"I bet," Rachel laughed. "Does your uncle have a trailer or a doublewide?"

"Uncle Terry has a big house on a mountain. He owns a string of restaurants around the country." Ronnie replied.

"We will have to go visit Uncle Terry sometime," Rachel giggled.

"He would like that," Ronnie said.

"What is it they would like us to do?" Jim asked.

"I can't really tell," Alex mused. "It looks like a confirmation of the facility, or a review of the profile and update to it. But they really aren't giving a lot of guidance. I would hate to rush in and find it is not something we should be doing."

"So?" Jim asked.

"For now, we will shelf this one and look through the stack of files that they threw me and go for something with some type of constructive endpoint. That is, unless Tarkington or someone special calls and says different," Alex completed.

"Maybe something with a beach," Jim laughed.

"I will take it under advisement." Alex got up and closed the file. "I am sure there is something with snow I can find."

"Brrr," Rachel grimaced.

Alex walked to the door of the mess hall and left for his office.

Chapter 4

Maria Juarez was well versed in moving. Her ex-husband was very good at finding clues and had nearly found her and the girls many times over the past 10 years. Her daughters, Margarite and Magda, were the highlights of her life, and she enjoyed every moment she had with them. Margarite was studying at a local community college. Magda was at band camp learning how to march and play a snare drum.

The modest house they had lived in, for the past 3 years, was being taken apart by movers. It swarmed with men in jeans and sport jackets. The Marshalls who would relocate her again.

They had picked up chatter about an attempt on Maria's life, and there was a lot of concern about both Maria and the girls. Maria because her ex-husband wanted to silence her forever. The girls because their father wanted them back.

About 10 years ago, a man had gone into Venezuela and rescued the girls. Their father had called, and she had never heard him that angry. He said he would kill her and strip the skin from her body when he found her. Several government groups recorded it all and had stopped a subsequent attempt, but no one realized his reach. A few days later, they were put in the witness relocation program. Since then, they had been in numerous houses and schools. Each time there was talk, then action as their location was leaked or discovered. Each time the Marshalls relocated them.

Margarite was easy to please. She was always doing her best or better to fit in and enjoyed spending time with her mother. Margarite was older when her mother and father split up. She had seen the worst he could be. When they were rescued, Margarite was critical to ensuring they would get out easily. She was even more critical to her sister being under control as Magda was a rebel, even at 5 years old.

The past 10 years had been a roller coaster with Magda. She wanted her father all the time, and then wanted to be a rebel, then wanted to be more. She was constantly at odds with Margarite and Maria. She was always looking for an excuse to start a fight or show them how important her father was in the world. Magda was intelligent and methodical. She could achieve anything she put her mind to, but she found that her favorite pastime was avoiding her intelligence and being less than cooperative with any type of authority figure.

Music had become Magda's passion. Initially, she was vocal, then angry, then brooding. As of late, she was addressing herself through music, speaking very little. When Maria and Magda were together, they would go for hours without a word. When Maria tried to speak to her daughter, she was not successful.

The movers were very good at their job. She wondered if they were used for government contracts all the time. Perhaps each knew the Marshalls on a first name basis, sending Christmas cards to each other.

"Ma'am," a voice asked, "we're finished with the bedrooms. Do you want to walk through and check them with me?"

Maria was suddenly out of her thoughtfulness. "Yes, of course."

She walked the rooms with the short non-descript man, who was checking things off his list. She looked at the empty rooms as memories being sealed away again. Her room was full of empty moments and quiet alone time. The outline of the bed was like a chalk outline of a dying life with no promise of redemption, save for two lovely daughters. It was sad to be moving again but necessary. Every move had a reason. Anything to keep Maria's daughters from the life their father led. Anything to keep them safe.

Maria nodded, and they left her room, entering Magda's room. It was a good-sized room with no bathroom or amenities but a good view of the front yard. As they looked it over, the man said, "We see the vent that was behind the bed looks a little screwed up. We will fix the grate, so there will be no issue.

Maria nodded. It was not her responsibility nor was it her house, but as she looked at the vent, she saw a glint behind the grate.

"Can you open the vent?" Maria asked.

"Sure." The man reached into a toolbelt and pulled out a nut driver. The driver was the right size, and he removed the screws, pulling off the beige vent cover.

Maria knelt and looked into the galvanized steel vent. She saw a stack of papers, rubber-banded together. Reaching in, she pulled it out and heard a clunk. She reached further and pulled out two cellular phones. The papers were neatly bound and were all open envelopes. The phones were older, Razor style phones. Both were off and still had plastic coverings on them.

Maria took the rubber band off and pulled out an envelope. Her heart jumped as she read the postmark, Venezuela. She opened the letter and read:

"My Dearest Daughter, I miss you too. Don't worry. I won't tell your mother you want to come back. I know she would not be happy. I have made mistakes in our life and am looking forward to making them right with you. Enclosed find enough money to get a plane ticket, an address book to get you here, and a new cell phone. If you call on it, we can continue our conversations. Love, Dad"

Maria's heart was racing. She flipped the envelope back over. The postmark was just two days prior. The letter was sent to a P.O. box local in Atlanta. Maria began trembling and pulled out her cell phone. She looked in her recent calls and clicked on Magda. The phone rang and went straight to voicemail. Maria fell to her knees. "No, no, no," she cried, "No."

Two Marshalls ran into the room. "What is going on?"

Maria handed them the letters and the phone. The older of the two, Milton Grimes, looked over the packet and paid close attention to the letter that Maria had opened and read.

"I guess we know where the leak came from," Milton said.

The second Marshall, Suzanne Krump, took the letter. She scanned it and asked, "Do you know where your daughter is now?"

"She is supposed to be at band camp," Maria sobbed, "but she is not answering her phone."

Suzanne pulled out her phone, walking away from Maria and Milton.

Shouts erupted from downstairs. Maria heard a box drop and the obvious shatter of glass inside. Milton drew his weapon, a Glock 22. The 40-caliber pistol was a solid weapon, and Milton had used it often. Milton moved Maria towards the back bedroom, further away from the stairs.

Suzanne was at the top edge of the stairs with her phone in one hand and her Glock 22 in the other. She peered around the edge of the stairwell. Shots pinged the wall with a loud chunk associated with each shot.

Suzanne was against the wall, crouching. She looked back down the hallway to Milton. He was crouched and aiming towards her. He motioned her back and moved Maria into the back bedroom. Suzanne backed up slowly towards Milton until they were side by side. Milton moved inside the door where Maria was, and Suzanne moved into the room across the hall. Both aimed their weapons at the stairs and waited. There was silence.

Milton scurried to the window on his knees and looked out to the front yard. As he looked, he saw a man in a black track suit and black tennis shoes, looking at a phone. The man was pressing buttons on the phone while looking at the house. Milton yelled to Suzanne as he stood and grabbed Maria. "Bomb," he called loudly but did not yell. "Get in the tub. Too late to run."

Suzanne was frozen for a second then ran to the hall bathroom. Milton grabbed Maria and ran to the bathroom attached to the master bedroom. He pushed her in the tub then jumped on top of her. Maria was shaking and bewildered when the world went insane.

The noise was much more than deafening. It literally echoed in Milton's brain. The tub lurched and pushed upwards as the room seemed to evaporate around them. Milton held the side of the tub and put his other hand over his head as splinters flew everywhere. Milton tried to shield Maria as she held onto him and the tub. A lurch threw his head forward, and he hit hard on the faucet sticking out of the prefabricated fiberglass wall. Milton felt blood on his face.

As fast as it began, it was over.

Milton's ears rang. Everything sounded muffled and almost "cloudy". He moved back and realized a four-inch splinter was protruding through his hand. It was not large, but it was not small either. The room was at an odd angle. The foundation had collapsed, and the second floor was partially on the first floor. Maria lay beneath him. Her eyes were closed, and there was blood on her face. Milton checked her breathing and pulse. She was ok.

Milton pulled himself out of the tub. As he shifted, so did the tub, sliding a few feet. Milton held on and tried again. This time the tub was stable. His ears rang. When he touched them, there was blood. He likely popped an eardrum. He could barely hear the sounds of sirens and wondered how far off they were.

A wall fell and crashed down a few feet from them. He looked back at Maria, and she was opening her eyes. There was a moment of terror, but when she saw Milton, she was not as anxious. Milton got out of the tub and steadied himself. The odd angles of the room were accentuated by flashes of light from shorting out fixtures and bare wires arcing.

"Are you ok?" Milton asked Maria.

At first, she looked confused, then Maria nodded her head. "Yes," she answered in a loud voice.

Milton pulled his Glock back out and surveyed the area. They were in rubble, but he didn't want to take the chance that someone would want to finish them off.

He motioned to Maria, "Stay down." He worked his way around the area the best he could.

Maria stayed hidden and peaked over the edge of the tub.

He heard a cough somewhere to his side and pointed the weapon with his good hand. He did not want to pull out the chunk of wood just yet, wanting to be sure there would be no more damage. But it hurt like hell. Milton worked his way through the rubble and found the other bathtub. The cast inserts of both were nearly indestructible, but the second bathtub was upside down. Milton holstered his weapon and used his good hand to pull up on the tub. It was far too heavy for him to move easily alone, but he was able to move it enough that he could see Suzanne. She was moving.

"You ok?"

"What?" Suzanne yelled.

"It will go away," Milton replied.

"What will go away?" Suzanne asked

"The ringing in your ears."

"I think I am hurt," Suzanne yelled.

"I will be back with help." Milton's ears rang, but he could hear a little now. First responders were rolling in. He moved to Maria and stayed next to her as the Fire department worked their way in the area. The Firefighters were methodical, testing each spot as they moved to where Maria and Milton were located.

"Are you OK?" one asked.

"I will be," Milton said, "Help my partner first and then check her out." Milton nodded towards Maria.

"Let's get you out of here," the EMT said.

"I stay with her," he pointed to Maria. "No matter what happens, I stay with her." Milton pulled out his badge and showed it.

Maria was sitting up then, "Magda. Margarite. I have to find them."

"We will find them," Milton said, "We will get you to a safe location. This time, it will stay safe."

34

The EMTs escorted Maria and Milton out through a maze of broken glass and splintered wood. Once outside, the air had a different quality to it, as though it were soothing the chaos in Milton's soul. Maria was led to the back of an ambulance, and a technician checked her. A second tech worked on Milton's hand. The wound was superficial. They removed it and put a temporary dressing on it.

"They'll want to clean and dress this at the hospital. Maybe get an x-ray and make sure the bone wasn't chipped." Milton was told, "Maria needs to be checked for a concussion, but she looks fine."

"What about Suzanne?" Milton asked.

"Suzanne?" the EMT replied.

"The Marshall in the other bathtub," Milton pressed.

"Umm, sir, I," the EMT stuttered.

"Spit it out, where are they taking her?" Milton fumed.

"Sir, the other woman died. There was a board through her chest and, well, when she moved, I mean, well, it was quick," the EMT said in a solemn almost apologetic tone.

Milton choked back the emotions flooding him and looked at Maria. "Let's get to the hospital." He got in the back with Maria and the tech.

Chapter 5

Alan walked to the driveway of the house with Melody. The dogs had disappeared into the brush as the car pulled up the long winding asphalt then gravel. Alan watched, putting his hand behind his back and under his black t-shirt. A Walther P99 9mm was tucked into his back pants. He touched the handle for only a moment.

The older Toyota Camry was probably a 2001 or 2002 but looked as though it was in good shape. The silver paint was dull but not rusting. The windows intact, and the tires he could see were fairly new. Toyota Camry's were those cars that drove forever, making them a car you see almost everywhere. Alan looked at the driver and pulled his hand away from the pistol.

He began walking forward as the car reached the garage area and turned off.

"Margarite?" he whispered to himself, a look of astonishment on his face.

"Alan?" Melody said, "You look like you've seen a ghost."

"Maybe I have," Alan replied as the car door opened.

"Margarite?" Alan asked.

"Alan," Tears formed in the girl's eyes, "You were impossible to find." Margarite ran to Alan and threw her arms around him. She was crying now and held him as though she would never let go. Alan was cautious at first but put his arms around the small girl and held her. She was so small. Margarite was wearing jeans and a tank top with a cotton shirt over it and looked grown up.

"How did you find me? Why did you find me?" Alan asked.

Margarite cried more, looking around, "Where are the dogs?"

"Mara passed away, a few years ago," Alan lamented. "Brahma followed her within a month. They were close and had grown up together."

Margarite cried more and tried to catch her breath. "No dogs?" Margarite sniffed. "That just doesn't fit."

Alan snapped, and Shiva and Vishnu ran to his side. They sniffed at Margarite but sat down and did not move.

"They're beautiful," Margarite sobbed.

Melody took control. "Why don't we go inside and figure out what's going on here?"

Alan shook his head, "Margarite, sorry, this is Melody. Melody and I, well, she is my girlfriend."

Margarite put out her hand, sniffling, "Good to meet you."

Melody put her arm around the girl. Margarite was 5'5" and was almost waifish with how thin she looked. When Alan had seen her last, she weighed 55 pounds or so. Now she was maybe 100, and her long black hair and dark complexion gave her an exotic beauty. Her simple outfit and the Converse "chucks" made her look complete.

They entered the spacious living area and Alan followed the two women inside. Melody immediately got a tissue from a countertop and brought it to Margarite. Alan sat down at the kitchen bar, and Margarite sat next to him while Melody made tea on the other side of the bar.

"Margarite, how did you find me?" Alan asked.

"It was hard at first," Margarite said. "I have been looking for years. I saw you in the fringe of a picture about an attack on a home in the area. I doubt anyone else would have noticed, but I was paying close attention to people who helped other people. I found the source, came to town and just started asking questions. A waitress said you lived in the area. The grocery said you lived in the hills. I went through the public records and found a few people who could be you. I was lucky that you were the first one."

"OK, why?" Alan asked as they heard the tea kettle start to whistle.

Margarite started crying again, "I need your help."

Melody listened as she went to retrieve the kettle.

Alan was still stunned by the girl's appearance, "My help? What's wrong?"

"Magda," Margarite said. "She was never happy. I think she has been talking to our dad. I need to find out if she has and keep her from doing something stupid."

"Why do you think that?" Alan asked.

"She has always been upset since you brought us home," Margarite began, "I mean, she was too little to see what type of person dad was. She didn't see him beat Mom, or any of the things he did to hurt people. She just wants a family, and she treats mom horribly to try to get dad back. Then a few months ago, things changed. She had money. She was being more secretive. She wouldn't talk to me. Really, she wasn't talking at all. I would ask her questions, and all I would get is crickets. Maybe not even crickets. All I would get was silence. Then a few weeks ago, I saw her using the phone. When I walked up to her, she hung up, and I saw it wasn't her phone. It was an old flip phone. I asked to see it, and she threw it into the lake," she paused, "I mean, who throws a phone in the lake if there isn't an issue? Well, who throws a phone in the lake? I started watching her, and she continued to act strange and out of character. Then a few days ago, she got really weird. She hugged me, then walked away like I was going somewhere, or something like that."

Alan listened. Melody poured hot water over teabags and handed a cup to the other two. She then took one for herself and sat on a stool across from them.

"Did you talk to your mom about this?" Alan asked.

"Well, no," Margarite said. "Mom would freak. I know she has nightmares about Dad all the time. She has not even dated since we have been over here. She just looks out for us. But I am worried something bad is going to happen. Magda is such a screwup sometimes."

"I think we should call your mom," Alan said. "I bet she is worried about you."

"Alan," Margarite said, "I am twenty now. I can take care of myself."

"Yes, you can," Melody joined the conversation, "and I bet this is frustrating you terribly."

"Yes, it is," Margarite said. "Mom treats me like a child as well. I am tired of being treated like I am some kid. You know, Alan, I have seen a lot." Margarite was suddenly stern, "I think Magda is talking to our father again. I have tried to call and I can't get ahold of her. Her phone is off. I am worried she is meeting him somewhere, or worse, going to Venezuela."

Alan looked at the floor. The situation bothered him more than he could relay. "I see," he finally replied.

"I see?" Margarite said in a disturbing voice. "I see? What does that mean? She's my sister. She has gone silent. I am worried. She is a pain in my ass, but I don't want her to get hurt."

"Slow down," Alan replied. "When did you hear from her last?"

"Three days ago. I talked to her in person when she hugged me. She was all over the place and was scattered. I was worried. I called her later that night, then again two days ago, morning and night Then again yesterday," Margarite said. "It goes direct to voicemail."

"Have you called your mom to see if she is around?" Alan asked.

"No, I didn't want to worry her."

Melody sipped her tea. "Where is your father?"

"I don't know, and I don't want to know. Probably in Venezuela, but I haven't talked to him since we left," Margarite began to tear up again. "I never want to hear or see him again."

"Margarite," Alan began, "is it OK if I call your mother? Just to see if she knows where Magda is now. I won't talk about you, but she might know, or maybe Magda is with her."

"I will call her," Margarite said as she pulled out her phone.

Margarite hit her "recents" and dialed her mother. The phone rang, and Alan and Melody could hear it ringing. There was no answer, voicemail picked up and began "The person at..." and Margarite hung up.

"Weird," Margarite said. "Let me try again."

Margarite dialed again, and there was no answer. As the voicemail message played, Margarite hung up and dialed again. This time the phone picked up.

"Hello," a man's voice came.

"Who is this?" Margarite demanded. "Where is my mother?"

"This is Atlanta fire rescue," the man said, "there has been an accident."

"An accident?" Margarite was frantic, "Is my mom ok? Where is she? How can I find her?"

Alan put his hand on Margarite's phone, "Let me talk to him."

Margarite was shaking and let Alan have the phone.

"Which hospital would they have taken anyone to?" Alan asked. "Piedmont? Thank you."

Alan hung up the phone and handed it to Margarite. "What now?" Margarite asked.

Melody moved over and stood next to Margarite. Alan walked to his computer, pulled up a few screens, and picked up his phone. He called Piedmont Atlanta Hospital.

"Yes, thank you," Alan began, "My name is Alan Jones, badge number 464317, can you please connect me to the ER?"

There was a pause, then Alan said, "Thank you."

"Yes, this is Alan Jones, badge number 464317 looking for a status on a Maria Juarez, female just admitted," Alan stated. "A Marshall, yes, please, may I speak to him?"

Another pause. Alan put the phone on speaker.

"Marshall, can you verify the status on Maria Juarez?" Alan asked.

"Who is this?" the voice asked.

"Sir, my name is Alan," Alan began, "How can I verify you are a Marshall?"

"Let me ask the questions," the voice replied. "Who is this?"

"I bet I can make this easy," Alan said. "Margarite is with me. She came here looking for help."

"What about Magda?" the voice asked.

"I can't confirm anything at this time," Alan replied.

"I can call through the office. If you can call in to the Chicago office, I will call in and get us on a secure line. Ask for Nancy Parker. Give me two minutes to set it up."

"Will do," Alan said. "Calling in 3 minutes."

Alan hung up the phone.

"What does all this mean?" Margarite was getting frantic again.

"It's hard to say," Alan began.

Melody cut him off. "It could be nothing, sweetie. Let's wait until we get all the information before we worry. We can listen in and let Alan find out about your mom. We won't let anything happen to you."

Alan sat at his computer for a moment and pulled up a new screen. He dialed the Chicago Marshall's office.

"Nancy Parker, please," Alan said in a polite manner.

"Hi, Nancy. A Marshall will be calling in and setting up a secure line for us to talk," Alan stopped. "OK, please put me through."

Alan put the phone on speaker again and set it on the counter. He sat back down with Margarite and Melody.

"Who is this?" the voice came.

"I know you will try to trace. You will not be successful," Alan said. "I am a friend. I am the person who brought the girls home, 10 years ago."

"How can I know that?" the voice replied. Alan nodded at Margarite.

"This is Margarite," Margarite spoke up then. "He is the one who saved me and my sister."

"This is Milton Grimes," Milton said. "I am with Maria. She is being checked out and then we will be moving. The house was compromised, and they tried to blow us up. Maria is fine. We are both a little banged up. Lost my partner today and need to deal with that too."

"What is going on?" Alan asked.

"Seems Magda has been in contact with her father for a while," Milton said. "She is likely on the way there."

"Can we confirm that?" Alan asked.

"Not yet. Still trying to clean up. You may want to dump her phone. They are likely tracking it." Milton said. "How can I get you?"

Alan walked back to his computer, opened a pouch and pulled out a phone. "Let me give you a number. We will sync up later."

Alan gave him a number from the back of the phone and hung up.

"Let me have your phone," Alan said.

Margarite gave him the phone.

Alan turned the phone off and put it in a pouch.

"Pouch is shielded, no signals. We will take care of it more later," Alan looked at Melody, "Up for a trip to Atlanta?"

"What about my car?" Margarite asked.

"We will take care of it and get you something down there for the time being, or the Marshalls will. We can work it out." Alan said.

"What should I pack?" Melody asked.

"Pack light. We will take the dogs. I guess we should call Jay," Alan sighed.

"You call him, we can take the truck, that way the dogs will have it easy." Melody said.

Alan picked up another phone and dialed a number as Margarite watched.

A voice said, "Relocation."

"Hi Jay, we need a ride," Alan said.

The voice repeated, "Relocation."

"Really? I still have to go through this? I have known you longer than Michael," Alan pressed.

"Relocation," came the voice.

"Wheels up in 2 hours," Alan said in an exasperated voice.

"Cargo?" the voice came.

"God! Ok. F350 Supercrew," Alan stated in a dry voice.

"Roger," the voice replied, "Proceed DUB 180."

"Out," Alan replied, and the phone went dead.

Melody came back in the room, "Jay coming?"

"Yeah, 3 hours. He still does the whole back and forth thing like we don't know each other. It is getting old." Alan stated with irritation, spraying from his words.

Melody started laughing. "That's funny." She giggled a little more, "Jay was telling me when we borrowed his plane to flip the "off" on a console because his IVRS system tracks where he is and takes care of calls. He hasn't answered that phone in a long time."

"Really?" Alan asked.

"Yeah, if it was him, he was pulling your leg, but I bet it was a machine you were just arguing with," Melody snickered and went back for a bag.

Alan went to a wall and moved a book, the wall opened to a small gunroom. He walked to a drawer and pulled out a harness and put it over his T-Shirt. He put his Walther in one side and picked up a second one and put it in the other. Alan pulled out a small bag and put four magazines in the bag. He then grabbed a Beretta 92F for Melody with a belt holster. It was like her service revolver. Alan grabbed a few magazines.

Margarite followed him into the small room. "Wow."

"Sorry, was in a hurry," Alan said. "I hope this doesn't bother you."

The room was covered with pegboard on two sides and drawers on the other. All were dark wormwood and the pegboard had weapons hanging from plastic covered hooks all over the wall. One row was long weapons, some were wooden with stocks and a whole wall was pistols in almost every size.

"Why do you need so many?" Margarite asked.

"Good question. I guess I don't, but almost every weapon has a specific use," Alan told the girl. "Sometimes you need size, sometimes speed, sometimes penetration. Sometimes you just want to blow something up. You can't use the same weapon and think it will always work exactly right."

Alan was finishing packing up and pulled two Glock 17s off the wall. He knelt and opened a drawer and pulled out two "K9 Pack" backpacks. The packs were made for dogs and Alan slid open a side Velcro and slid a weapon into each pack.

"The dogs need guns?" Margarite asked.

"No, but I might, they just carry an extra each," Alan replied.

"Alan," Margarite asked with a tear forming in her eyes again. "Do you think my mom will be ok?"

"She will be fine. We will see her soon and get you somewhere safe," Alan told her.

"You know, I feel bad, but it is Ok if Magda goes to live with our father," Margarite said, "She just makes mom and me sad all the time."

"You don't mean that," Alan stated. "She is just a teenager, and things happen to teens sometimes. Maybe they go a little crazy, or maybe they see the world with different eyes, but someday she will be your best friend."

"I don't know," Margarite whispered.

"I do," Alan reassured the girl, "it will all be ok."

"What's that red light?" Margarite asked.

Alan turned and looked at the red light blinking on the wall. "It's a notice. I should have put your phone in the bag sooner."

Chapter 6

The evening air was crisp in Kentucky. The hills were a beautiful sight and sunset had been a stunning view across the edges of the mountains. Abby and Michael walked the area they could through paths cut into the hills and laughed, told jokes, and enjoyed themselves. Abby was getting cold. Michael took off his denim shirt and put it around her. His black Under Armor shirt was fine for the not-too-cold, not-too-warm eve. As they arrived back at the small motel, they went to the modest room and closed the door.

The room was clean but a little dated. The bed was comfortable, and the décor was acceptable for a motel.

"This is such a quaint little place," Abby said. "It has character."

Michael looked around, "Yep, probably something from a Cary Grant movie."

Abby started laughing.

"Actually, this is all pretty modern and well put together. The bed frames are well done, and everything is as it should be in a much bigger hotel."

"Wow, Michael, you should be a hotel motel reviewer," Abby laughed.

"I have stayed in enough," Michael replied. "I could be like Jay and say, 'I was in this hotel once and I found a bed with a bar next to it.' Then tell cool stories about the places that people laugh at."

"Have you talked to Jay lately?" Abby asked.

"Not really," Michael said. "You would know if I did. I got an email from him about getting a second big plane. He was wondering if I would be using it."

"What did you say?" Abby asked as she sat down cross legged on the bed.

"I told him I was retired, but I could use his service sometimes." Michael sat on a desk chair near the bottom of the bed.

"You know? Your retirement seems pretty busy," Abby chided. "We are on the go a lot, and retired people shouldn't be on the go like we are, right?"

"Well," Michael said in a pompous voice, "I am an ex-assassin and there are some provisos that seem to pop up with my ex-profession." Michael looked to the ceiling and seemed to count his fingers with a silly smile on his face.

Abby laughed again. "I bet there are" she began, "Actually, I know there are. Who in the world would have found you to kidnap you? To fight in an arena? That's insane."

"I think the insane part was thinking they could beat you," Michael laughed.

"Well, you know that's true. It did let me see our Michigan house though. I am glad we got to spend time there."

"Me too," Michael said, "The house was empty for too long. Was nice to get some use out of it."

"Any more houses I should worry about?" Abby asked and reach over, still cross legged, and punched his shoulder.

"More houses? We need to worry about the house here." Michael replied.

"Yeah, I miss Kentucky sometimes. Now I miss Dubois, and Ivel, and" Abby took a deep breath," well? We need a schedule."

"We do not need a schedule," Michael said. "A schedule is where people find you. I would rather not be found."

"I know, but I hate that we can't use the houses," Abby replied.

"We will use them, but one of the reasons we have them is to stay off the grid, not become predictable," Michael said.

"Predictable?" Abby grinned. "Are you saying I am predictable?"

"Umm, never?" Michael laughed in a nervous voice.

Abby leaned forward on her knees again, still sitting Indian style and hit Michael on the arm again. "That's right and don't you forget it."

"You hit me," Michael said.

"You are mine," Abby giggled.

"Does that mean," he paused, a twinkle in his eye suddenly, "you are mine?"

It was the blink of an eye and Michael pounced on Abby. She fell back as he grabbed her with gentle force and leaned her back, still Indian style but flat on the bed."

"Wow," Michael said looking down, "flexible, this could be interesting."

"You know it," Abby said as she grabbed his head and pulled him down to kiss her. The kiss was soft at first but gained intensity. Michael and Abby both began to pant.

Michael stopped and pulled away just a little. Abby looked up at him. His blue eyes were full of passion, rage, and a hundred other emotions. "I love you," Michael said.

Abby just looked at him for a minute, soaking him in and all the complexities that was Jonathon Michael Masterson. "I love you, Michael, and I adore you."

Michael lowered himself to the bed and Abby held him tight.

Chapter 7

Milton walked into the emergency room as the doctor explained things to Maria. "You have a slight concussion. It is nothing to worry about. I am hopeful the ringing in your ears will go away in the next several days. It's a miracle that you didn't burst an eardrum."

"Thank you, doctor," Maria said.

"The nurse will be in with some paperwork and a prescription. Then you can go," the doctor stated as he left the room.

"Margarite is OK I think," Milton said.

"Where is she?" Maria asked in an excited tone. "How do you know?"

"She is with the man who saved her," Milton stated.

"Alan?" Maria asked. "How did she find him?"

"I wish I knew," Milton replied. "We are going to meet her in Atlanta. He is bringing her to us."

The thin curtain surrounding the area in the ER let sound pass through easily. They both heard the sound of automatic gunfire and Milton looked out of the curtain. "We need to go, now."

Maria allowed herself to be led out of the area and Milton looked for an exit. He drew his weapon as he motioned people to the ground or under cover as he walked in a crouch.

Gunfire erupted again, behind them. Milton motioned Maria forward while he waited. Security rushed into the room they were just in and one of them fell backwards in a hail of staccato sounds and a spray of blood. "Stay here," Milton said to Maria and a few people around her, kneeling and murmuring.

Maria nodded.

Milton worked his way forward. The rooms were like a maze, and there was one way to the ER from the previous room to where he was at now. Opposite the hall, where the security guard was laying in his blood, was the actual main portion of the hospital. More security would come, but they were not trained for this type of situation or they two that had come forward had been so caught up in the adrenaline rush that they made a mistake.

Milton heard the sound of curtains being pulled back. He looked around the corner and pulled back in almost a single motion. The man in the black track suit was in the area Milton and Maria had just been.

Milton heard another curtain being pulled back and screaming. Kneeling, Milton fell to the floor, pushing outwards with his gun forward in a two-hand grip. The man did not see Milton right away and Milton fired the Glock 22. Two shots rang out. The first hit the man in center mass, the second was in the forehead. The man fell to the ground. Milton rose, still covering the area in a two-hand grip, partially kneeling.

Security guards were running up to him, yelling "Freeze."

Milton pulled back his jacket as he lifted his weapon, pointing it towards the ceiling. He showed them the badge "US Marshall."

Both men kept their weapons pointed at Milton. The bigger of the two said to the second, "Check it out."

The second security guard walked up and looked at his badge. "Other ID?"

"Hang on," Milton said. Keeping his weapon high, he reached into his back pocket with two weapons trained on him. He pulled out his wallet and handed it to the guard closest to him.

The guard went through the wallet and found the ID. "He is legit."

"How do you know?" Milton smiled.

"15 years in the FBI, thank you," the guard stated.

Behind Milton, there was a unique click that was the chambering of a shotgun. Milton turned towards the sound and saw another person in a black track suit, raising a 12 Gauge pump shotgun. As Milton raised his weapon, he wondered who would be faster. Shots fired, and both security guards hit the man three times each. The shotgun clattered to the floor, and the man collapsed. Two more guards joined the others. They fanned out towards the ER.

"Step back, sir. We will handle this," they said to Milton.

Milton moved back to Maria. "As I was saying, they are coming to us. We need to get you to a safe house. I have a number to call him and he me. It will take them a while to get here."

Maria was shaking and in near shock, "Whaat?"

"I need to get you away from this. Somewhere we can hold out and be safe." Milton replied as he ushered Maria away from the chaos. Behind him, the sound of fast footsteps and control being regained as police converged on the ER as well.

Chapter 8

Alan pulled Margarite into the gunroom and started to grab a rifle from the wall. Stopping, he instead grabbed a different rifle. The P90 was Michael's choice. Alan was never a huge fan, but he knew the weapon was resilient and had a 50-round magazine. He pulled out 2 magazines, put one in his back pocket and slapped the other on the P90.

"Melody," Alan said, "We have company."

Alan handed Melody the bag that contained her Beretta, and she took it out immediately.

"I'm going to walk out front to check it out," Alan said. "Close Margarite in the room and stay aware."

"Where are the dogs?" Melody asked.

"Probably in the woods waiting for me to tell them what to do."

Melody nodded and grabbed Alan, kissed him, "I love you."

"I love you, too," Alan said, lost in the moment. He snapped out of it and walked out the front door.

No one was evident. Crouching behind a woodpile, he worked his way outwards.

There was a snap behind him. Alan turned to see a man who was glancing down at the twig he had cracked. The man was carrying an AK-47 and started to swing it towards Alan. Alan fired the P90 into the man's chest. The effect was intense knocking the man backwards, but Alan was not sure of the penetration. He crawled to the man who was writhing in pain.

"How many?" Alan asked.

"Fuck you," the man yelled.

Alan pulled a knife from the sheath and checked the man's chest. The vest he wore had protected. It looked like one bullet had gotten through and grazed his shoulder. Alan asked again. "How many?"

The man started to talk, and Alan put his hand over his mouth. He grabbed the man's hand and put it on the ground. Alan pushed the knife through it, pinning the man to the ground.

"How many?" Alan asked again.

The man reached for a weapon on his chest, but Alan was over him and he was prone. Alan took the weapon and put it in his pocket, sitting on the man's other arm. Looking at the man's chest, he saw a large army dagger. He took it and, with no thought, pushed it through the man's other hand and into the ground. The man started to scream, but Alan put his hand over his mouth again.

"How many?" Alan asked and took his hand off his mouth.

"Two more," the man said.

"Why are you here?"

The man looked at him and Alan pulled the knife from the man's left hand.

"The girl," the man said.

"Thank you," Alan said. He pushed the man's knife through his head directly between his eyes. The knife stuck deep and the man's astonished look stuck. Alan closed the man's eyes and pulled his knife from his right hand.

Alan clicked a few times with his mouth and waited.

A howl erupted about 100 feet to the west of him, another about 50 feet to the south west.

Looking around, he waited for a moment. He did not have a vest on and wondered if he should take the one on the corpse next to him. He looked at it and realized that was just not going to work. The vest was far too small for him. He kept waiting and a few minutes later saw a man come out of the bushes whispering for Miguel. He realized he must have Miguel next to him.

Alan watched and took the P90, aimed and squeezed off two rounds in the man's head. He dropped hard.

Alan looked at the body next to him, "Well, Miguel, you have company. Your friend is with you now."

Alan waited and looked out. The third was not having it. Alan whistled and ran across the drive. Shots rang out, bouncing off the ground as he jumped behind a woodpile.

More shots. Alan stayed behind the woodpile as his new assailant emptied a magazine. Alan looked as the assailant walked towards him, dropping a magazine and putting another in. It was mere seconds and Alan saw the Shiva running fast from the right of the gunman. He jumped at him and as she passed his shoulders clamped onto the man's vest. The momentum spun him backwards, but Shiva pulled harder and spun him completely around.

The AK-47 fired in thin air and the gunman went down hard. Vishnu was there before he could move and had the back of the man's neck in his jaws. The man could not move. Alan walked out. The man was panting but not foolish enough to try to move. Alan took the AK-47 and threw it to the side. "Any more?"

The man was panting, closed his eyes and shook his head no.

"How many know you are here?" Alan said.

"No one. We followed the girl's GPS," the gunman replied.

Alan walked over, picked up the AK-47 and looked at the weapon, "I have a friend who collects these from the men he kills. He has quite a few. I never much liked them. Who sent you?"

The gunman thought for a moment, "Her father. He just wanted her brought back. Who are you?"

"Just some scary guy," Alan said.

"You know he will kill you for this when he finds out," the gunman spat.

Alan looked around, the woods were dark and quiet. The normal sounds shattered by all the gunfire. The silence was deafening. "How will he know?"

Realization hit the gunman, he started to struggle just as Alan snapped his fingers. His struggle ended as the dog snapped his neck.

Alan walked inside to the girls. The gun safe was closed and Melody was pointing at the door. "Let her out," Alan said as he picked up a cloth and wiped his knife clean.

The two dogs walked in the door and sat near Alan. Alan leaned against the granite kitchen counter. "I am too old for this."

Melody opened the gun safe, and Margarite ran out. "Is it safe?"

"Yeah," Alan said, "safe for us. I really need to put in a cellular and GPS jammer. They said no one knows they are here but I'm not sure I can trust that. Let's pack up and get out of here."

"Aren't you forgetting something?" Melody asked.

"No," Alan said as he grabbed a bag.

"We have bodies in our drive," Melody said with a smirk.

"Oh," Alan said, "I will call and have a cleaner come out. I don't remember the number; but it is in my phone."

Margarite looked on. "Is it that easy to get rid of someone?"

Alan shrugged, "I have no idea, I rarely use them. I am sure it is easier than anyone thinks, but who knows. People disappear all the time and no one knows."

Alan kissed Melody and took the bag out front.

"What was that for?" Melody asked.

"Just because," Alan said as the door closed.

"My mom?" Margarite asked.

"She will be fine," Melody replied. "Let's pull the truck around and get your stuff."

They walked to the garage and the Crew Cab F350 that waited for them. It was jet black. Melody pressed the garage door button and waited for the door to open. "Hop in."

"It's only a few feet," Margarite said.

"Yeah, but I am sure Alan is cleaning up a little. Let's just drive around to your car."

Melody backed the truck out and swung it around to the front of the house. Alan was moving things out by one of the woodpiles while the dogs ran around in circles.

"Are those bodies?" Margarite asked.

"Probably," Melody said, "but you don't need to think about that."

"Have you ever seen a dead body?" Margarite asked.

"I was an army investigator before Alan and I met. So yes, I have. Perhaps too many." Melody replied.

"Can I go see?" Margarite asked.

"Umm, how bout we don't and say we did?" Melody said. "Let's get your stuff."

For a teen, the car was surprisingly clean. There was one bag in the trunk, and it, too, was well put-together. There was also a small bag of dirty clothes that Melody insisted they take. It was only minutes as they loaded the back of the big truck. Melody opened the back of the truck. The bed was crisp and clean as though new. Melody loaded the girl's bags into the back, and it seemed to be still empty, the maw of the truck waiting for more.

"Help me out," Melody said. The two girls walked to the house and retrieved the other bags, then walked them to the truck bed and loaded them up.

Margarite looked for Alan and didn't see him. The dogs appeared and disappeared in the woods, watching her like ebon guardian angels. "Let's close up the house, ok?"

"I know you are trying to keep me busy while Alan takes care of the bodies, but I am an adult. I can handle it." Margarite said.

"Yeah, I know," Melody replied as she swept her long dark hair back. "But there are some things you shouldn't have to handle."

Margarite studied the woman before her. Melody was tall, but she seemed small next to Alan, everyone did. There was a twinkle in Melody's eyes but also something that was knowing, well prepared, and something else.

"Shouldn't we try to see everything we can?"

"No, sweetie," Melody said, looking down at the young girl as they walked into the house. "I think you will find, when you get older, there will be things you wish you could un-see." Melody paused for a moment, "Life and death are things to be experienced. Not things to be seen but instead, things to be lived. As I investigated murders, I always felt the person would have liked to see one more day, one more moment. Thinking about death, or dwelling on it, takes away the fire in life. Wouldn't it be nice if you could just focus on life for a while?"

Melody was checking windows and doors in the house. Margarite followed almost mindlessly. She would have seen a lot if she had been paying attention, The impressive bedroom with an overly large bed stood in the room. Margarite smiled at the size of the bed; she expected as much. The guest room, a room for the dogs full of toys that Melody picked up and put in baskets in the corner, a small gym filled with weights and mirrors. Instead of seeing any of her surroundings, Margarite was just following and watching Melody. "So how do you face problems without looking at the bad?"

Melody stopped, "You don't need to run away from the bad, just don't run towards it either. I am sure you are a strong young woman. Don't try to grow up too fast just to prove you can."

"Thanks," Margarite said.

"For what?" Melody asked as they reached the garage door again. She pressed the button and closed it.

"For not calling me a little girl," Margarite replied.

Melody stopped, turned and reached out her arms. Margarite walked to her and Melody hugged her. "You are a wonderful young woman with the world in front of her."

Alan poked his head in the door, "Are you ready?"

The girls smiled and broke their embrace. Melody motioned to the bag with weapons in it by the gun safe. "Do you need that?"

Alan smiled. Margarite was impressed with the big smile. Alan laughed then and said, "I think we have established that I may need that." He paused for a moment, "Actually, we do need that." Alan picked up the bag and carried it out front.

Melody looked around the front room of the house. It was always so alive. Alan was full of life, and the dogs made him act like a young man. He seemed to be tied to them. Their exuberance to please him was only matched by his exuberance to take care of and please them. Melody felt so much a part of this. It had opened to her a short time ago, making her feel so welcome and so much a part of this pseudo family.

Melody smiled and armed the alarm system at the door. It was not a simple alarm like most residential homes had, but instead, it armed a series of countermeasures, just in case. Alan had said it best once when he showed her how to arm the system, "Best in case of what?" he had asked as he wiggled his eyebrows. The system armed, Melody closed and locked the door then walked to the truck with Alan and Margarite.

Alan took the driver's seat, Margarite the center front, and Melody sat in the passenger seat. The dogs ran to the passenger side of the car. Alan said, "sook," to them and the dogs took off in front of them. Alan put the truck into gear and descended the hill of his house at only a few miles per hour. As they moved further down the hill, they heard a single bark in front of them. Alan sped up until they reached almost the end of the drive. There was a white Chevy van with power company logos on the sides. Alan got out of the car and Melody pulled out her weapon. Alan drew his as well, moving up to peer in the passenger window. The dogs ran up to the side of the vehicle. Alan slid the side door open and Shiva jumped in the van. Then turned and came out wagging her tail.

"Maybe he was telling the truth?" Alan said. "Any more?" Alan asked the dogs as they tilted their heads side to side trying to understand, then ran to the door on the truck. "It appears we have the pup report and the area is clear. Either that or they want a cookie from downtown."

Margarite giggled.

Melody was happy to see that Margarite was not in shock about the events she had just gone through. Being locked in a gun room then brought out to an area she knew was covered in dead bodies, well, that wasn't for the weak. Margarite was a very mature young lady and had an inner toughness probably born of their unique situation.

Alan opened the back door and the two dogs jumped in. Margarite looked back and Vishnu licked her face with a giant slobber covered tongue.

"Aren't you lucky?" Melody said, "Doggie kisses."

Margarite giggled as she tried to wipe the saliva from her face.

"I hope Jay can make it on time," Alan said.

"Is the plane nice?" Margarite asked. "Will we get good seats?"

"You could say that," Alan said, "As comfortable and as roomy as we have now with lots of room to stretch."

"Do you still have your plane?" Margarite asked.

"Yes," Alan said, "It is a work in progress. It runs sometimes. And well," Alan thought for a second how to say it, "sometimes it tries to run. I spend a lot of time with it and haven't used it much since I flew you out of Venezuela. After we got picked up, I had to fly back down and take the long way home over Mexico and up through Texas to Kentucky. That's where I lived at the time. It sat there for a while because I was just too busy. When I moved up here, several years ago, I flew it up here and it was a little persnickety. Actually, it tried to dump me out of it a few times. But I got it here and I tinker with it from time to time."

"Why don't we fly your plane?" Margarite said.

"Because we want to live," Melody whispered.

"I heard that," Alan said, "and I agree. She is not in the best shape."

The roads were good. And the dogs watched from side to side as they drove. Alan knew if someone was watching, they would alert him in an instant. As they came over a hill, the semblance of a city came into view. The quaint town of Dubois.

"Have you rescued anyone else since us?" Margarite asked.

"Not any little girls," Alan said, "You were a special case."

"Does anyone else ride the dogs?" Margarite asked.

"Umm, no," Alan laughed, "but they try to ride me occasionally. Vishnu wants to be carried sometimes. Such a baby."

Margarite giggles turned serious, "Do you think Magda is ok?"

"Hmm," Alan said, "Melody, know anyone who can trace last tower on her phone while I drive?"

Melody smiled, "Of course you know I do. Let me make a call."

Melody pulled out her phone and called a number. "Ronnie, its Melody, and yes I'm fine. Can you trace last tower used without going through all the red tape? Do we need some red tape? Let me give you a number." She read Ronnie the number. "Let me know if you can find anything, I will be on this line as long as I can be."

Alan looked over, "Ronnie? From Tarkington's group?"

"You know it was," Melody said. "I worked with them for a little while. I trust them."

"I know," Alan said, "I was just curious if you would use them or the army."

"Army asks more questions," Melody said.

They pulled into the airport and before them was a very big plane. The C130J Hercules was a masterpiece of aviation that could carry troops, supplies and in this case a big truck. Alan pulled up to the back of the plane and got out. He walked to Jay and put out his hand.

Jay was thinner than Alan had ever seen him. He was not tall by any means but not short. His long grey beard made him look like a short Santa Claus that lost his belly.

"Wow, you've lost weight," Alan said.

Jay moved his hand aside and gave Alan a big hug. "We don't shake hands, we hug," Jay laughed. "Where's Melody?" Melody got out of the truck followed by Margarite, "Wow, you have a family now."

Jay walked to Melody and hugged her as well. "Glad you are still with this brute; he needs a cleanup job."

"Good to see you, Jay," Melody laughed, "This is Margarite. She is going along for the ride."

"More the merrier," Jay laughed. "The Happy Scotsman loves passengers. I remember picking up Alan a long time ago in France. I was at a bar, Willy's Wine Bar. It is famous for being, well, a wine bar. Anyway, I was talking to this beautiful French girl," Jay winked at Margarite, "and this big lug comes in and drags me to the airport. Good thing too, I heard later that that French girl's husband showed up at the bar. Was good I was long gone."

"Well, you had too much wine. She was not worth the trouble," Alan laughed.

"Where to?" Jay asked.

"Atlanta. Then on station until I can figure out where I need to go next." Alan said.

"That bad?" Jay asked.

"Maybe," Alan said.

"Her sister?" Jay asked.

"Yeah."

"How do you know my sister?" Margarite asked.

"I flew the bigger plane that picked you up in Brazil. You may not remember. You and your sister were exhausted. I flew you to Florida. You both spent most of the flight curled up with his dogs."

"I think I remember," Margarite said, "It was a long night."

"Shall we load this beast?" Jay asked.

"I've got it," Melody said, "You guys get out of the way."

"I guess we've been told," Jay laughed.

"How's Janet?" Alan asked.

"She is doing pretty well," Jay replied. "We spent a lot of time in Puerto Rico recently. She had so much fun but burned herself bad. They make sunscreen for a reason. When we got home, I told her to rest. I had been on the road a few days when she called to say she was taking a charter to Alaska and back and would be a few days. We are meeting back at home, next week."

"She has really been picking at you with this diet, huh?" Alan smiled.

Melody had the truck in the C130J and was already pulling the straps on the wheels.

"We are taking the truck and the dogs and all? That's cool," Margarite said.

"Yeah," Jay said, "and one of the dogs might be the copilot."

Jay looked back to Alan, "Yeah, she is on my butt all the time. I have lost a lot, but God I want a cheeseburger."

"If you are good, we will get you one," Alan said.

"Naw, she would kill me. Besides, it isn't awful to eat well." Jay looked at the truck, "I guess the dogs are with you?"

"Yeah," Alan said, "We are all going to Atlanta."

"Oh," Jay said, "I heard all your fun comments on the machine. You were talking to a machine, you know."

"That's what I am told," Alan replied.

"Well," Jay chuckled a little, "I thought you might want to know. Let's get this thing in the air. This runway is a bit short, but they take bets on whether I can make it every time."

In the cockpit, Jay sat down and began flipping switches. The mighty engines began to spin up and Jay pulled on his headset. "Tower this is GYza55 Heavy, what are the odds on me this time?"

"Even money," the tower replied. "You keep making it."

Jay flipped a switch and the back doors began to close until a light came on confirming their lock.

"I appreciate the confidence," Jay replied, "GYZa55 Heavy requesting permission for takeoff on runway one."

"Gyza55 Heavy, the pattern is clear, good luck," came the reply.

"Guys, strap in. I hate being even odds," Jay replied.

The plane moved around and lined up with runway one as Melody, Alan, Margarite and the dogs got back into the truck.

"Truck strapped down good?" Alan asked.

"Yeah, why?" Melody asked.

"May be a fun ride," Alan said as the plane lurched forward.

In a few moments, the plane began to move into the air and banked hard both right and left. The dogs steadied themselves. The three people held on tight, and soon the plane was well into the air. When the flight started to smooth out, Alan opened the truck and stepped out.

"Wait here, just in case," Alan said as he closed the door.

"You done?" Alan said as he entered the cockpit.

"Yeah, just made it look like we were lurching a bit, will fix my odds," Jay laughed.

"Only you would try to fix your own odds," Alan said. "Listen, we had a bit of an incident at the house. A few men were following Margarite's GPS, and well, they ran into me and the dogs."

"I bet that was fun," Jay laughed.

"It was," Alan said, "You know a cleaner? I left some presents at that house and would hate for the buzzards to get them first."

"Let me get to autopilot altitude and we will make the call," Jay replied, "Might cost a few dollars."

"No issue," Alan said, "I can handle the cash, I just don't do the work as much anymore."

"Maybe you should?" Jay said. "remember when we were in that bar in Morocco? You said you loved helping people that couldn't be helped by others. You have a knack for it. You also drank a whole bottle of Macallan 18-year-old Scotch. I almost cried."

"Maybe," Alan said, "But I enjoy my time with Melody, and I would rather spend the time with her.

"Now you sound like Michael," Jay said.

"Maybe that's not so bad," Alan replied. "I am going to check on the girls."

Alan walked back to the truck strapped into the cargo bay. In the front seat, Melody and Margarite were asleep. As he looked in the back, Shiva and Vishnu were asleep as well. Alan was glad they were getting their rest now. He was worried it might be hard later.

Chapter 9

Michael and Abby were back at the house site, watching as the last of the rubble was cleared. On what was, and would be, the driveway of the house, a large table had been set up and several men were gathered around the table. The plans were relatively straightforward but used a variety of different materials. One of the men looked at the list.

"You really want to use steel beams for all the runs. A central steel beam would do well, and you could save a lot of money using wood beams as the actual supports." the man said.

"Good idea, but I want the floors to all be able to handle excessive weight. I would like to get this back to where it was before. I used outside contractors then. I decided I trusted you all and you should get this work."

David spoke up, "We want to do this to the specs he has. Y'all are kin or friends and I know I can trust you. We need to build this like it was ours."

"None of us could build a house like this," the man said.

"This is Tom," David said, "Tom is my cousin on my moms' side. He is a good guy."

Michael nodded, "If you take care of me, I will take care of you. It's that easy. I want my house back and am willing to pay."

"Hey," a man said, "Name's Phil. We can do this, but it will take a lot to get this type of material here. I don't know where we can get this door you have on the front. It is not like any I have seen."

"I designed it," Michael said, "If it is set right it can hold back a tank. I will give you the supplier who makes them for me. They are in Garrard county."

"If any of you want out, just say it. The rest of us will pull it off or I will do it alone rather than bring someone in from outside," David said.

There was a mumbling for a moment.

"We can do this," David said.

Everyone nodded or said yeah, "We will get it done, Michael."

The men started looking at the plans in more depth. David walked to the side and motioned for Michael and Abby.

"Sorry about that," David said. "Not too trusting, you know."

"I know all about it," Michael said. "How much you need to get started?"

"I don't rightly know," David replied. "This is a big job."

"Which bank do you use?" Michael asked.

"People's on 23." David stated.

"Meet me there at 1:00," Michael said, "I will put enough money in your account to get started and cover payroll for a while. You can submit bills to me. I will walk through them."

"I have a cousin, Sue Ellen," David says, "She says you have done some good around here. Helped out some people who needed help, but I should be scared of you."

"Scared?" Michael asked.

"Well, she says you are a scary-as-hell shot. Before the house was gone, a bunch of guys got killed up here," David said. "She says you scared them to death just by looking at them." David paused, "My other cousin, old man Wallings, says you are a super good guy but to never cross you or I might just disappear."

Abby laughed, and David looked over at her.

"Michael, we haven't known each other for long. You ain't gonna kill me or my kin, are you?" David asked.

"No," Michael said, "I just want to get my house fixed and enjoy my retirement."

"Yer awful young to be retired," David said, "What line of work were you in?"

"I was a retirement specialist," Michael said. "I helped people retire."

"Well, OK," David said, "Old man Wallings trusts you, so I will. Sue Ellen likes to gossip. I believe him over her every day and twice on Sunday."

"Works by me," Michael said. "See you at the bank in a few hours.

"See you then," David went back to the table where men were working over the house plans.

Chapter 10

Milton drove up to a house on the east side of Atlanta. The drive had not been long, but Milton had turned multiple times to avoid potential tracking to tails of any type. The home could have been any home from the suburbs, but it had a black CTS in the driveway. Milton parked and walked around to help Maria out of the car. They walked to the dark brown front door framed by white vinyl and black shutters. White picket fence lined the front lawn and the house was easily 6000 square feet at a glance.

Milton watched the street as he led Maria into the house. Milton knocked and a woman in a dress and apron answered opening the door only a little. Milton could smell cookies from somewhere inside. She saw Milton and opened the door wide. Behind the door were desks and people scattered everywhere working. A young woman walked up to Milton, "Sorry to hear about Suzanne." she said.

Milton looked at Maria, "Bad news travels fast."

A big man walked to Milton. "What the hell is going on, Milton? I don't lose agents."

Milton nodded at the man. "Maria, this is Anton Kolchak. I report to him. He is going to be able to help you."

"How did they find her?" Anton asked, "She was bulletproof."

"We aren't entirely sure, but the youngest seems to have gone rogue and he somehow found her." Milton said. "Then the oldest found the man who originally saved her."

"Ahh crap," Anton sighed, "We are going to end up with CIA in this again, or worse."

"Worse than CIA?" Maria asked, "I thought the CIA was good?"

"They are the good guys, but they walk in shadows like the damn devil. DEA has been worse already, my phone has been ringing off the hook from some new person in charge." Anton replied. "Any lead on the youngest?"

"Not so far. Her phone is off. Waiting on the last known location but you know how those justice people are," Milton replied.

"Justice," Anton growled, "We are the Justice department. Get a judge on the phone and get it done. Miss Juarez, we will find your daughter."

"When is the agent or ex-agent supposed to be here with the oldest?" Anton asked.

"He didn't give a time, just that he would find me. He gave a number, but it is off and shielded right now." Milton said.

"Is she clean now?" Anton asked.

"I believe so," Milton said, "No phones or tracking devices of any kind."

"Have everything scanned, make sure. I don't want this house going the way of the last one you two were in," Anton said. "Then get her in a room upstairs until we hear from this wolf guy."

"Wolf guy?" Milton asked.

"The code name for this guy who saved the girls was Silent Wolf. Sounds like a Saturday morning cartoon. Just make sure we get the girl and then let him disappear again before this gets out of hand further than it already is."

Milton led Maria upstairs. The first room was full of tech gear and two guys who looked like they should be in a nerd movie. "We need a scan," Milton said.

One of the guys took off a set of headphones that had been covering one ear and pulled out a wide wand. He said nothing as he wandered the wand up and down Milton and then looked at the screen to the right of him. "You are clean."

Maria stepped forward and the man began scanning her. After a few seconds he noted, "Left pocket has a tile in it."

Maria pulled out a home key with a small square attached. "Is that good or bad?" Milton asked.

"It requires a person using the tile to be close. It does not do GPS on its own. At least this one doesn't. It won't work in this house; you could have been tracked on the way here," the tech explained.

"What do we need to do?" Milton asked.

"Well, if it is being tracked, you can send it off somewhere to throw people off or crush it," the tech replied.

Milton took the tracker and smashed it under his boot, "That work?"

"Yep," the tech said, "but if someone was tracking it- and it is doubtful- they would know where it was seen last."

"I guess we'll take that chance," Milton said.

As they headed back downstairs, Anton met them with a small woman in a dark brown blazer, jeans and a black cowboy hat.

"A little early for Halloween," Milton said.

Anton rolled his eyes. "Milton, this is Jamie Hurst. She is your temporary new partner."

The woman was petite with long auburn hair pulled into a ponytail. Her outfit was something that could be worn to a western bar, but it was her eyes that stood out. They were a brilliant shade of green. Jamie put out her hand, "Pleased to meet you."

"Anton," Milton said, ignoring her hand, "I just lost a partner and..."

Maria shook Jamie's hand, "Thank you for helping me."

"Exactly, no lip. Jamie is temporary unless you two work out to be a good team. You need somebody to watch your back and she needs experience."

"You give me someone green?" Milton asked.

"Not exactly. She was top in the Navy. Gunner or something. She worked her way through and got good marks for it. You could use someone who will have your back."

"I'm not sure I have time to…" Milton began.

Anton broke in again, holding out an envelope. "Here is an address you can use. Get this woman and her daughter there and then find this other daughter. We promised to set them up in exchange for testimony that Maria here," he nodded at Maria, "gave Justice. We need to hold up our end. I have already talked to the Attorney General and he was pissed we allowed this to happen. He is blaming me," he fumed for a moment, "and well, mostly you. Now we have to fix it."

"Ok. What about the older daughter and this guy coming here?" Milton asked.

Jamie took the envelope that Anton was still holding out and put it in her inner jacket pocket. Milton looked and noticed the outline of a large silver weapon, but he couldn't tell what.

Anton continued, "Now I expect you to get out of here and get to this new safehouse. Start setting up a new identity. All the papers are in there. Get some groceries, make some cookies, but keep this situation a lot less visible." Anton looked down at Milton with wide eyes. "A lot less visible!"

Jamie walked to the door and still had not said a word. Maria followed her.

"Do I have any choices in this?" Milton asked.

"No, not really," Anton replied. "You pretty much need to solve all the stuff that fell down and find a way to make it right."

"If I can't?" Milton asked.

"I am reminded of the movie *Roadhouse*. You know, that one with the skinny guy, Patrick something. I think he said in the movie, 'there's always barber college' or something like that. The point is, don't mess up and it will be fine. Mess up, and well? It won't be so fine." Anton said as another man in a black suit walked up to him. "Now get that car off my pretty city block where we are just a happy family waiting for cookies."

"What is it with the cookies?" Milton asked.

Anton laughed, "They make people smile."

The door closed behind them and they made their way to the car. "We should take this and trade it."

"If we can get your charge to the safehouse, I will swap the car out and return," Jamie said. "That will free you up to get things in place. I can also pick up food for dinner."

"Wow," Milton said, "Full service."

"Look," Jamie said with her green eyes seeming to flare, "I heard you in there. I know you don't want me, and it has been a few hours since you lost your partner. We need to get you both somewhere safe, and get things calmed down. You can whine about me being too small or too cowgirl later, but the job is number one."

"I like her," Maria said to Milton.

"You would," Milton replied.

Jamie walked to the driver's side, "Keys?"

"I drive," Milton said,

"Not today," Jamie replied again. "Anton told me to take care of you. It is what I am going to do."

Milton threw the keys and Jamie plucked them from the air. She got in and moved the seat forward while Milton opened the back door to help Maria in. The engine started as Milton got in the car. Jamie began driving as soon as the door closed.

"Seat belt," Milton laughed.

"You will get it on," Jamie said as she turned out of the street onto a main road.

"Do you know where we are going?" Milton asked.

"Heritage Parkway area. Close to the airport. Close to shopping. A nice little neighborhood that we can get lost in for a while," Jamie replied. "By the way, I read your file. I really didn't want you either. I am trying to learn what it means to be a Marshall, and you have been skating for a while. Sure, you are good at your job, but divorced, no kids, no real life, you don't take pride in anything."

"Wow," Milton replied, "You got all that from a file."

"Called your ex too," Jamie said, "Not for work but did a survey about marriage. She still thinks about you but said you were 'shut down' and not 'engaged' in the relationship. I told her she had a chance to win a free set of knives."

"Just who do you think you are?" Milton asked.

"I am a person who is putting her life in your hands," Jamie stated dryly. "In the service, I know just about everyone has my back, but out here people have hidden agendas and all sorts of baggage. I am not interested in that. I want to do the job and get it done."

"I really like her a lot," Maria said.

Jamie looked back at Maria, "I'm sorry about your daughters. I was reading up on you as well. Your ex sounds like a real piece of work. I am surprised no one has terminated him."

"He is very well connected. At least he was," Maria replied, "He can get anything he wants just by asking."

"How did you two meet? There wasn't much in the file," Jamie asked.

"My mother," Maria recounted. "She gave me to him. She could no longer pay her debt, so I was used as payment for it. He married me almost right away and made me his. I was young at the time. Barely a teenager."

"I read that," Jamie said. "The records in Venezuela are not very good. There is an age problem according to them. You and Margarite are pretty close in age."

Maria bowed her head. "As I said, I was very young when he took me."

"Don't worry, Maria," Jamie stated. "You won't have to worry about him now. We will get your family back together and try to make it a happily-ever-after scenario."

Milton rolled his eyes, "How long have you been doing this?"

"Six months, if it matters," Jamie replied.

"In six months, you can give someone a *happily-ever-after*?"

"Matter of details, sir. We will make sure the details are right and follow up regularly. That will make sure it is good," Jamie replied.

"Got it," Milton said as Jamie pulled on the expressway.

It was quiet for a while. Jamie was concentrating on driving through the series of stop and go, rubber necking traffic jams on the expressway and finally pulled off on a side series of roads and weaved through them with expert efficiency.

Milton was thinking about his ex-wife, wondering if Jamie was right about him.

Maria was worried about Magda. Margarite would be fine, she was made of different stuff, but Magda. Magda was so impressionable.

"Do you think Magda is ok?" Maria asked Milton.

"I think so, yes," Milton replied. "Your ex has gone through far too much trouble to hurt her."

"There are many ways people can be hurt," Maria said.

"Truth," Jamie said as she drove towards the safe house.

Chapter 11

The Happy Scotsman was a flying taxi service for those who could both afford it and knew Jay from his previous line of work or were ex-military. Jay had put the plane together after he left the service because he enjoyed flying. At first there were just a few clients, but they had paid so well and given such good tips that Jay kept refining the plane and his offerings constantly. It wasn't very long before he had bought a few additional planes, but his most enjoyable was the Scotsman and the abilities it offered.

The modifications done to the plane allowed him to service more customers which created a word-of-mouth network that kept him busy and in fuel always. Alan had met Jay while he was in the service. When Jay went freelance and got the Scotsman, it made sense to use him.

"Still got that little plane?" Jay asked.

"Yeah, she runs now but I don't take her up enough," Alan replied.

"You and Melody doing good?" Jay asked.

"Yep," Alan replied.

"You always were a short talker," Jay said. "Do I need to start singing?"

"Do you want to start singing?" Alan asked.

Melody walked up to the cockpit, "What's going on up here?"

Alan reached up and held her hand, "You were asleep, we were just talking."

"No, I was talking, he was giving me those short little answers that make you want to scream." Jay stated. "I was in a bar with a guy like him once. A great Malt Bar in Wisconsin, and I was talking to this guy about Airplanes and he might as well have been saying 'yes they go up and down'. Of course, the guy had about 10 drinks too many, but I was trying to talk, and he was just lumbering along in the conversation. Yeah, that's it. You lumber Alan," Jay laughed, "I bet I could have a better conversation with your dogs than I can have with you sometimes. At minimum I could giggle as they cocked their heads back and forth." Jay looked back from the wheel, "What do you see in him, does he talk to you?"

"He is sweet, and he is always talking," Melody said, "I have had some of the best conversations of my life with him when we were driving around in his car. I guess you have to get to know him."

Alan reached up as Melody knelt a little. He kissed her.

"Maybe that's it," Jay said. "If I kiss you will you talk to me more?"

Alan laughed. "Maybe."

Jay was serious again. "We have about another hour or so to go before we get to Atlanta. How long do you want me to hang around once we get there?"

"Not sure," Alan said. "I have enough on account with you for a few weeks, right?"

"I really don't care about the money with you," Jay said. "I am just trying to decide if Janet should fly down here or if I will get to head home soon."

"I can let you know tonight," Alan replied.

"That will work," Jay said. "There is a Taphouse in the airport I can hang out in for a little bit. Tell a few stories. Laugh a little. I can work on a few upgrades on the plane too."

"Maybe this is all a red herring," Alan said, "Maybe Magda will show up and we will head home with the dogs tonight."

"Yeah, sure," Jay said, "By the way, I had the cleaner put the cleanup of your house on my tab. I will let you know when I get the bill."

Alan laughed a little. "You're right. It would be a little too much to ask for this to be a red herring."

Melody snapped her finger on Alan's head. "You think?"

Alan looked up at her. "Wishful thinking you know."

"Meanwhile here in the real world we had a stack of bodies removed from the house and have a scared little girl with us, thinking she will lose her mother and her sister," Melody stated.

"Yeah," Alan replied. "I guess Michael doesn't get all the fun."

"This is fun?" Melody asked. "Fun was what we were having before."

"Are the dogs ok?" Alan asked. "I should give them some water." Alan stood. Melody grabbed him by the neck and kissed him. He put his arms around her and pulled her close.

"Sorry about all this," he whispered to her.

"It is fine, we will solve it," Melody replied. "I knew your life was unique when I started hanging out with you."

"Hanging out?" Alan asked.

"Yep," Melody replied. "Until you put a ring on it, we are hanging out."

"Got it," Alan said. "Be right back."

"Are you getting a ring from back there?" Melody called after him.

Alan looked back and smiled, then went to the truck.

The plane sped on towards Atlanta.

Chapter 12

Alex and Jim were walking towards his office on the campus of the Bluegrass Army Depot when they heard his phone ringing. After five rings, Alex said, "Voicemail time." Jim laughed as they continued their paced walk forward. Seconds later, the phone began ringing again. Both men look at each other and picked up the pace. Alex fumbled with the lock on his screen and got it open, slapping the speakerphone button on the Cisco phone.

"Brown," he said.

"It should be, because that's the dimwit I called," the voice replied.

The voice belonged to General Samuel Tarkington. His group took care of issues no one wanted to talk about and had no official classification. Alex reported directly to the general and took care of older problems that resurfaced. Many of these "problems" were directly related to a time period when Tarkington had a series of assassins working for him dealing with worldwide espionage, and worse. Even though it was not a prescribed practice to hire assassins to deal with "problems", sometimes it was necessary. Tarkington was a "get the job done" type of guy. His involvement in multiple high-profile issues was never advertised but administrations knew who was behind many critical resolutions and made sure he had enough freedom to deal with the issues in the way they needed to be dealt with.

Only once recently had Tarkington gone too far. His language was always colorful and edgy, but after confronting the president with a series of expletives that could make sailors dive from their ships, the president had given Tarkington an ultimatum, clean up his language or clean his desk. The result had been quite entertaining for everyone who was used to Tarkington's salty ways.

"Yes, sir. What can I do for you?" Alex asked.

"Have you gone through all those files I gave you to review?" Tarkington was always direct and to the point.

"Yes, sir." Alex stated. "I am trying to determine which will be higher priority and start working them."

"Look back through them for a Maria Juarez," Tarkington said. "Witness protection and the Marshalls have been attacked. A real well? A real firestorm has hit the fan so to speak. We are on the fringe of this, but my expectation is as Alan Spears gets involved, we may end up a focal point."

"Dog guy's last name is 'Spears'? I think I may giggle myself to death looking for the point," Jim laughed.

"You didn't tell me you had a clown in the room," Tarkington said.

"Sorry, sir," Alex said. "Jim and I ran to the room and I hit speaker."

"I need you to get in touch with Anton Kolchak with Justice to determine if any of the issues we had not tied up in our files are coming back to haunt us. Then I need you to determine if we need to get involved for any creative solutions to the problem." Tarkington said.

"Do you have any history outside of the files on this one, sir?" Alex asked.

"None at all," Tarkington stated. "Spears was contracted outside of us. He and Jay McCloud took care of the operation. This was in a period when he was not so positive about the government as a whole. All we know is he was able to get in and extract the two young girls from a secure facility in Venezuela. In the process he may have ruffled a few feathers, but human casualties were limited or covered up."

"Understood," Alex said. "We will start with Kolchak and see where it goes."

"One other thing," Tarkington said, "I keep tabs on McCloud, and he visited Dubois today. My sources say Masterson is somewhere in Kentucky. Spears and McCloud may already be involved."

"Ya know," Jim injected, "Dubois is an awfully small town for all the action it gets."

"Review the file, determine if we need to consider a course of action, and solve this if necessary. It may be nothing, but an agent has died, and the Justice department will be out for justice," Tarkington noted.

"So how in depth do you want us?" Alex asked.

"How many things have you done as leader of this team so far?" Tarkington asked.

"A dozen or so different items," Alex replied.

"Exactly," Tarkington injected, "Figure it out. If you can't, use the goofball next to you and figure it out together. Make it work. Use whatever you need to use but I am telling you to figure it out."

"Goofball, I like that," Jim said.

"You know exactly the words I would like to use right now," Tarkington quipped, "so don't get too lost in liking it."

"I love you, too," Jim replied.

"Brown, make this happen. Close it up. At least this one won't involve Masterson," Tarkington barked before the line went dead.

"He makes me feel so warm and fuzzy inside," Jim laughed.

"Yeah, right," Alex countered, reaching into his desk to rifle through several files. "Get this copied, we will meet on it with everyone in an hour."

Jim opened the file and looked it over. "Not much here. Seems like this is a Justice issue, why involve us?"

"Not sure," Alex replied. "When I read it over there was a lot of redacted information I had to request. The redactions didn't offer any real clarification. In fact, I am not sure why it was redacted except for names and dates. It's not like we don't know the players. It's not like we haven't been involved with the ones we know."

"Look at this," Jim said. "The DEA was poking around here and lost four people. Looks like the four tried to get to a warehouse and disappeared. There is no definitive outcome."

"If I remember right you will see a lot of those in that report," Alex stated.

"I will make the copies and let the team know," Jim said as he stood.

"Jim," Alex said as Jim began to turn away, "You know I could get you released from this duty. Tarkington ordered you back in when we were after Masterson in Kentucky. I could get you removed now, and you could go back to your retired life. Fast cars, fast women, and no more Tarkington."

Jim turned, looked at Alex and sat back down. "Is that what you want? Me gone so Tarkington doesn't get too riled when I poke him?"

"No," Alex lowered his head, "I want this team to always work, but who am I to decide your fate?" Alex looked back up, "We have been friends for a long time. To me that means something."

"Yeah," Jim replied, "It means something to me too. When I was joined to this team, I was not happy. Somewhere along the way I found a family here. Rachel is hard core, but she needed me to put her in her place. Ronnie is so naïve it scares the hell out of me, and he needs me to help him grow up. Barbara needs someone to keep her from turning Ronnie into a raging hormone machine. Terry needs me to someday make him laugh. You need me to keep Tarkington from driving us all insane and to be your voice of reason." Jim paused, looked at the door, "Lisa needed me to love her, and then to avenge her. Family means more than blood. It means something deeper. And I have it here, so this is where I belong until I'm dead or you find someone better."

"Really, you were doing so good, then 'Starship Troopers'?" Alex mumbled.

"Well, I didn't want to be too serious. After all, I am the clown of the bunch too," Jim began. "I will get these copied," Jim said as he stood, "then we will meet and decide if we want to go kick some ass or go get a coffee."

"I vote the coffee," Alex laughed.

Jim turned to leave again.

"Jim," Alex called after him.

Jim turned again, "Yeah?"

"Thanks."

"Sure," Jim replied as he left the room.

Chapter 13

Michael and Abby arrived at the worksite and the men were already there. The men were throwing knives at cards on a tree that had fallen in the explosion the year before. Michael got out of the DB9 and walked over to the small group. He watched the different knives fly across the room and embedded themselves in either wood or the cards.

"What's the game?" Michael asked as Abby joined his side.

"Blackjack," one man said. "Hit 21 without going over."

Michael noted the cards were from a small deck, maybe an older Ryder mini deck. "Who's winning?"

"Tom has 20," another man said as he pointed to the man who was obviously Tom. "He usually wins. You have to be really lucky to get 21."

Michael looked at the tree, the aces were all on smaller branches. The size of the sticks holding them were small, and there wasn't a clear picture of the backing. The face cards, 10s, and all the other cards where on the trunk of the tree. "How many knives?"

"Two," Tom said.

"What do you win?" Michael asked.

"Respect," all the men said at once.

Abby smiled and winced as Michael pulled the two Kunai throwing knives from his belt. He spun them on his finger by the rings on the end of the knives. Each of his hands seemed to have a slow-moving propeller on it until Michael threw them in rapid succession. The first knife pierced the center of the King of Spades, and the second knife fell just off dead center on the Ace of Spades that hung at the tip of the 4 aces.

All six men who had been working walked to the tree. The knife through the King was perfectly placed. They looked to the Ace of Spades and saw the knife was dead center in the middle of the one-inch stick holding the Ace, just to the side of dead center.

The solid black Kunai knives hung in the tree as Michael walked up and pulled them from the cards.

Tom, who was usually the winner, held out his hand. Michael shook it. "I can respect that," he smiled. All of the men gathered their knives and walked to the worksite.

David was starting up the bulldozer to finish clearing the site and the group of six additional men busied themselves clearing small rubble and assorted brush from the area. A deep foundation was evident and had been poured towards the base of the hill in the hollow.

Michael and Abby helped to clear rubble and soon the door in the side of the mountain was clearly visible. The small group of men that David had assembled worked hard and fast. They were far better workers than most Michael had seen. Michael was far more used to the men and women who ignored work ethics and instead did as little as possible to just get by. Michael had recognized a long time ago that most of the men and women of Appalachia were driven with an intensity many would never know. It seemed they had a need to prove themselves, not once, but constantly. It was one of many reasons that Michael built his first house in Appalachia. He felt that if he could be accepted that he could protect them, and they would protect him.

A beam protruded from the top of the door. It was only a piece, but it was clear that a support beam had been attached there once.

"David," Michael called out as the men gathered around. "This is the main beam support. The beam behind it is driven 15 feet into the mountain. It is hardened steel and held its shape even in the explosion. This is the center beam point to lock into and build from."

"You guys seeing this?"

They all looked and examined the beam a few feet higher than they were.

"What's in the room?" one of the men asked.

"Shh," Tom chastised.

"No," Michael said. "Fair question. It is a vault. Right now it has a limited number of weapons in it. I left them here because I knew no one could get in."

"Why you telling us that mister?" another man asked. "I hear you are someone weez should be scared of."

"I am trusting you," Michael stopped. "I am trusting you so you will trust me to not be the monster the rumors say I am."

The men looked at each other. "How we going to get the beams down here?"

"David here is the proud owner of a Link Belt Crane that will be delivered tomorrow. The prefabricated beams will be here as well along with the welding and power equipment to begin building the frame of the house," Michael said. "After we are done, maybe you can build for other people, the way I know you will build for me."

David took off his American flag hat for only a moment. Putting it back on, he walked to Michael and shook his hand. "Yeah," he said. "We'll do this."

Chapter 14

The Happy Scotsman landed in Atlanta's Hartsfield Jackson Airport and was directed to a large hangar alone on the edge of a field. Jay had arranged for the hangar when he knew their destination, knowing it would allow him to not be as conspicuous as he usually was at airports. The Happy Scotsman, with its overly impressive Scotsman in kilt painted on the side, was a media magnet and drew questions almost everywhere. In this case, Jay had taken the better part of being less obnoxious, and instead, deciding to hide.

"Airport exit is to the west," Jay said. "I will stay on station until I hear from you."

Melody hugged Jay and then Margarite shook his hand. "I will see you guys again," Jay said. "I am gonna pull out the bed and sleep for a while."

"I will be in touch, Jay," Alan said. "It shouldn't be long."

The three got in the truck along with the dogs. The dogs looked out at Jay through the window.

"Stop looking at me like that," Jay said. "I am not a tasty meal."

Both dogs licked their lips and then started panting, making it look as though they were smiling.

Jay laughed. "Stupid animals."

The gate fell backwards on the Happy Scotsman. The big F350 backed out of the plane. Once on the tarmac, the truck drove to the exit and left the airport through the gate.

Jay closed the tail of the plane and headed to the beds near the cockpit.

Alan and Melody watched the road as they worked onto the back streets of the airport. Alan took the phone out of the envelope and dialed the number Milton had given him.

"We are in Atlanta," Alan said as the phone answered on the other side.

"We need to meet up," Milton said.

"Where?" Alan asked.

"755," Milton said. "A little restaurant."

"I'll find it, when?"

"One hour," Milton replied.

"Good. One hour at 755," Alan repeated before he hung up.

"Where are we going?" Melody asked.

"A little restaurant called 755," Alan said.

"Want me to look it up?" Melody asked.

"No, I know where it is," Alan said as he smiled at Melody. "It actually isn't that far. A lot of industrial in the area. We will want to keep our eyes open. This could be a trap, but I doubt it."

"Do you think my mom will be with them?" Margarite said.

"She may be," Alan said, "but I want you to sit in back between the dogs when we get there. I don't want anything to happen to you."

"But if my mom," Margarite started.

"Let us check it out first," Alan said in a stern voice.

"It will be ok," Melody assured Margarite. "It won't take long. If they have your mom with them, we will get her and move on. If it is the Marshalls, maybe you will get a new house."

"And Magda?" Margarite asked.

"We will figure that out after we know what's going on," Alan said. "Please?" Alan asked softly.

"OK," Margarite sighed.

"Good," Alan said. "Now we have to stop over here in the field for a second."

"Why?" Margarite asked.

"In case the dogs have to well, you know," Alan replied.

Melody and Margarite laughed. "Potty?" they giggled.

Chapter 15

"I don't like it," Jamie stated. "We should get backup. A sniper or two, maybe SWAT. This is not a good idea."

"Maybe," Milton agreed, checking his weapon. "But maybe this will be a positive move for us. We will have two of the three back together. We can work to find the third more effectively if we get them under control."

"I don't like it," Jamie said as she pulled her ponytail apart, tightening it.

"If it looks like there are any issues, we will just leave," Milton noted. "It is a busy place, busy area. Too many people for anything really out of line to happen."

"Depends on what you consider as *out of line*," Jamie replied.

"Will Margarite be there?" Maria asked.

"Yes," Milton replied, "At least as far as we have been told."

"Then I want to go," Maria said.

"Absolutely not," Milton replied.

"Out of the question," Jamie stated.

"I am going," Maria said. "Call your supervisor, but I need to see Margarite."

"I am not up to the fight right now, but you have to do as I say," Milton nodded to Maria.

"I will listen, I just need to see my daughter," Maria was adamant.

"We will take you," he stopped, looked at Jamie, "we will take her."

"We'll play it your way, Milton, but I am not happy about it," Jamie said as she checked her weapon again.

The three had settled into the suburban home. The car was in the garage waiting for them, still ticking from cooling down from the drive around the city. As they entered the garage, Milton hit the garage door button and waited while the insulated two car garage door rumbled to the up position, seeming to buck and jump along the way. He looked out of the home, cautious from his last day.

Jamie had gotten into the driver's seat. With one last look, Milton got in the passenger side while Maria slid in behind them.

"Seatbelts," Jamie said.

"Yes, mother," Milton chortled as he put his belt on.

Jamie started the car and backed out of the garage. Milton picked up the remote on the dash and pressed it. The door closed as fitfully as when it had opened.

They drove down the street and out the small circular road area of the small subdivision.

"If this goes well, we may go back to the house," Milton stated. "It will be safer."

"You know, Anton would have given you time off after Suzanne," Jamie said. "There is no shame in admitting you are emotionally compromised."

"I am?" Milton asked. "I am happy to know that now."

"I know you have lost partners before and been shot four times but that does not mean it does not hurt," Jamie said.

"You've been shot four times?" Maria asked.

"Well, technically, we were blown up today, Maria, so completely different," Milton laughed.

"It's not a joking matter," Jamie said. "There are far more suicides with servicemen and public service professionals. We are public service professionals."

"It's not far down the next street," Milton said as he ignored the statement.

"I know. It is on a side street though," Jamie replied as she turned down the next street.

Milton pulled his weapon, looking at the chambered round again.

"If you are nervous, I can leave you here and walk in to determine the situation," Jamie stated.

"I am not nervous," Milton said.

"It is ok to be nervous," Jamie said.

"Do you have an off button?" Milton asked.

"No, sir," Jamie replied. "I offer suggestions all the time. We have arrived. There seems to be no one here."

"Back in so we can move fast if we need to," Milton said.

"We really should have called for backup," Jamie said.

A rather large F350 truck pulled in the lot. They could hear the sound of the diesel engine as the truck backed up a few dozen feet from them at a different angle. The truck was jet black and could have been driven off the showroom floor the way it sparkled.

"Maria, stay in the car until we get things figured out," Milton stated.

"Ready?" Milton asked Jamie. "Keep cover on me. I will meet this guy."

"OK," Jamie said, "We can still call for backup."

"It will be fine," Milton said as he opened his door and stood behind it.

Jamie opened her door and stood behind it, drawing her weapon and putting it on the door handle. Through the slot, the door acted as a holster. She could pull the weapon quickly but show both hands.

From the truck, they saw a woman open her door and stand behind it while still perched on the running board. This allowed her to be hidden and off the ground. When the driver door opened, a huge man stepped out and looked over at Milton and Jamie.

"How are we going to do this?" Milton asked.

"ID would be good," Alan stated.

"Meet in the middle?" Milton asked.

Alan walked over between the two vehicles. It seemed a little silly as it was only 30 feet or so, but Milton walked over as well.

"You know I can put you under arrest," Milton said, "so don't try anything."

Alan smiled. It was a broad knowing smile. "I doubt you want to do that. You don't know who you are dealing with and you need to know more. I know a little about you, but I need to know more. I know nothing about your partner. I do know Maria. You should ask her if she remembers me so we can get on with this and start looking for Magda."

"Show me the girl," Milton demanded.

"Show me your ID," Alan stated.

Milton was watching this man whose arms tensed slightly, looking as though they could snap him in half. He reached for his wallet and the girl on the truck tensed. Looking back, he could see that Jamie was also tense.

"Someone is going to get hurt if we can't get past this," Alan said. "I am going to grab my ID. We will show them to each other."

"OK," Milton said and pulled out his wallet and showed his ID. Alan did the same. It was a service ID, but Milton had never seen one like this.

"Now," Alan walked back, "follow me and I will show you the girl."

"OK," Milton said as he walked a few steps with Alan pacing him until they reached the back doors of the massive truck. Alan opened the doors and Milton looked inside. Margarite was there between two exceptionally large black German Shepherds. "Are you ok?" Milton asked.

"I'm fine," Margarite said, "Is my mom with you?"

"Yes, honey," Milton said looking at Alan, "Let's go see her together."

Margarite slid towards the door. The dog on that side of her jumped out to the ground. As Margarite got out, the second dog jumped out next to her. Milton began to walk towards Margarite and one of the dogs curled its lip.

"Let's just all walk over together," Alan said.

Milton considered the two dogs for a moment and didn't move.

"If you draw this will be bad," Alan said. "I am one of the good guys. If you are as well, Maria will be in the car and we can move on."

Milton walked back to their car, opening the back door. Maria stepped out and Margarite ran to her with two black guardians by her side. Alan clapped and the dogs ran back to him and stood by his side. The two women hugged, and Maria was crying. "I thought they would get you."

"Do you remember Alan?" Margarite asked.

"Of course," Maria replied. "He rescued you both for me ten years ago."

Jamie and Milton began to breathe a little easier. Milton turned to Alan. "Alan, huh? You could have said that on the phone."

"I have a stack of bodies, or did have a stack of bodies, at my house that wanted to kill this little girl," Alan said. "I think my caution is deserved."

"My ears are still ringing from the house they blew up around us, so mine is too," Milton said.

Alan reached down and rubbed Shiva on the ears. He motioned to Melody who made her way over to them as well. "I'm Alan, Alan Spears. This is Melody. Margarite came to us looking for Magda and help."

"Why you?" Milton asked as Jamie walked to them.

"I saved the two girls when they were 5 and 10 about ten years ago. She had said I was the only one that had ever defied her father and had not died. She explained that she feels that Magda has been in touch with her father. At about that time, all hell broke loose, and I had to pay a big cleaning bill to get rid of bodies." Alan watched the two women talk to the side of them and looked down at the dogs, made a gesture and the dogs walked over and sat next to the girls, watching everywhere.

"I think we should go back to the house," Milton said, "Try to figure this out."

"Good idea," Alan said, "I'll follow you. No disrespect but the girl rides with us."

"None taken," Milton said.

"Margarite," Alan called out, "Come ride with us over to the house."

"OK," Margarite hugged her mom and ran to the truck. The dogs following on her heels.

The drive was very uneventful. This time, Milton drove. "What did you think? You were awfully quiet."

"Seems innocent. The girl is fine. We will have to see how this goes. You know you may be compromising this safe house? Right?" Jamie asked.

"This will be worth it if we can get ahead of losing Magda," Milton replied. "Think about it. This man has firsthand knowledge of the girls and of their father."

Maria started in with a force that she normally did not use, "He is a good man. He saved my daughters from the monster that stole them from me. He was humble and asked for nothing. And his love of animals shows what type of man he is to people."

Jamie sighed. "I really can't argue about that. Those dogs watched us and him every instant. I am sure they would do anything for him, and it sure looks like he would do anything for them. Normally, that would do it for me."

Milton nodded. "I am amazed by the control of the two of them. I will be interested to get their stories."

"Me as well," Jamie replied. "We have a little to do, but as I think about the animals perhaps it will be a good move on our part to engage." Jamie paused, then spoke again. "Did you call in and follow up about Magda? Do we have any idea about the phone last location?"

"No," Milton said, "Why don't you call in. We have maybe two minutes until we are at the house. Maybe they have an update."

Jamie pulled out her phone to call Anton.

Glancing in the mirror, Milton asked Maria, "Do you know anything else about this man?"

Maria sighed. "We went to the state department, your people, and they would not get involved. We asked many people and I asked dozens of people, and we got nothing. We even talked to mercenaries, and they laughed at us. They knew my husband and told me anyone who took the job would die. We ended up talking to this man in a government agency that had no name. The man had a strange name that I do not remember. He recommended this man, Alan, who came to see us and talked to me about my daughters. At first, he was not wanting to get them, but as I cried and begged, he looked over things with my caseworker, then he said he would do it. He took clothing and I remember his dogs were not black, but black and tan."

"Do you know if he worked for the agency?" Milton asked.

"No," Maria said, "I do not think he did. The agency man spoke of him as," she paused, looking for a word, "freelance or free agent. He also spoke of a second team that would take care of my husband and bring him to justice."

"Do you know who that was?"

"No," Maria said. "I never found out. They sent some people in who did not return. After that, since I had my girls, they left my husband alone. We ended up in witness protection after Alan brought the girls back and I got no more information on him. Now I feel I should have paid more attention. Alan brought my girls back. He is a good man."

"Assuming you were told about everything, you think they were going to try to bring your husband back on US soil?" Milton asked.

"The goal was to make certain he was prosecuted for all of the things he had done. The drugs and human trafficking were part, but there were many murders that were uncovered during the investigation," Maria stated. "My husband was a bad man. He took me very young. After he took me, I had a child," Maria bowed her head. "I am told I was not the first nor the only one he took."

"I am sorry I asked so many questions, Maria," Milton said. "I was not your Marshall when all of this started."

"There was talk about killing my husband for some time," Maria continued. "The man from the agency said that he had a person that could," she searched for a word again, "eliminate the problem. But your people from the DEA said they wanted him alive, and the Marshall who helped me wanted to capture him. He went with the team to get him and was never seen again."

"I have never heard that," Milton said, "I will have to look into it."

Milton drove into the neighborhood and to the garage of the new placement house. He pressed the garage door button and waited as it rolled up."

Milton pulled into the garage and turned off the car. The three got out and waited as the big F350 pulled into the driveway. Jamie was still on the phone, listening. After a few minutes, she walked to the back of the garage and began talking.

The F350 turned off and the two dogs jumped out first. They ran both directions and the door closed for a moment. When the dogs returned, Alan, Margarite, and Melody got out of the truck and walked in the garage. Panting dogs followed them in.

"What was that all about?" Milton asked.

"What?" Alan asked.

"The dogs?"

"Oh," Alan replied. "They checked ten houses in both directions for anyone who could be out of the ordinary."

"How would they know what is out of the ordinary?" Milton asked, a questioning tone in his voice.

"They wouldn't," Alan said. "They would identify potential issues and come back to alert me. People who are potentially trouble are different than those who are not. They can't talk or judge people, but they can inform me if people are close more accurately that any surveillance."

"How long does it take to teach that?" Milton asked.

"A while," Alan admitted. "Takes patience and the ability to help the dogs understand what you want from them. Dogs just want to please the owner. They are like young children that want to be happy and want their owner to be happy. I just give them guidance. They see no right or wrong with anything unless you instill it."

"Are you some kind of dog whisperer?" Milton asked.

Maria and Margarite were petting the big dogs, rubbing their ears. The dogs enjoyed the attention.

"Something like that," Alan said.

"I have news," Jamie said as she put away her phone. "The phone in question was used in Atlanta in the proximity of the airport," the group all looked on, "then 7 hours later in Venezuela. Shortly after it was turned on, the phone was not online anymore. This could mean the battery was removed, it was shielded, or it was destroyed."

Maria started crying, "No, not my baby."

Margarite put her arm around Maria, "Don't worry," she said. "I will go get her."

"Out of the question," Milton jumped in.

Melody said a simple word, "Stop."

All of them looked at her. Margarite and Maria in tears, but everyone else was not used to hearing her speak. Alan smiled.

"Let's go inside so we can discuss this please," Melody said. "Outside is not the best choice."

Alan smiled again. "Good idea, we need to decide who and how this is going to be handled."

Melody ushered the group inside the door. The dogs waited until last. Alan waited. As she pressed the garage door making it close, Alan stepped out and kissed her on the forehead. "I love you," he said, and they walked into the house together.

Chapter 16

Alex's cell phone rang just as the group was sitting down to discuss the file. Jim, Rachel, Ronnie and Alex sat around a table. Barbara and Terry were on the way and would be on site within minutes. The time was spent talking about various items not related to any file.

"This is Alex. Alan? Do you have a last name?" Alex asked the operator on the phone.

Jim laughed, pointing to the file. Alex rolled his eyes and covered his phone. "That would be a big coincidence."

"Which is about what we always seem to run into, right?" Jim replied.

The operator came back on the cell phone, Alex nodded then looked at Jim. "She said, 'he said we hung out in Michigan'."

"Told you," Jim laughed.

"Put him through," Alex said. He set the phone on the table and pressed speaker.

"Alan?" Alex said.

"Yes, Alex. Is this line secure?" Alan replied.

"They said it was when they transferred you to me," Alex said. "You are on speaker. I am in a meeting that may be pertinent to you."

"I am about to be in one of my own," Alan said. "You know I don't ask for much, and my dealings with Tarkington are more superficial than Michael's. Still, I was aware of most of the dealings between them and some of the other interests that Tarkington took."

"We are aware of that," Alex replied, "and Tarkington has never said anything really negative about you. What is it you need Alan?"

"There was a target I worked as a favor to Justice and Tarkington brought me in years ago. I am not sure if there is even a file on your side. It dealt with retrieving two young girls from Venezuela and getting them home. After I succeeded there was a possibility of a second operation. Can you see what you can find for me on that? Ask the old man, he should allow me access. I also need to know current intel on the people in that file. Specifically, a Carlos Juarez." Alan stated.

Jim laughed under his breath and Alex shook his head, "Funny you should call," Alex said. "We have the file on the desk in front of us and were about to review it."

"Really?" Alan replied. "What brought it to you."

"Apparently, there has been some trouble in Justice. Tarkington called and asked us to review the situation," Alex replied as he leaned on his hand. "This is quite a coincidence."

"Umm, that's for sure," Alan said. "What have you found?"

"Nothing yet," Jim said, "Hi, Alan. We were about to meet. Where are you, how did this get to you?"

The line was silent for a moment.

"I have several people here too, including Melody," Alan said, "Can I put you on speaker here and we discuss this for a moment?"

"Yes," Alex said.

There was a brief pause and a sound that indicated a sliding cell phone or other outside noise. "On our side I have Melody, Milton Grimes, Jamie Hurst, and Maria and Margarite Juarez."

"The dogs aren't there?" Rachel asked in a joking tone.

"Of course, they are," Alan replied, "but I will translate for them."

Rachel laughed but Alan glared a little.

"On our side, you have Jim, Ronnie, Rachel and me but Barbara and Terry will be joining at any minute. We can go forward without them," Alex said.

"Well," Alan stated in a somber tone like an overworked mortician, "We just got word that the second daughter is almost certainly back in Venezuela. We think Carlos manipulated her into coming back, but it is hard to be certain."

"I want my baby back," Maria wept.

Melody took control of the call for a moment, "We know the girl is probably south. We have Maria and Margarite, the other daughter, and Justice has some artifacts that suggest an ongoing collusion. I have not reviewed those yet. There have been a lot of attacks so far, including bodies in Atlanta and in Dubois."

"Someone attacked you?" Jim asked. "How did the dogs take it."

"Someone tracked the girl using her cell phone. We were not a target; in fact, we were an unknown. It was obvious they were not prepared for us. There were three attackers who were heavily armed. One divulged they were there only for the girl. He expired as well," Melody said.

"I miss you," Rachel said. "Mel, you make death sound like a symphony."

Melody continued, "We tried to question one of the men. We don't think they called in location on us nor do we think there were more in the area."

"How do you know?" Alex asked.

"The dogs swept the area," Alan said. "They came back with nothing."

"Sniper?" Alex asked.

"Doubtful," Alan replied, "We would have been dead."

Melody cleared her throat, "We arranged transport and brought Margarite to Atlanta. We are trying to determine next steps. We believe Magda is in Venezuela, and we believe that she is being used as a gateway to Maria and Margarite. Mostly, Maria though for revenge."

"This is all true," Maria said, "but there is also another possibility or at least an additional one." Maria paused and tears formed in her eyes.

"My poor daughter." She wiped her eyes a little. "My mother was Alexis Alexandra Juarez. She was married to Carlos as well. When she stood up to him and tried to leave, it is true she was killed, but Carlos then took me as his wife."

"How old were you?" Melody asked.

"I was 12 years old at the time Carlos took me. I was pregnant and had a child a year later at 13 years old. From that time on, I attempted to protect my two girls and ensure they were safe from the monster who killed my mother. When I left with the girls, he found us and, because I was so well protected, found a way to take the girls. I knew if I did not save my precious Margarite and Magda that they would have suffered my fate. I was a slave to Carlos and did his bidding until the day I took the girls and left." Maria whimpered some, overcome with emotion. "When this man saved my girls, I had new hope and did not expect to have another problem. Now that he has Magda," she paused again, "I know what is in store for her."

There was silence on the phones for a moment.

"That's just sick. Call Tarkington, let's go down and kick this guy's ass," Rachel said.

"Not that easy," Alex said.

"The hell it isn't," Rachel said. "We cover that man's ass; it is time he gives us the ability to take care of this guy and save that little girl."

"Relations with Venezuela are tough right now," Alex said, "We will have to go in and try diplomatic measures first. Inflation is out of control and people are in chaos. We also don't know what we would be walking into and at least one team was lost trying to get to them."

Jim was reading the file. "Maria," he began, "I am reading this file and I have your birth certificate, as well as Magda's and Margarites. Something does not add up. If you were 13 when you had your first child and these dates are right well…"

Alex looked at Jim, "Yes, what?"

"Open your file," Jim said, "There is no way Margarite is Maria's daughter."

"What?" Margarite said.

Maria started speaking in Spanish rapidly. Margarite replied in tears, yelling.

"What is going on?" Alan said.

It was Maria who spoke, "Yes. It is true. Margarite is not my daughter. When my mother was killed, I was 12 years old. When I was 13, I had a daughter and five years later Alan rescued my girls from Carlos. Margarite is as much a daughter to me as Magda, but Margarite is actually my sister. I knew if I did not save her as my daughter and Magda as my daughter that the Justice department might leave Margarite behind. I have kept my silence to keep her safe as I knew at ten years old Carlos would have made her his wife."

Jim closed his file. He looked at Alex, then at Rachel and Ronnie. "Alex, I agree with Rachel. I say we go take care of this in person. This type of scum needs a special ass whoopin'."

Rachel nodded. "Damn straight."

Chapter 17

Magda woke in a lavish bedroom. She looked around the room. The canopy bed was done in white silk. The dresser and the entire room were clean, white, and decorated in white.

Magda remembered arriving at the airport and walking through the terminal until she saw a man holding a sign that simply said "Magda". She had gone to the nicely dressed man in the black suit with the clean black hat. She remembered walking to the big limousine and asking where her father was and why he wasn't there. The man had reassured her and told her he was taking her home. Getting into the back seat, she thought she smelled something sweet. Then there was nothing.

She reached to her side for her cell phone and it was not there.

Magda took the covers off of her and saw she was dressed in a white satin skirt with a flowing satin top. She remembered her mother wearing a dress like this a long time ago. Then the memory was gone. She realized she had no bra nor panties on, and her nail polish had been removed. For the first time since she began talking to her father, she was afraid. She stood and felt a little dizzy. The sweet smell was still there, but it was not overpowering. Magda looked for her bag in the room, opened the closet. There were clothes, all new and still with tags, but nothing that was hers was anywhere to be found. She searched the drawers of the dresser and divan, and there was nothing there. In one drawer, a collection of perfumes but none of hers. It was as though Magda had been teleported to a new dimension, and she was no longer a part of her old world.

She walked to the door and opened it to a long hallway. She remembered playing here when she was a child and looked up and down the hallway. She remembered laughing with her mother and sister running down the hall. She walked down the hallway a little and saw a chair, an antique chair sitting in the corner. She remembered her mother crying in that chair. Why was her mother crying? She strained and could not remember.

Magda heard footsteps in the hallway and a man turned the corner. He was not a big man, nor was he small. At 5'10 he was considered normal for the country he called home. He was dressed in white pants and wore brown sandals. A white cotton shirt was draped over him and was mostly open in the front. His dark hair was now greying, and a few wrinkles had found their way to his face, but he was otherwise the same as Magda remembered tucking her in the day they left.

"Hello, father," Magda said.

The man smiled, "Magda, Mi Amor." Carlos Juarez walked to Magda and hugged her. The hug was firm and powerful, and he did not let go easily.

"We have so much to do, so many things to talk about, so many things. How are you feeling? Are you hungry? I can have the cooks make you something," Carlos said.

"Where are my clothes?" Magda asked.

"Those clothes were old and worn, the pants were not fit for my lovely woman with holes in them. They have been discarded," Carlos said.

"You threw away my clothes?" Magda fumed.

"Yes, yes," Carlos replied, "it is time now for a new life. Time now for you to take your rightful place as the Madre de la Casa"

"Dad," Magda was irritated, "where is my cell phone, my things. What have you done with my stuff?"

"It is in the past," Carlos was sickeningly sweet. He reached out and played with Magda's long hair, "We did not want our enemies tracking you. It is no more. My men have deleted your social media and eliminated your phone. You are free, mi amor. You are free to begin a new life here at this house with me."

"I wanted to see you," Magda said, "I did not come down here to stay. I have a life. I have a sister. I have friends."

"You will make new friends here," Carlos said, "and perhaps Margarite will join us. I have sent my men to bring her here as well."

"What?" Magda said, "No, she can't know I am here. She hates you."

"She will grow to love me as her mother did, as her sister did, as you will," Carlos replied.

"What are you talking about?" Magda said.

"Once we had her cell phone number, we tracked Margarite with no difficulty. My men were sent to bring her home," Carlos replied.

"What about my mother?" Magda asked.

"She is of no consequence," Carlos said. "She crossed me and no one alive can cross me and live."

"What have you done?" Magda panted.

"I have," he paused and thought for a moment, "I have taken out the trash as American's say."

Magda swung away from her father, "I need to call my mom," she cried out. "I want to go home now."

"No need," Carlos said, "My men reported blowing up your house over a day ago, your mother, well, I am not sure if she is dead or not, but I am sure she will be soon."

Magda's tears began to flow.

"Why do you cry my daughter?" Carlos said in a soft voice. "This is the way of the world. In time, you will accept it all. For now, you must rest. Get to know the house again. You are free to enjoy all the pleasures our house can offer. Then, three days from now, you and I will be casada."

Magda struggled to remember the language she rarely used anymore, "Casada?" she repeated, then the realization dawned as her memory pulled back that word. "Married?"

"Of course," Carlos said. "I love you and will keep you safe for all time."

"Married?" Magda said again as she considered the words and the life she had inadvertently chosen.

Chapter 18

The crane was delivered mid-afternoon and David was overwhelmed with the newness of the vehicle. He had never had a new car, nor bulldozer, well, really much new other than clothing and the occasional cell phone or television. The crane was bright yellow and as crisp as a new dollar bill. David took no time at all to begin learning how to use the big crane. But his experience with heavy machinery was significant and in under an hour he was using the machine like it had been his for a long time.

Tom and the group of other men were busy setting the mounting points for the beams and framing that would arrive sometime today. Much of that was still intact from the explosion. Hardened steel that held its own even under duress. Some of it was due to the shaped charges that had been built into the house, focusing on the structure but protecting the gun room and much of the core of the house.

The men worked hard, and the eyelets were cleared, and then the concrete cleared and cleaned. Several of the men made trips back and forth to huge dumpsters where scrap was placed, ready to be removed later. Michael was impressed, but not surprised, at the tenacity of the small group of workers. Abby left for a while to pick up pizza for everyone. A small pizza parlor in town looked good and Abby brought back 5 pizzas, ice cold water and cold Mountain Dew, Pepsi, and Ale-8.

It was more than enough food. Abby loved Ale-8 and had not been able to easily get one in some time. While they had been in Michigan, Abby had found a small candy store named, The Lakeside Emporium, and there she had found specialty drinks from all over. It was a pleasant surprise to find Ale-8 and have a few back at the house. Michael was not so thrilled with Ale-8, but he did drink it from time to time.

Abby popped the top from her Ale-8 and began drinking. The men looked at her and laughed. "Only a Kentucky girl would down an Ale-8 like that."

"Born and kinda raised here," Abby said. "Dad was at Fort Knox when I was born. Spent a lot of time in the state and went to school in Louisville."

The men chuckled.

"What's so funny?" Abby asked.

Michael had a slice of pizza and watched.

"Just expected you to be more of a city girl than anything else," one of the men said.

"Really?" Abby replied in an indignant tone.

"Sorry, ma'am," Tom said. "You have the fancy car, the fancy house, and the fancy boyfriend. We just expected you to be, well, you know, soft."

"Soft?" Abby asked.

"Uh oh," Michael said.

"A girl like me is soft?" Abby asked.

"Well, yeah," a big man at the table replied. "We don't mean nothing by it. We just don't see many city girls who could hunt, fish, and work with us. Girls from around here, well, they know the world a little better." The man took another slice of pizza and put it on his plate. The makeshift table was made of plywood and his paper plate was bright white against the wood finish of the table.

"I get it," Abby saw Michael smile as he shook his head. "We city girls are for what?"

"Well, ma'am," a skinny man said, "you are girls to look good. I mean no offense, ma'am, but you look like one of those girls in a magazine. All perfect and pretty and wearing that perfume you can only get at a big store."

Abby stood and walked over to Michael, looking directly in his eyes. He stood looking down at her with a slight smirk.

The big man who had spoken a moment ago had finished another piece of pizza in only a few bites and put another piece on his plate. He looked up at her as she faced away from him, staring into Michael's eyes.

"How do you like your pizza?" Abby asked not looking away from Michael.

The big man answered right away. "Martha's is really good. They give you such big pieces of pizza. I love 'em."

Michael closed his eyes and snickered.

"Maybe I should cut it for you," Abby said as she spun around. She had pulled one of Michael's Kunai knives from his belt. The knives were slid into the leather belt and normally looked like extra loops. She threw the knife. The blade spun as it soared across the distance going through the pizza and into the plywood underneath, dead center of the slice."

The other men at the table kept eating and were silent. Abby walked over to the big man and pulled the knife from his pizza. The man was still and stared into her crystal blue eyes as she slid her finger along the edge of the knife and licked the pizza residue from her finger.

"Good pizza, isn't it?" Abby said as she picked up a napkin, cleaned the blade and walked back to Michael.

The big man gulped. "Yes, ma'am," he said in a much more respectful tone. "Thank you."

"I can respect that," Tom laughed, and the other men started laughing at the big man. "Phil," Tom said, "She owned you."

She slid the blade back in the leather holster in Michael's belt.

"You are so bad," Michael whispered. "I love you."

An 18-wheeler broke the mood as it pulled up to the upper lot. David walked to the top where the crane waited and now all the steel beams to continue to work on the house.

A small man jumped out of the cab as the crew reached the summit of the hill. Phil was still eating pizza.

As David signed paperwork with the driver, the driver looked at Phil, "That looks like good pizza."

"There's plenty down there if you want some," Abby said. "Cold drinks too."

"Just don't ask her to cut the pizza," Phil said.

All of them men laughed as the truck driver tried to figure out the joke.

Chapter 19

"Let me get this straight," Tarkington asked. "You want to get involved in this little melee because the man is a sick f…" Tarkington paused, "A sick individual?"

"Sir," Alex said, "It is apparent this man has taken a US citizen and has them in a foreign country against their will."

"You will have a hard time proving that," Tarkington said. "The girl is his daughter, it could be argued there is no issue with anything he is doing, it is a family matter."

"Well, he killed at least one government agent in Atlanta. It could be called terrorism," Alex said.

"That too is a stretch without proof," Tarkington said.

"Isn't that what we do? Stretch the situation so we can solve it?" Alex stated.

"From time to time, we act on the edge of the written law to ensure the safety of the American people," Tarkington said. "I used the plural in that case. This man is a pain in the ass, but he is not threatening anything but our sensibilities and our moral code. If we opened that up, we would need to nuke most of the third world. Alex, I know this has you on the edge, and I asked you to look at it in case we could help, but we need some type of case so we don't end up with another grey file that may be audited in the future. Your purpose is closing down those grey files, including this one."

"What you're saying is we let him go?" Alex said, "We walk away and let him do what he wants and kill who he wants?"

"No," Tarkington said, "but let's say there is a discretionary fund, like the one I give you, that has no audit on it. Let's say there is a private contractor available that could go in and take the girl back, maybe someone who has been there before and has a personal interest in getting her back. Let's say that that person leads this man to a neutral or pro American country, and we have jurisdiction. How many counts is the DEA waiting to take him on?"

"I understand," Alex said.

"Do you, you little..." Tarkington paused again. "Do you Alex? I don't think you understand the trust I have put in you. After all, you can engage a team that is pretty diverse and that has handled some serious issues. You even know someone that would eliminate this issue more efficiently than just about anyone on the planet and still you look for more approval. You know you had that, or you wouldn't be where you are right now. You want brownie points, join the Elks lodge, you want my respect, eliminate the situation without compromising the United States of America in any way."

"Yes, sir," Alex said.

"Good talk," Tarkington said. "Now get the damn job done."

Alex hung up the phone. He sat in the room with a group of people that were waiting for action.

"Jim," Alex said, "get Alan on the phone. You and I need to talk to him alone."

"On it," Jim picked up the phone and dialed a number.

"Ronnie," Alex continued, "find me the most likely spot close to the Carlos Juarez estate in another country that we can have jurisdiction in."

"Yes, sir," Ronnie said and left the room.

"Rachel," Alex continued, "I need to know how many men Carlos has at his location. Try to confirm the girl is there. Call in a favor for a drone or satellite picture, just get me intel. Find a way to find out. Then get our gear ready for a trip. We will need weapons and enough ammo to deal with a whatever you find."

"On it," Rachel said and left the room.

Barbara and Terry remained.

Alex nodded to them. "Get the plane ready, we are going to South America. When Ronnie gives you a location, set it up."

"It will be ready," Terry said as he left the room with Barbara.

"I have Alan, Melody, Milton, and Jamie on the phone," Jim said.

"Jamie and Milton," Alex said, "you may not want to stay, up to you, but whatever I say stays between us."

"Go," Milton said.

"What is it?" Alan asked.

"Alan, I would like to contract you to get Magda back. We are verifying she is there, and we will work out a way for you to get her and be followed to the border where we will be waiting." Alex said. "My team is working out the details."

"Contract me, huh?" Alan asked. "From Tarkington?"

"No," Alex said. "From me."

"Why don't I just go get her and take care of this?" Alan said, "This is personal to me you know. He sent men to my home. He put the love of my life in danger."

"Why go alone when we can work together? Me and my team will be flying down as soon as we get all the intel," Alex said.

"You do that," Alan said, "I will contact you when I am on site in Venezuela."

"Wait, wait," Alex said, "If we coordinate, we will..."

"No waiting," Alan broke in, "this girl needs to be out of the situation. I can deal with this. I will deal with this and you let me know where to lead him to, but it will be once I know the girl is safe."

The phone went dead.

"Idiot," Alex said, "He will get himself killed."

"Will he?" Jim asked. "He has been there. He is a pretty adept individual. I wouldn't want to meet him in an alley and smush his cookies accidently."

"Sure," Alex said, "he has been there. Carlos knows that too. How long do you think Carlos has been thinking about whoever liberated his kids the first time?"

"You have a point," Jim said. "We'd better get there."

"Yeah," Alex said. "Help Rachel, let's get this show on the road."

Chapter 20

"Alan," Melody said. "Why don't you wait for Alex and his group to help you set this up."

"No time," Alan said as he held her, "You heard Maria. This girl has days before her life is ruined. I will be home in a few days and the girl will be safe. Jay will fly me down. I will exit wherever Alex and his group are set up. We can end this."

"Alan," Melody pleaded, "You are too close to this. I love you. I don't want to lose you."

"You won't lose me," Alan said, "Shiva and Vishnu will take care of me."

"I love them, too," Melody said. "They need you too. Wait for Alex."

"How about this?" Alan said, "I will head down and wait for Alex." Alan paused, then continued, "if he can get there in time."

"God you are stubborn," Melody snapped.

Alan hugged her and she tried to push away. "I will be ok." Alan said. "The dogs and I have done quite a bit together. It will not be an issue."

Melody slowed her struggles and put her arms around Alan, "Promise me you'll come back."

"I promise," Alan said, "I will be back." Alan said in his best Arnold Schwarzenegger voice.

Melody looked away.

"Get a plane home if you want or I will have Jay fly back here with the truck after he drops me off. The dogs and I will find our way home."

"I will wait for Jay," Melody said. "I will get a hotel by the airport and wait."

"I love you," Alan said.

"I love you, too," Melody replied. "I will get an Uber from here. I want to talk to Maria for a few."

"Those things aren't safe," Alan said.

Melody smirked. "Get going before I make you stay."

Alan kissed her then he and the dogs headed out to the truck.

Melody came out of the house and walked to the truck. "Alan," she said, "are you sure?"

"The dogs will take care of me," Alan laughed. "I will be home soon."

Alan got in the big black F350 and started the truck, as he backed out, he blew Melody a kiss. She smiled a fitful smile and watched him drive away.

Alan picked up his cell phone and dialed Jay.

"Alan, that you?"

"Yeah," Alan said. "Fuel up to go to Venezuela. You will drop me and the dogs off in air somewhere close to Canaima."

"You aren't going back there," Jay said, "They almost got you last time. That was 10 years ago, he will be ready for you this time."

"I doubt it," Alan said, "You don't have to land. Alex will set up an exit point for me."

"Alex can't go in Venezuela, that country is way too hot for US entry."

"I will lead Carlos to them, and they can clean up," Alan said.

"Alan, I know you are good, but this is," Jay searched for a word, "well this is crazy," Jay said.

"Do you tell everyone that?" Alan said.

"Of course not," Jay said. "Most people I couldn't care less, but I would rather see you with Melody for a long time."

"The dogs and I will be parachuting in," Alan said. "Can you see if anyone has the harnesses for a loose drop and the releases. Also, I will need a GPS. I didn't bring one. Do you have an extra?"

"Of course, I do," Jay said, "I'll make a call to a group that works out of Atlanta. They might have harnesses but jumping with two dogs? That is not something I have ever seen. You're a big guy, Alan, but two hundred-pound dogs and you on one chute. That will be a big chute."

"Where can we get one? Fast?" Alan asked.

"What is the hurry?" Jay asked.

"We are on a tight timetable, a little girl is in the balance," Alan replied.

"Not your little girl," Jay said. "Slow down."

"Do I need to get another plane?" Alan asked.

The phone was dead for a moment, "No, Alan, I will make some calls and get the fuel for a run to South America. I will set us to refuel in San Juan. It will allow some leeway from customs and questions."

"Good choice, Jay," Alan said, "There is a tack shop in San Juan I can send specs to for the harnesses for the dogs. If I do it that way, we can have them deliver to the airport. I will call once I get to the plane."

"OK," Jay said.

"Jay," Alan said, "No one flies better than you. Thank you. Sorry I was short."

"We will have time to talk in the plane. Maybe you can bring me a cheeseburger." Jay replied.

"I will be there in less than 30 minutes," Alan said.

Chapter 21

The trip to the airport from Richmond, Kentucky was full of discussions for Alex and his team.

"We have minimal intel on the actual house. It is way off the beaten path at the edge of the rainforest. No cameras, no active surveillance unless it is requested." Rachel handed out some printouts. "I had a buddy in the DEA that ran a sweep there about six months ago and this is what we have." Rachel waited for them to look for a moment, "The whole compound is well fortified. My guy said it has been for a long time except they cut back the woods a little further and built four towers on the corners of the estate. You can see them if you look." Rachel pointed on the map Alex was holding, "My guy wasn't sure what else they added but there are some weird new towers in the woods. His guess was infrared and camera in the woods, but he said it would be hard to handle with all the wildlife. Lots of new tech though that can look for people instead of animals."

"What else?" Alex asked.

"If you look at these old maps," Rachel handed them around, "there used to be access roads in the area. Those have been eliminated. It looks like the bulldozed everything and let nature take it back. One way in, one way out, about a ten-mile hike to get in from any road now. That may not be too bad, but there are these." Rachel handed out some additional printouts, "These boxes are used in the states to track highway weather, snow, rain, traffic and all that stuff. These are placed pretty tight on the road. If you used any road coming are going Carlos will probably know you are coming before you do."

"Sounds pretty grim," Alex said. "Your pal in the DEA have any suggestion on getting in?"

"He suggested an Abrams or at least a Sheridan," Rachel replied. "The last time they ran a drone over they estimated 30 men on patrol in the area."

"We're almost to the plane, sir," Ronnie said from the driver's seat.

Alex turned to Rachel "We'll talk more in a minute. Based on what you know now, how will Alan fare? You know, if he goes in?"

"I don't know, sir," Rachel said. "You know me, I love a good fight but I'm not sure I would walk into this. Alan is a real badass. That stuff we did in DC, well, you know, Alex, he was majorly kicking ass. I normally wouldn't bet against him. And those damn dogs of his are a living forcefield. But I would say he would have just about zero chance in this unless..." Rachel paused.

"Unless what?" Jim asked looking at the map.

"Well, the eastern side of this compound is 60 miles of pure hell to Guyana. Three days in a good march but coming in from that side is less monitored. Would just have to be a group that could deal with all of the challenges," Rachel said, "Still, I doubt one man could do it, but we may be able to skirt the lines a little because," Rachel paused for a moment, "There's nothing there."

"How did Alan do this last time?" Jim asked as Ronnie pulled up to the airplane in the hanger.

"He used a service road to hide a jeep, went in through the jungle, and got back to his plane at Canaima. He flew it to Brazil and Jay ran him home. It shows in the file he picked up his plane, a week later, after Jay dropped him off and ran it through to Kentucky. I'm not sure if he flew it home or they loaded it on that beast Jay flies." Rachel said, "Anyway, that avenue is dead."

"Any way we can get him an Abrams?" Jim laughed.

"My grandpa has a Sherman," Ronnie said, "We could probably use it if we asked."

"He was kidding, Ronnie," Rachel barked.

"Oh," Ronnie said, "Ok."

As the group gathered bags from the glossy black Suburban, Jim whispered to Ronnie, "Does your uncle really have a Sherman?"

"Yes, sir," Ronnie replied.

"Cool," Jim laughed.

The group got on the Gulfstream G650 and took their seats in the back. Alex spoke to Terry as the door closed. "Everything set?"

"We are set," Terry replied, "We will be on our way momentarily. Barbara will copilot so you guys will need to take care of yourselves until we are on our way. Tarkington is being picky about a replacement."

"Why?" Alex asked.

"Ever since we lost Lisa, he has been picky," Terry stated. "Melody leaving the group has made him even more so. We will find someone though. It won't be long."

"We can talk later," Alex said. "I need to be aware of these things so I can push him."

"Sure," Terry said and walked into the cockpit.

The group sat in the back as the Gulfstream taxied and took off from the Bluegrass Airport. The sleek craft rose to 10,000 feet in a matter of moments. As they leveled off for a slow ascent, Alex turned to Ronnie. "60 miles to the closest place in Guyana?"

"Yes, sir," Ronnie said, "Rachel and I talked. There is little we can do to get any closer. It is just too far. I am worried, sir. I was reading about Venezuela. They will kill anyone who is on their land. They may even kill US citizens. The State Department really doesn't want anyone going there. I have nothing else, sir."

"We set course and wait for Alan to call. Looks like we will get a little heat for a while." Alex said.

"No beach though, huh?" Jim laughed.

"No, no beach. I doubt there is much of anything," Rachel replied.

"Find us a place to lay low. A hotel or something. We may be there for a while," Alex said.

"Anyone bring a deck of cards?" Jim laughed as he lay back in the comfortable Gulfstream chairs.

Chapter 22

The frame of the new house was beginning to take shape. The thick beams were attached to the ground and then to each other creating a latticework that would be strong and durable. The design would handle anything up to an explosion. The design was obviously very solid as the main studs that had been anchored deep in the ground had survived the previous explosion when Michael believed the location to be compromised.

The team of men set the beams and then bolted them down one by one. Abby and Michael were in the middle of it all helping where they could. They helped guide the beams, set them, and Michael welded some of the beams when they needed it using an arc welder attached to a generator high on the hill.

David turned out to be seriously adept at the new crane and was able to drop and set beams with accuracy that many people would not understand. An observer might think setting beams, or using a crane in general, an easy task, but some men take a significant amount of time to understand the dynamics of the sway. Being able to place the beams where a worker wanted them was as much an art as a skill.

Abby's phone rang. She walked away from the site off the foundation.

"Yes," Abby said.

"Abby," came a voice, "Is that you?"

"Mel?" Abby asked, "Is that you?"

"Yeah, it's me," Melody replied. "Do you have a minute? I am sorry I used your number. I know you said only in an emergency, but I was struggling with who to talk to. You know your dad and the team he assembled better than I do."

"What's going on, Mel?" Abby asked.

"Alan got involved in something he thought he solved years ago," Melody began, "Now he is off to Venezuela to save a girl that has been kidnapped. Alex and his team are going to be one country over waiting for him, but this is major, Abby. He reassured me, but after he left the more I thought about it, the more worried I became."

"Alan is a professional," Abby said. "He has been doing this type of thing for a long time."

"Abby," Melody broke in, "I know how good he is. But he is one man with two dogs in the Venezuelan rainforest saving a girl in a fortress in the middle of nowhere and expecting to get out. We know he has killed, but he tries to avoid it. I am worried this is going to backfire on him."

"Why worry?" Abby asked. "I don't worry about Michael."

"Michael would topple the world to get back to you, and you to him." Melody said, "But Alan cares. Alan cares about people. About getting things right about me and about his dogs. He is not as committed to one thing as Michael. That's where I think he could run into trouble."

"What would you like from me?" Abby asked.

"Will Alex make sure he is ok? You know Alex. Will he have Alan's back?"

"I don't know Alex that well," Abby said. "I met him when you did in DC. I knew of him from Michael's interaction with him in Kentucky, and in Texas. I hadn't really talked to him until DC. Michael trusts him, which is tough for Michael, but I'm not sure he would trust Alex having his back in a situation like that," Abby stated.

"Why?" Melody asked.

"Because Alex would follow the rules," Abby said. "He would certainly want to help but he is career. He will follow god, country, and dad, first, then whoever he is protecting unless he was ordered to keep someone safe. I don't know, Melody. Do you want me to ask Michael?"

"No, Abby," Melody said, "I am sure it will all be fine. I haven't known Alan long enough, and maybe I am being silly."

"Silly?" Abby said, "You? You're careful, and I appreciate that."

"Maybe I am too careful," Melody replied. "I just want a long life with Alan."

"I know," Abby said. "Listen, I will talk to Michael, see what he thinks. No arguments. If he is concerned, maybe he can call Alan."

"Don't worry about it," Melody said. "This is on me. I will be fine. Thanks, Abby. I will talk to you later and let you know how it goes."

"Talk to you soon," Abby hung up.

Michael was wiping off his brow as he approached Abby and hugged her from behind. "Slacker," he laughed.

"Michael," Abby said, "That was Melody. She is worried about Alan going to Venezuela."

"What?" Michael said. "Why is Alan going to that part of the world? It is pretty much a country full of starving people and corrupt politicians at the moment."

"She said something about him saving a girl from a fortress in the middle of the jungle," Abby said. "She is trying to hide it, but I think she's scared."

"Juarez, I bet," Michael said. "We were still in college when he came up. Had two daughters that someone saved. I guess it was Alan. They were going to send in a sweeper team to take care of it, but it got too hot. The political climate was better than it is now. He was well protected and locked in with the government along with several drug kingpins."

"Did you get sent after him?" Abby asked.

"No. Another target came up that was more difficult, and they sent me there. They sent another team in. When the team was lost, they set Juarez aside as a target. I think the DEA oversaw it. They wanted him to come out of country so they could get him, but he never has, I guess." Michael recited. "I am sure everyone would be happy if they got him and put him away for a long time. I would guess Tarkington told them he would only send me if they wanted him dead."

"Do you think he will be ok?" Abby asked.

Michael looked at the Kentucky countryside beneath them. "This place, I love it. It is thick and with the home advantage pretty much no one can sneak up on you. Where Juarez lives is a lot thicker, a lot deadlier. I wouldn't want to go in unprepared. A lot of potential traps to walk into," Michael said, "It is good that it is Alan, the two dogs give him an advantage. They will adapt to the area faster than he can. I would say it is about even."

"Alex is backing him up with the team," Abby said.

Michael grinned. "That gives him a little more chance if Alex falls asleep. Jim will break the rules, Alex will only bend them."

"What do you mean?" Abby asked.

"Your dad always gave me parameters when he sent me somewhere alone. He would tell me not to go into some area and a whole bunch of stuff he would have to say, then I would go in, deal with the problem, and leave and would be rewarded. He says that stuff so he has deniability and can keep the country safe, but Alex sees his words as law, and won't break them even when Tarkington thinks he should."

"Can you tell Alex that?" Abby said.

"He's a good guy. I am glad he is out there, but he won't believe me," Michael replied.

"Can you try?" Abby pleaded.

"Hmm," Michael held Abby for a moment, "you know I can't resist you, well, much."

Abby hit Michael in the chest, "Much?"

"Sometimes I have to keep you safe," Michael said. "You know what I mean."

Abby hit him in the chest again, "Can't resist, much?"

"You know what I mean," Michael said. "I will call Alex. Can't promise anything, but I will call."

Abby put her arms around the back of Michael's neck and pulled him down for a kiss. "Resistance is futile." She said as she kissed him.

Michael smiled and kissed her back. When he broke the kiss, he looked down at her, "I will call. Can you make sure these guys don't bolt themselves to the floor or anything?"

"You bet," Abby said and walked back over to the worksite, looking back halfway to smile.

Chapter 23

Alan paced up and down the cargo area in the C130J Hercules. The plane had been in the air for an hour, and Alan was troubled. The dogs watched him from inside the big truck strapped to the cargo bay floor. Alan walked back to the cockpit, where Jay was reading a book and checking the autopilot occasionally.

"What's wrong?" Jay asked, setting down his book.

"I was thinking about it," Alan said, "you may be right. This may not be my best move."

Jay sat up. "I can turn around if you like. Let Alex and his team take care of this."

"I can't do that either," Alan said. "Maria and Margarite are counting on me."

"To die?" Jay asked.

Alan looked at him in a stern manner. "No," he paused, "I won't die. I can pull this off."

"I am sure you could if you had more time to plan and more assistance," Jay retorted. "This is not like you, Alan. Rushing in and not doing all the homework."

"The girl," Alan said. "He will take her soon, I don't know when, but he won't wait for long. Can you imagine the damage that will do to her if her own father makes her..." His voice trailed off.

"That's not your responsibility," Jay said. "By what you have said, she made some bad decisions. That put her in this mess, not you."

"She's a kid."

"She's not innocent to the situation," Jay replied.

Alan looked out at the clear blue sky in front of them. The powerful drone of the engines filled his ears and vibrated all around them. "Yeah, you're right. Still, I have to do this."

"Why?" Jay asked.

"Because it's the right thing to do," Alan said.

Jay reached down and pulled up the headset that dangled around his neck, "Hmm, incoming for you."

Alan sat down in the copilot's chair and put on a headset; he keyed the microphone. "Alan here."

"Alan, this is Alex. Contact me when you land in San Juan," Alex said.

"Why?" Alan asked.

"I will fill you in then," Alex said.

"I have a sat phone. You can encrypt the transmission," Jay said.

"Number?" Alex replied.

Jay gave Alex the number.

Jay reached to his side and pulled out the small Iridium phone. "It will auto-encrypt if it can. I am betting they use the same type of technology."

The small phone rang. "Yeah," Alan answered.

"Alan," Alex said, "We have been looking at this every way we can. It is a no-win situation. You might get in, but you won't make it out."

"Why's that?" Alan said as he pressed the button for speaker on the sat phone.

"The roads you used last time have been removed. There are new positions everywhere monitoring the area. New camera towers and just towers. Jim thinks some are automated gun towers. They expanded the yard, and we think they have added more people," Alex said. "Maybe 30 or more."

"Not good news, Alex, but I was just discussing this with Jay. I have to go in," Alan stated.

"Why?" Alex said, "Let's take some time and plan this out a little better. Get a group to go in."

"That little girl will be raped within a few days if she has not been already," Alan said, "Jay has already said it is not on me, but I would remember it for the rest of my life."

"She's not your little girl," Alex said. "She was just a job. Our number one rule is don't get personal, and you are obviously way on the personal side here."

"Maybe she is personal to me," Alan said. "Maybe I have taken too many things personally for a long time. Maybe that's why I wanted out. I can't be Michael and divorce myself from it all. I have to do this, Alex."

"If it's suicide?" Alex asked.

"Then it's my death," Alan replied.

"The dogs," Alex said.

"Nice try, Alex," Alan said. "They would survive without me in a rainforest. Probably would get fat on snakes or squirrels. Who knows? They may have a taste for sloths or who knows what. They would be fine without me."

"How long til you get to San Juan?" Alex asked.

Alan looked at Jay, "About an hour."

"We will meet you there and at least get you all the intel," Alex said.

"Might see you there, who knows," Alan hung up.

He stood looking out the front window for a few minutes. "Maybe I should write a note to Mel, just in case."

Jay shook his head but just flew the plane.

Chapter 24

Maria and Margarite were in the living room, talking, when they heard the glass break in the house. Jamie showed up in the living room first.

"Garage," she pulled her weapon and checked the doors and windows.

Milton rushed into the room as Jamie ushered the girls to the garage. As he looked around, he drew his weapon, expecting the worst.

The smoke grenade went off with a loud pop, and smoke began to fill the living room.

Melody was at the garage door waiting for them. "What the hell?"

"Who knows?" Milton said. "They are tracking one of them somehow."

The front door slammed open as the frame cracked. The lock shattered from an impact. A big man, probably 6'4", pushed through the door and swung an MP5 from side to side. Jamie let loose with her Glock 21, hitting him four times in the chest, he stumbled back but did not fall. "Body armor," she stated.

"Duh," Melody snapped, drawing her Glock 27, "I was already at this party at my house." Melody fired shots in pairs of two, four times, as the big man swung his MP5 to bear on them. The last pair caught him in the face and the MP5 sprayed the room as he fell. Melody dropped the magazine and slid another into place. "What are we doing? I only have one more magazine."

Jamie opened the garage door, and the door exploded inward. Large pieces of the garage door landed on top of their car.

"Guess we need another car," Jamie said.

Milton took point, facing the living room while Melody and Jamie covered the windows, Margarite and Maria huddled in the center.

Milton looked at Maria, "Your ex-husband is a major pain in the ass."

Lasers flashed back and forth across the room in the smoke. Melody stepped up. "Thank you for showing me the way." She opened fire on the origin points of the LASERS, and the weapons fell to the ground. She didn't know if the men went down, but she wasn't waiting to find out.

"Protect them," Melody said as she ran to the first man, picked up his MP5 and pulled two magazines from his vest. Staying low, Melody went down where she had shot at the other men. She came to the first one and fired into his head twice. Then scurried to the second, shooting him in the head as well. Both were darker skinned men, but that could have just meant they tanned often. Coughing from the smoke, Melody searched the second man. She pulled his ID, then pulled his MP5 and two more magazines. Melody made her way back to Milton.

Milton crouched by the kitchen counter. "We have to get out of this house."

"Why?" Melody said.

"The last time I was in this situation was less than two days ago. They decided to blow up the house," Milton said.

"Good reason," Melody said, looking at the doors. She handed the other two MP5s to Jamie and Milton.

"Out the front or try the back?" Melody said.

"Front is more likely clear," Milton said, trying to see through the smoke. He coughed twice, "At least we will be out of this crap."

Melody nodded and headed to the front door. Jamie followed, and Milton ushered the other two women in front of him. "Stay low," he said.

As Melody exited the door, gunfire erupted. She dove into the bushes as she turned and watched bullets rip up the white siding in the house. Jamie walked out and opened fire on the Black Escalade in front of the house. Melody crawled behind bushes until she was at the end of the house and as Jamie pulled back into the house Melody opened fire from the edge of the house.

The staggered fire approach would not work for long with the limited ammo they had, so something had to happen fast. Jamie stepped out and began to fire but was met with one gunman opening fire on her. As they stopped shooting Jamie opened fire again and Melody ran to the Escalade. At the front of the vehicle, she stopped. Peeking first, she swung around to the far side and opened fire on the two men huddling there. She hit them each multiple times and they fell to the ground writhing.

Melody approached as she looked inside of the car. Nothing.

She knelt by the men as Jamie reached the car too.

"Check out the car," Melody said.

The man was panting. One of the shots had missed the vest and went through his chest. "Who do you work for?" Melody asked.

The man spat at Melody.

"Sure, ok," Melody said, digging her finger in his wound. Blood welled up and covered her hand in short order.

The man screamed. "How about now?" Melody asked. He spit again. She wiped her face and hit him in the head with the MP5. He was out.

"Car's ok," Jamie said. "Holes in it but the tires are good, and it is still running."

"Milton," Melody yelled, "we are leaving. Wanna come?"

Milton ushered the other women out to the car. "Dumb question," he said. "How am I going to explain two houses in as many days? God this is not good."

Jamie was at the wheel and Melody in the passenger seat. Milton pushed the women in the backseat and got in behind the passenger seat, watching the house as they left. "Floor it," Milton said.

As they left the neighborhood, Milton laughed, "At least the house is still in one piece."

They turned the corner and the last thing they saw was the house exploding in a plume of flames and smoke.

Chapter 25

The table was set in the design of kings. The ornate dining room was as Magda had remembered it, but now the linens were far crisper. The silverware polished to a shine that reflected any light in the room with a vigor that could only be considered brilliant. The room had the touch of class that homes only see when the owners are genuinely interested in the details.

Carlos Juarez sat at the head of the table; Magda was placed at the far end. There were three seats on either side between them and only one additional plate set at Carlos right. A beautiful woman in a floral gown came in and sat to the right of Carlos and several women walked in with the food.

Salads, a pork roast, and a variety of vegetables were brought in and arranged on the table. Magda sat at the table in her white satin shirt and pants.

"I'm not hungry," Magda said.

"Of course, you are," Carlos replied with a slight jingle in his voice. "You need to keep your strength up." Carlos paused, "Where are my manners? This is Blanca, she has been taking care of me and the house while you and your mother have been gone."

"Did he force you to come or just buy you?" Magda asked.

"What a horrible question," Carlos inject with the same sing song voice, "You came here of your own free will, so did Blanca. She has kept me and the house in perfect working order and will continue to assist you as long as you want."

"Don't worry, Blanca," Magda said, "I will be leaving soon. You can have him and this house to yourself."

"No no," Carlos said, "You mustn't say such things, my darling Magda. You are mine. You will always be mine. You cannot leave me now that you have returned to our wonderful home."

"Oh, yes," Magda said with spite dripping from her voice, "I will be gone as soon as I find a way."

Carlos stood and walked to the end of the table and stood over Magda behind her chair. He put his hands on her shoulders and began massaging them. "My dear Magda, if you try to leave my men have been instructed to bring you back, and as they do, they are to use whatever force they feel necessary. Think well how you might fare with my guards. Perhaps they will only use chloroform on you again, or perhaps they will be more forceful. You will not leave here, ever." Carlos slapped Magda lightly on the face from behind. "Do not test me."

Magda held the side of her face, "Then I will be your battered daughter. I am not staying with you. You are a sicko!"

"We shall see," the levity in his voice gone. Carlos walked back to the head of the table and sat next to Blanca. He turned to the young woman in the floral dress. "You will teach her to behave or you will both suffer." Carlos stood and threw his napkin on the table. "I am no longer hungry," he said and walked down the hall.

Blanca stood, her long black hair shimmered in the light. She was maybe 30 years old and stunning in her own way. She nodded to a woman in the room and several women came in and began picking up the plates and clearing the table.

"What's your story?" Magda asked. "Where did you come from?"

Blanca nodded to a woman picking up a plate. "This is my mother, Sabrina. She has been here for some 30 years. She was still here when your grandfather was alive. Think back, you may remember me. We played together from time to time, but it was frowned upon by Carlos. Your family was not to mix with the hired help. When you escaped, Carlos killed all of the guards but one. Then began to hire new help. We were one of a few that stayed. Two weeks after you left, he made me his choice for the bedroom. I was 14 at the time. I have been his ever since. He will not let you leave, nor will he tolerate the things you are doing for long."

"Whatever," Magda said, "I will say and do as I please."

"Mama, aqui," she said, and the older woman walked to her. "My mother once thought she could speak as she saw fit. When Carlos announced he would take me, she protested." Blanca opened her mother's mouth. "As a punishment for her defiance Carlos cut her tongue out. Do not think for a moment he will not do such to you. He has done far worse. It would be better if you did as I did and learn to make him happy so that one day when he is finally no more that all this will be yours." Blanca's mother bowed her head and went back to work.

Magda wore a face of shock. "What does he want from me?"

"Why a son, of course," Blanca smiled. "Someone to take his place. Your mother gave him daughters. Your mother's mother gave him daughters. I have given him three daughters. If he gets a son this will cease. Perhaps it will get better, or perhaps not."

Magda stood and slapped the glass from the table. It landed with a crash against the wall and shattered. "I will not sleep with my sicko father so he can have a son. That's just wrong."

"You act like you have a choice," Blanca said as she turned and looked out of the window. "I tried to resist the first time, so he had my mother hold me while he raped me. If there was a way to be rid of him, I would have done it long ago. If there was a way to escape that would leave me and my mother alive, I would do so."

"Where is your dad?" Magda asked.

"He was a guard when you escaped," Blanca replied, "Carlos put a bullet through his head while my mother and I watched."

Chapter 26

Alex answered the satellite phone on the first ring. "Yes."

"Hello, Alex," Michael said. "I need to speak to you for a moment. Can we encrypt this call?"

"Michael?" Alex asked. "How did you get this number?"

"Unimportant," Michael said. "I understand Alan may be going into Venezuela."

"I am not sure where you are getting your information," Alex said. "Maybe you should call Alan. Why would you call me about it?"

"Alex," Michael said, "I think our relationship is beyond games. Well, I thought it was beyond games but still you are playing the good little soldier."

"Sorry, Michael," Alex replied. "Hang on."

Alex pressed a button on the phone. "We are encrypted. Old habits die hard. I still worry about Tarkington and you being involved in anything."

"I am not involved," Michael stated. "No one involved me. I am looking into a potential problem for a friend."

"I can guess who," Alex said.

"Doesn't matter," Michael replied. "Is Alan going after Juarez in Venezuela?"

"Yes," Alex replied, "I voted against it. I tried to talk him out of it. I actually begged him not to go. We met in San Juan and I tried again. He is headed there now to jump out of a plane with two dogs strapped to him to face an army."

"What do you think his chances are?" Michael said.

"I am thinking about 60-40 against," Alex said. "I give him that just because of the dogs."

"I am thinking more along the lines of 90-10. I am willing to bet there are snares everywhere after his last visit to the Juarez house."

"Maybe so," Alex said. "I will help all I can."

"How?" Michael replied with virtually no tone inflection. Alex knew this tone. He had heard it before and argument or cover up might not work in his favor.

"We will wait at the border and take Carlos as he chases Alan to us," Alex said. "If necessary, we will find our way into a secluded spot if we will not be detected."

"Of course, you will take Carlos into custody," Michael stated.

"That is the plan," Alex replied. "DEA and a host of other agencies want him."

"If Alan kills him?" Michael said.

"It would be fine as long as it was warranted."

"Warranted," Michael stated. "I was asked to clean that up when I was in college. No one wanted him dead then either. I read his file then, it was worse than you are probably being led to believe. At the time, it would have been easy for me to eliminate the situation. Ten guards and him and a few staff members. I would be willing to bet he has doubled that amount."

"Tripled," Alex broke in.

"You are letting a man with two dogs who tries not to kill or only kills when it fits his moral code go in to try to get a girl out who went there of her own free will?"

"I am not letting anyone do anything," Alex said in an irritated voice. "I am getting a job done I was asked to do. He went without us because this girl will probably be made into the new house mother pretty quickly."

"All the more reason to terminate him," Michael said.

"Not my choice," Alex said.

"Has Tarkington gone soft?" Michael asked. "I was always given the choice to do as I see fit. I was told what was asked to be done but also told that it was more of a guideline than a rule. Tarkington never once pushed back if I decided it was better to terminate an objective. If I thought a situation was compromised, I could clean the area from a distance, and not think a thing about it. I was paid and paid well to think as much as act."

"I have seen part of the ledgers," Alex said.

"I am sure Tarkington trusts you or you would not be in the position you are in. You just need to rethink. When I say that, Alex, I put the emphasis on think."

"I have been in the service for a lot longer" Alex began stating with indignity.

"You are not in the service, Alex. Only on paper. You are part of a team created to try to catch me, and your team has been involved in some serious situations. If people had to die, they had to die. In the end, it was your choice and Tarkington would have been behind it." Michael stated with the same consistent tone of voice. "Oh," Michael said, "When you try to lecture someone about how long you have been doing something, I suggest you compare what you have done, and how you have done it. How many tours have you done? I know, remember? How many confirmed kills? How many people have you saved? Think about when we first met. A man filled with vengeance sent you in to try to do his dirty work. I am standing where I saw you for the first time. You, Mark, and your team coming right to me. All that training, how did that turn out for you Alex?"

"You know what?" Alex said, "Sometimes your attitude can really piss me off."

"Good," Michael said, "Or maybe not. I don't get pissed off. Well, not often. I eliminate problems, and when I do, I make decisions without malice or vengeance or delusions of morality. I do what is necessary."

"I have seen you be moral," Alex said as though he had caught him in a lie.

"Perhaps," Michael replied, "but only when it comes to people close to me."

"Why did you call, Michael?" Alex asked.

"After we first met, Alan lifted a weight from me that I had been holding onto for some time. He gave me a necklace he had made from a shot I missed. A shot I thought I did not miss." Michael said. "I am trying to decide how much that shot was worth. How much a friend's request means to Abby and I."

"What's that mean?"

"I'll let you know," Michael replied. "For now, I think you need to think about your position, and all that it means."

"I think you know I think about it every day," Alex replied.

"I know you do, Alex," Michael said. "But sometimes you have to stop thinking and start acting."

"Like I said," Alex replied, "sometimes you really are a pain, but I get what you are saying."

"I don't like this at all, Alex," Michael stated, "This is a job for a sweeper team, or someone like me. It is not a job for someone like Alan, but perhaps I'm wrong."

"Ouch," Alex said, "that must have hurt."

"Really?" Michael said. "Have you seen me shoot, Alex? Do you think I picked up a rifle the first time and put 100 out of 100 within 1 cm of bullseye? I had some skill, maybe more than most people, but it took a lot of shots to get me where I am. If you are never wrong, it is likely you are never right. I will not walk the path of that person who thinks they are right, even when they have not considered the options."

"What does that make me?" Alex asked.

"In my opinion? Safe," Michael said.

"Safe?" Alex said. "I have never thought of myself as safe."

"When it comes time, will you pull the trigger or follow orders?" Michael stated. "I will do what is necessary. I think Jim would as well. You will weigh the choices and chose the one that will not endanger as many people, or you."

"I think I do the right thing," Alex said feeling attacked. "It's not like I shy away from a fight."

"Never said you did," Michael was direct. "Unless it is a fight inside your mind. This is far too deep for a conversation on a sat phone. Perhaps over a drink someday. Perhaps not. The reason for my call was Alan, and I have my answer. Thanks, Alex."

"What was your answer?" Alex said.

"I'll talk to you another time." Michael said. The line went dead.

Jim studied Alex with care. "I am guessing that was our friend Michael. He said something that got to you."

Alex stared at the floor of the plane, speeding towards Guyana. "Just a few things to think about."

"What did he want?" Jim asked.

"He has some concerns about Alan," Alex replied.

"Don't we all. But what made him call and why did he call you?" Jim asked.

Alex seemed to snap out of a small dream. "You know, I'm not really sure. Maybe some kind of insane pep talk?"

"Do you feel peppier?" Jim asked.

"Not really," Alex said, "I feel like I got chastised by a man at least ten years younger than I am."

Jim laughed. Rachel moved over to the two of them.

"What's so funny?" Rachel asked.

"Alex just got chastised by Michael," Jim laughed.

"He teaching you how to kill people?" Rachel stated in a serious tone. "If so, maybe you should listen."

Alex smiled as he looked at Jim, "...and now this?"

Jim laughed, "She has a point, you know."

"What is it with you guys? I have been around the block a few times." Alex replied. "I mean, we do well as a team, right?"

"We do exceptional as a team," Rachel said. "You always push us to where we are going. We mesh better than anyone I have worked with at the base, or anywhere else. When it comes to the tough decisions though we stand out while you temper us."

Jim nodded at Rachel. "You and Ronnie are the control rods of our team, Rachel and I are the reactors, and Terry is a long-distance solution."

"What about Barbara?" Alex asked.

"She is good, but more of an outsider. Even though she works to make us a good team, I can't imagine her wailing on some idiot like Rachel would." Jim considered for a moment, "Lisa was in between as well. She would have done anything you asked. Melody was a thinking reactor. I would not want to cross her. She would have it all figured out and then would systematically tear you to pieces."

"What's wrong with being a little less aggressive?" Alex asked.

"Nothing, unless it's time to be aggressive," Jim said.

"You pretty much saved me," Rachel added. "Well, you and this doofus. I was a bully and a clown and people for sure didn't like me before. When Jim put me on my ass, my world changed. Then you pressed me to use my anger in the right way. Jim keeps teaching me, and someday I will be able to beat him." Jim raised an eyebrow. "But I don't need to any longer. I am comfortable with myself now. When I let loose it is not to prove something to myself. It is to do the right thing."

Alex considered for a few moments. "When Michael was talking to me about my need to "rethink". Maybe he meant how I saw it all. Then again, this is a killer that has quite a few kills."

"A lot more than we are aware of I am sure," Jim said. "He does have a code, but I would not want to be on the fence if he was considering me. Even in hand-to-hand, he is formidable. With one of those pistols or rifles he uses; I feel a little naked."

"We need to rethink," Alex said. "What is the right thing to do right now? Not the safe thing to do."

"We leave that to you, boss man," Jim chided. "We're just the hired guns."

"Yeah," Rachel laughed and flexed her biceps showing definitions in her arms. "These guns don't run!"

Alex smiled a little.

"Lighten up, Alex," Jim laughed. "Being too serious will kill you. We trust you."

"I hope I can live up to that for you," Alex said, "and for Alan."

Chapter 27

Alan readied himself at the back of the big C130J. He had dressed in standard camo, not the current digital camo that was regulation. Instead his camo was brighter like the leaves and edges of the rainforest. Alan checked his harness again and made sure the parachute and backup chute were tight and his pack was loose to the back of him. He was taking a chance and had never jumped in this configuration with a pack. He guessed he was jumping out of a plane with 220 pounds of extra dog and 150 pounds of equipment. His tethers were tight on the pack and he checked the double harnesses of the dogs and the panic releases on each of them. The tack designer had done a good job in San Juan, building the rigs exactly as Alan asked. They would be supportive and comfortable to the dogs. When they landed, they would leave them.

Alan had told the man to make another set, stating he would pick them up later if this worked. The older leathersmith had looked at him and asked for Alan to prepay.

Alan had laughed and handed him the money for another set but understood the caution. Now here is he was, about to make a jump that would land him in the record books if anyone saw it.

"About the only clearing I see is coming up in about two minutes. You want me to circle or are you ready?" Jay said over the intercom.

"Open the doors," Alan said.

The two dogs were unaffected by the shift as the doors opened. They had both jumped many times with Alan. He leaned down and clipped two clips on the right of him to Shiva, and on the left of him to Vishnu. When he stood, he lifted the dogs off the ground in their harnesses. Their feet dangled. Shiva's legs moved as though she were swimming for a second and then she stopped. The dogs were calm.

Both dogs wore goggles and padded shoes. Both dogs were panting lightly, looking as happy as if they were sitting on a comfortable couch. The drone of the engines was more powerful with the doors open and Alan looked out and saw miles upon miles of forest below. At 8000 feet, he was lower than he usually jumped but far within guidelines and could handle the jump very easily. That was without all the things he was carrying.

The lights went off in the back of the C130J and a red light lit above the door.

"Be ready," Jay said over the microphone. "Check in on landing with four clicks to verify. Stay radio silent, I will relay status."

"I could just use the sat phone," Alan mused as he adjusted his goggles.

The light in front of him turned amber. The dogs licked their lips and kept panting. Alan moved to the edge of the ramp and held the strap above him. The wind whipped across them. Alan reached down and petted each dog one at a time.

The light above them turned green. Alan jumped away from the back of the plane and into the fall.

The straps holding the dogs shifted and both dogs were under him as he floated down with his body forward. The jump would be short, maybe 15 seconds before he would open. He turned to get his bearings. Below, he saw the clearing. A patch of what looked like grassland from this height. He would be about five miles from the house and was hopeful he would not be seen. He was certain, however, that someone would hear the plane, but knew planes were over the area often.

Alan looked at his altimeter and, as they reached 5000 feet, pulled the cord. The big chute opened wide and there was a sudden jerk. Both dogs were panting and watching the ground come up with a look of almost anticipation. Alan was on target for the dead center of the clearing and dropped his pack from the tether. It strung down behind him and stretched out about 30 feet. The pack hit earlier and was behind him as he pulled the parachute cords hard slowing their decent even more. Alan bent his legs and caught himself and the dogs. He knelt down right away.

The harnesses were fitted with quick releases. Pulling them, the dogs were loose and turned to him. In a few quick motions, the para-harnesses were off, and the dogs wore their standard vests.

Alan looked around. There were in tall grass, perhaps five feet tall in the middle of the rainforest. Alan stowed his parachute and took out a small shovel. He dug a shallow hole, putting the harnesses and parachute in the hole to cover them. Already covered with sweat, Alan stood and looked at the landscape.

"Voran," Alan said, and the two dogs ran in different directions. He waited. A few moments later, Shiva was back at his side. Vishnu returned a full minute later, carrying a dead Coral snake. The dog dropped the snake and waited patiently. Alan made a hand gesture and they began to move into the thick forest. Alan pulled a GPS tracker from his vest and noted he was 4.1 miles from the estate. They needed to be closer to be able to get in at night and escape at the break of dawn. Alan pulled his sat phone out as he walked and called Jay. The phone rang and Jay picked up. "Yeah," Jay said.

"We made it. We are fine," Alan replied.

"No radio?" Jay said.

"It was easier to call don't you think," Alan replied. "We are going in. I will call Alex as we leave."

"You sure you want to do this?" Jay asked.

"Goodbye, Jay," Alan replied as he hung up. He put the phone in a top pocket, sealed it and began a steady run.

The dogs were always somewhere between 20 and 40 feet ahead of him. They sniffed and paid attention better than a team of minesweepers and a dozen additional soldiers. Alan was proud to have trained two such amazing animals. They were by far the best he had worked with. Alan smiled as he ran. After they covered the first mile, he stopped and called them back.

The dog's tongues looked like something from a cartoon they were so large. Alan knew it would take some time for them to really acclimate to the hotter temperatures. He took out a silicon collapsible bowl and filled it with water from his canteen. The dogs took turns lapping up the water. Alan waited for them to cool off as he too sipped the water, looking at the dense foliage and the small pathways between. Monkeys darted from tree to tree. Alan was amazed at how little attention these animals paid to him. Instead the animals kept a wary eye on the two dogs and Alan wondered how many other predators were in the area. He knew there were many, but his concern was only with Jaguar and Cougar for now.

When they began running again, Alan had to slow down. The dogs could navigate more easily than he could as they dove from side to side. Alan removed a machete and began hacking away so he could follow. Several times he had to stop as he worked his way through the dense undergrowth. Howler monkeys echoed in the distance. It took twice as long to get the second mile. The dogs were less tired this time as they were moving much slower. He was doing more work hacking down vines and ferns that slowed him, and they were waiting. The pace was much steadier now and not as hurried.

Alan's chest vibrated. He reached in and found his sat phone. It was blinking "No Service,". Pulling out his GPS, it too was struggling to maintain a signal. Alan reached into another pocket and pulled out a sheet of paper Alex had given him. He noted the map on the paper and checked his position on the GPS. A tower was installed close to his location and he now knew it was likely a signal jamming tower.

Alan considered disabling the tower for a moment but thought better as he realized it could be detected and could be seen as an intrusion. The next two miles would be more difficult as they worked their way in. He was sure that Carlos Juarez had set up more than just signal jammers and he would need to pay close attention to avoid detection. The dogs were at his side. He pulled out the water dish and they sat for a moment.

"Well, guys," Alan said, "this may have been a mistake." He rubbed their ears and the dogs pushed into him for attention. "I wonder what we will find from here."

Alan heard a familiar snap and a few minutes later Vishnu trotted up with a dead coral snake and dropped it at Alan's feet.

"I guess I was wrong, if something happens to me you two will get fat on snakes, eh," Alan laughed. The two dogs wagged their tails at Alan, waiting for his command.

Alan made a gesture and the two dogs became alert and walked much closer to him. The last mile they would be more cautious and define their path out of the estate, hoping they found everything along the way. Alan and the dogs proceeded into the dark forest, ready for anything.

Chapter 28

Anton Kolchak was not happy.

"Two houses in as many days?" he barked at Milton.

"It was not my fault," Milton said. "We scanned everything. We were not tracked."

"So, you are saying one of our people is a leak?" Anton grumbled.

"I'm not saying anything," Milton replied. "We were attacked. Someone knew exactly where we were."

"How about her and the guy?" Anton pointed at Melody who stood in the center of the main room of the Marshalls' command center.

"She is clean too. And the girl, Margarite," Milton replied.

Anton paced. "Any ideas?"

Jamie shrugged, "I hate to say it, sir, but your idea of someone being a leak is all that fits."

"That's just swell," Anton said.

"We need to get someone else involved to get you off grid," Anton said. "I don't need another house being smoked. I need some answers. Any of you have an idea.?"

Melody raised her hand.

"Not in preschool, girl. Open up," Anton said.

"I will take them," Melody replied. "I know a place. We will be off grid and it's not too far from here. No one will know where we are going. We can dump all the electronics here and check in later."

"Really?" Anton said. "Just how will you do that?"

"I have my ways," Melody said, "I can contact you through General Samuel Tarkington's office. I know he does not have a leak."

"Think you can lose everyone?" Anton asked. "No place on earth is tech free anymore."

"Leave that to me," Melody said. "I have as much at stake now as anyone."

"How's that?" Anton questioned.

"Her boyfriend is heading to Venezuela to get the other girl," Milton said.

"Do you think maybe I should know that too?" Anton was obviously angry.

"We just got here," Milton said.

"Well get out of here, like now," Anton replied. "Before I end up in a blown-up house. Find a way to check in while we figure this mess out. I may lose my job over this. Don't think I'm going down alone."

"Yes, sir," Milton said.

The four left the house and went to the car parked in front. "That was a short visit. We should do it more often." Melody said. Melody looked in the back of the car and found a small plastic bag. "Cell phones, pagers, and anything electronic goes in here."

Maria and Margarite had nothing. Alan had taken Margarite's phone and Maria's was lost when her house had exploded. Milton pulled his cell phone out and put it in the bag, Jamie did the same.

"What are we going to do with them?" Jamie asked.

Melody tied the bag in a knot and threw it at the door of the house. "Leave them here, of course."

Jamie shook her head and got in the passenger seat car. "I'll drive," Melody said, claiming the driver's seat. The Crown Victoria was spacious but was not really comfortable for five. "We have a stop to make."

Milton sat in the back with Margarite and Maria. All were tired from the ordeals of the day.

Melody drove to a convenience store only a few blocks away. She came out carrying two smartphones. Once in the car, she broke one open and handed the other to Jamie. "Get it activated."

They sat in the convenience store parking lot for a few minutes. When Melody had her phone working, she looked up a local car rental company and called. "Do y'all accept cash for rentals?"

"Of course, I got a credit card, but I don't want my husband finding me ya know. I will leave the card but y'all won't charge it or nothin 'til I get to my destination?" Melody said in a thick southern accent. "Can you pick me something big so I can bring my family with me?"

"Aww, thanks," Melody said. "I'll be there in a few minutes."

Melody put the car into gear. "They have an Escalade. We will have room and it won't be trackable. We can dump this car in a mall parking lot along the way."

"This phone is ready," Jamie said.

"Thanks," Melody used the phone to dial a number.

A voice answered. "Samuel Tarkington's office."

"Sarah, it's Melody," Melody said. "I was hoping I could talk to the general."

"Let me check, Mel," Sarah replied. "One moment."

The phone played a nondescript version of some pop song turned into nonsense, for just a moment. "Melody?" Tarkington said. "Tired of being in the woods with Grizzly Adam's big brother?"

"Nice to talk to you too, sir," Melody said.

"Why the call?" Tarkington replied, short and to the point.

"I need some help," Melody stated. "I am taking a few people to a safe location, and I need a go between to Justice. I was hoping I could use your office to keep anyone from tracing us."

"Let me guess," Tarkington grumbled, "Juarez."

"I guess you know all about it by now," Melody said.

"More than I want to. I should have handled it before as I wanted. Those Justice morons are always trying to play an angle. God, they want to follow the rules all the time. Now we have a mess bigger than anything I could have made."

"Don't sell yourself short, sir," Melody replied.

"Very funny," Tarkington said, "Sure, keep in touch through Sarah, but make sure the damn lines are secure."

"I will do so, sir," Melody replied.

"I will see if she can get some updates on that man mountain of yours," Tarkington stated.

"I would appreciate that, sir," Melody said.

"Are you set for money? Safe place?" Tarkington asked.

"I have plenty of cash, and safest place I know," Melody said.

"Talk to him or her?" Tarkington asked.

"Who?" Melody replied.

"That's what I thought." Tarkington grumbled again. "Check in when you arrive and dump this phone. The line was not secure."

"Dumping it," Melody said and turned the phone off. As they were driving, Melody took the chip out of the phone and put it in her pocket. Then she threw the phone out the window.

"That will get expensive," Jamie said.

"Not too bad. There always seems to be a special going on," Melody laughed. After driving a few minutes, she pulled into a small strip mall. "Jamie, wait here and keep the motor running, I will go get us a car and drive back here. Then we can drive to somewhere that won't tow or pay attention to the car."

"OK," Jamie said and got out of the car. Melody got out, putting a purse over her shoulder and walking towards a second strip mall about a block away. As she walked, her swing became more predominant.

Jamie laughed, thinking how Melody was "getting into character". Looking around, she thought about how vulnerable the world was with all the cameras everywhere. A person could be tracked by their face without their knowledge, or worse. She studied the cameras in the area and wondered where they could go that the world was not watching them always.

After about 15 minutes, a black Escalade pulled in next to them then drove off. Jamie fell in behind it and followed Melody to a huge auto repair shop. Melody pulled up to the front and Jamie into a parking place. Melody walked into the shop and returned a few minutes later. "Keys?" she said to Jamie.

Jamie gave them to her, and Melody took them inside. After just a moment, she came out and got in the driver's seat of the Escalade while the others got comfortable.

"I asked them to check the car. Told them we were going out of town for a few days, and we will be back in a week," Melody said. "Asked them to park it out back to keep it safe. It will be ok. We have this truck for a week. Everything will be over by then, one way or another."

"Now what?" Milton asked.

"Now we go for a drive," Melody pulled out into traffic and headed north.

Chapter 29

The last mile was treacherous and full of unexpected twists. The dogs had found the first snare and as they progressed came upon numerous animals trapped in different types of traps. Some were alive, but most were dead which told Alan they were not paying as much attention to the traps. But they were still out there. The satellite phone was now useless, but the GPS still functioned. Alan had checked the map Alex had given him and it was obvious the intention was a web of jammers that would keep anyone from communicating close. With less than a mile to the house, Alan's sat phone beeped, He checked it and found he had signal. Looking at the map and the web of small towers, he surmised the tower where he was had malfunctioned, giving a small window of communication.

Alan and the dogs had gone through one canteen full of water but now the dogs were stopping occasionally to get water from many of the large leaves where it pooled from the near perpetual mist in the rainforest. Alan too began drinking from the leaves to ensure he would be able to conserve water for the longer trip out. Alan watched the dogs. They avoided some leaf types, and he made sure to as well.

Alan sat down in the brief satellite opening and dialed Alex. The phone rang and then answered.

"Alan," Alex asked.

"Yeah," Alan replied.

"We've been trying to get you." Alex said.

"That web you saw on the map, the web of towers, it's signal jammers. I am in a hole right now. I doubt I will see another. I am less than a mile from the house. I will camp out tonight and go in about 4 AM, get the girl and head out. It will give me the advantage of early morning and then daylight."

"Listen, Alan," Alex said, "You don't need to go in. We will find another way. I don't want something to happen to you."

"Afraid of what Mel will do to you?" Alan laughed.

"Maybe a little," Alex said. "But really, Alan, we can get a team in and end this."

"Would be a political incident, don't you think?" Alan said, "It is better this way. I will take care of getting the girl. He will chase me, and then it will be time for you to come get me."

"How long did it take for you to get there?" Alex asked.

"From the clearing," Alan replied, "5 hours. We have a rhythm now and will make better time going back."

"4 or 5 miles in 5 hours?" Alex stated. "It will take you a week to get out."

"We will make it."

"No, you will not," Alex replied. "Here is what you are going to do. Look at your map. There is another clearing next to a river, 12 miles out directly east of the clearing you landed in. Find it on the map."

"I see it," Alan said.

"We will get two helicopters and come in there," Alan said.

"Won't that get you in trouble?" Alan replied.

"Won't know until I do it," Alex stated. "I will expect you tomorrow at sundown."

"I will be there," Alan replied.

He hung up the phone and turned it off. It was the last mile. Alan pulled out his Glock 17, checking the path and the barrel. The weapon was resilient and was a match for the UDP-9 9mm rifle he carried. The advantage was one Michael and he had talked about. He carried two weapons, one for short range and one for longer range but they used the same round allowing him to share ammunition in a pinch. The UDP-9mm offered the added benefit of using the same magazine, and Alan had a considerable number of mags with him.

He checked the rifle. It too was in good working order, chambered and on safe, waiting for the conflict that may come.

Chapter 30

Blanca knocked on Magda's door.

"Go away," Magda said.

The door opened and Blanca walked in and closed the door behind her. Magda was sitting cross legged on the unmade bed.

"What do you want?" Magda asked.

"I have been asked to tell you of your duties," Blanca stated. "It gives me no," she paused, looking for the right word. "It gives me no good feeling to see you here."

"Sure," Magda said, "You liked it better when he was all yours."

Blanca lowered her head. Her long black hair was perfect, and her nails were long and painted a bright red. She raised her head and Magda saw the tears.

"No one should go through what I have gone through," Blanca said. "No one should face this monster."

Magda softened a little. "What am I supposed to do."

"You will take my place as mistress of the house," Blanca sobbed. "You will spend your nights at his side as he requests or leave him if he requests. The house will be your responsibility. You must ensure it is managed well and that all of the women are ready for him at any time. He will ask for you as he likes. He will take you when he wants. Do not make the mistake of saying no. It is not good. If you say no you will be punished. I said no and it took weeks for my face to heal. Carlos takes the women here as he wants them, he is truly a pig. He has grown tired of me and now I am perhaps once per week, but you will be used for weeks before he begins to tire of you."

"I can't do it," Magda said. "Not going to. I will stab him the first chance I get."

"He will expect that, several have tried. Their bodies were dumped in the forest to feed the animals that are close."

"I am just supposed to lay there? Not happening," Magda replied.

"Oh, he will expect you to struggle, or become involved, or do something." Blanca replied. "The day after tomorrow, he will wed you. It is not a real ceremony, but he thinks of it as such. It makes him feel better for the things he does to us all. You and I, we will be the lucky ones."

"How so?" Magda said, "I do not feel so lucky, right now."

"The other women here, since he does not use them as often, or at all, they are used by the guards. It is not good." Blanca said. "I once resisted, and he gave me to them for one night. It was not a night I wanted to repeat."

"What if I escape in the night?" Magda said.

"Likely the Jaguars will kill you, or worse. There are snakes and other animals that are as bad. If you escape, I will likely be killed as well, for allowing you to escape."

"We should go together," Magda said. "I can take you to the states, you can start a new life."

"I am of no use anymore to a new country or a new person. I am ruined," Blanca said. "I cannot let you go."

Magda walked to the woman who still stood at the door, "No, you could start over, have a family, find a life."

"I am ruined, my child," Blanca said, "My mother would be killed, my daughters, if they still live, will be killed as well."

"Your daughters," Magda asked.

"Yes, I have had three daughters and they were taken away from me at birth. All to keep me from running. Carlos blames his leniency for allowing you to escape. He will likely take your children as well and if you leave and use them to get you back. If I am good, he will let me see them. It has been months now." Blanca lamented.

"I will help," Magda said. "We will get your daughters and get out together."

"No," Blanca was more adamant, "You will take your place as the lady of the house and perhaps I will get to leave someday."

"You really believe that?" Magda asked, "You showed me your mother. You want to be the woman with no tongue watching her children be abused? Do you?"

Blanca turned, "Breakfast is at 7 each morning. You will be dressed and ready for breakfast at 6:15, and we will walk your duties," With that, Blanca left, closing the door behind her.

Magda sat brooding for a moment and considered the last few days. Her life was now different. Her life was no longer her own.

Chapter 31

Alex and his team landed in the western most airport of Guyana. The actual airstrip was little more than a paved road. The landing was smooth, and they taxied to one of four large hangers where the Happy Scotsman sat idle. The plane had been backed in and the nose protruded slightly from the hanger even though it was far too big for the structure. The small Gulfstream fit easily next to the C130J. Terry swung the plane, so they too were nose forward, ready to take off in short order if necessary.

Alex looked out the window and saw Jay coming down the ramp to the ground to meet them. Barbara opened the doors of the Gulfstream and the group deplaned and stretched. When Terry stepped out, Jay called to him. "Terry, you still flying that Tylenol?"

"It will outrun that pig," Terry said.

"Maybe," Jay said, "but I can almost fit your plane in the back of mine."

"True," Terry said as he walked to Jay. They shook hands. "How ya doin Jay?"

"I am doing good," Jay replied. "I was hoping to find a bar in this one-horse town. Haven't taken the time yet, may need to now that you are here."

"I am sure another bar will mean another story," Terry laughed.

"Did someone say bar?" Jim asked.

"I'm in," Rachel said as she walked up. "Did you find a bar yet, Jay?"

"I was just telling Terry I had not found a bar yet," Jay said, "but I am hopeful for some good tequila and rum. Guyana has great rum. I was in a bar once in Georgetown. They brought me this 21-year-old Rum, El Dorado I believe. I remember the bartender kept making different rum drinks for me. She finally made me a drink with rum and vanilla ice cream.

I had four of them. Woke up the next morning with a hangover and the bartender."

Jim, Rachel and Terry laughed.

Alex joined them. "Jim, find us two helicopters. Rachel, find us a real weapon. M134 or something we can mount. Get it here fast. We're changing tactics. Barbara, can you and Ronnie set us up a table here somewhere. Let's change our plan before we lose this asshole again."

"On it," Jim said.

Rachel walked away, already dialing on her phone. Barbara and Ronnie found a few sawhorses and began setting up a makeshift office.

"What can we do?" Terry asked.

"Make sure you both can fly a chopper. If Jim finds them, you two need to get them here," Alex said.

"I may be able to help. Let me get into the Scotsman and make a call. I met a guy in a bar in Georgetown that had a fleet of MD500Es in the country. I have his info on my phone," Jay said and began walking to the ramp to the big plane.

"Jim," Alex yelled, "go with Jay!"

Jim hung up his sat phone and began walking to the Scotsman.

Rachel walked to Alex, "I got 2 if you want them, they are in Georgetown. We could take the Gulfstream and be there and back within 2 hours."

"It's going to be dark in an hour. Who is going to sell it to you now?" Alex asked.

"Police in Georgetown seized two as part of an arms bust with our DEA. DEA is willing to give them to us," Rachel replied.

"I wonder why they would just give them to us? Take Terry and Barbara," Alex said. "Get it done."

"I need to learn to fly," Rachel said. "Barbara, you're with us." Rachel said as they walked to the Gulfstream."

"I will shave some time," Terry said.

"Jim and I can fly a chopper. We will get this to work." Alex said.

Barbara walked up to Terry and Alex. "What's up?"

"You are running to Georgetown with them," Alex said. "You'll be back soon."

Barbara's auburn hair swung in the wind as she turned and headed to the plane that Rachel was entering. Terry followed. Within moments the engines were whining, and the plane pulled out of the hanger.

Alex smiled a little. A plan was forming in his head as he walked to the makeshift table Ronnie and Barbara had set up. Ronnie was setting up computers and pulling extension cords.

"Power's working, sir," he said, "I thought we could use it. There's a Wi-Fi connection here too, but I'm not sure I trust it. I will see if it gets us out and bridge off of it with an encrypted VPN."

"Good work, Ronnie," Alex said. "See if you can get us a secure link to Sarah."

"Will do, sir," Ronnie said. "I will have it up in a few minutes if we can get out."

Jay and Jim walked down the stairs from the Happy Scotsman, laughing. "Two MD500Es are inbound. They will be here is about an hour. I told them we would pay for a week. I hope that's ok with you."

"Fine," Alex said, "Help me with this map." Alex was spreading out a topological map of the area.

The table was soon covered with the map. Alex pointed to several locations. "We are here," Alex said placing a rock on the airport they were at. "Carlos is here," Alex said and placed another rock there. "The 12-mile clearing is where we are going to pick them up," Alex placed a third rock.

"In, out, and gone," Alex noted. "If we need to, we will move up to the 5-mile clearing. How will we be for fuel?"

Jay looked at the map, "Gravy, we'll have a lot of leeway if we need it."

"Let's hope we don't need it," Alex said.

"What am I missing? Is there anything between us and those clearings?"

"A lot of trees," Jim said.

"A few animals," Jay added.

"A few people maybe," Ronnie said. "but nothing to worry about."

"Research it. Make sure," Alex said. "Terry, Barbara, and Rachel will be back in a few hours. We will take off at 0400 and head to the clearing."

Chapter 32

It was dark and getting late. Very late. Melody had been driving for six hours up I-75 then across a series of two-lane and four-lane roads in the middle of nowhere. As they passed Knoxville, Melody refilled the tank on the big Escalade and bought another pay-as-you-go cell phone. Then she called Abby to tell her they were on their way there. Abby had said she would set up hotel rooms for them where they were staying.

Melody had been appreciative. Then she removed the chip and destroyed yet another phone. Milton had remarked she made the most expensive phone calls of anyone he knew. Melody laughed but retorted with, "I am not getting another house blown up."

Maria and Margarite spent the drive talking about their mother, and Margarite was immediately forgiving of Maria's silence. After all, by taking all of the heat, Margarite had been spared many of the horrors she now knew her sister had experienced. She also had the benefit of some of a childhood in the states, having gone to school and college here would give her potential opportunities. Her business degree would get her somewhere. She was wondering where that would be at the moment. She was now an aunt instead of a sister, but it felt no different. Magda was her sister as far as she was concerned, and Magda was with her father. All of the theories of what would happen next were not good.

Maria was positive and uplifting for a woman who had been in two houses that had been destroyed over the past three days. She assured her sister this would be over soon. They didn't know Melody, but Melody seemed to have their best interest at heart. She was definitely aggressive in making things happen. The two remarked on the sights as they drove through the mountains in Tennessee and again as they went through the mountains in Kentucky. Even in the dark, the countryside was stunning. The carved-out roads made them both wonder what incredible machines could have ripped a mountain apart.

After weaving in and out of the mountains they pulled into the Alpine Motel and were not sure what to think. The drive there was nearly desolate and there appeared to be nothing on either side of any substance. A gas station, a car lot, and a few businesses but they were scattered. Milton actually asked, "Are you sure we're in the right place?"

"Yep," Melody said, "We will be here for a short time and then move on depending on how they want to direct us."

"You trust these people?" Jamie asked.

"I trust Abby with my life. And she trusts Michael even more," Melody said. "We had a bit of an adventure together. She is a formidable woman. Michael, well? I will let you decide."

Melody parked and got out of the car, stretched and waved at the hotel. Abby came out a few moments later followed by Michael. Milton, Jamie, Maria and Margarite exited the car. They were all tired.

"Mel," Abby said, "It is so good to see you." She looked at the group, "We got you all individual rooms. I hope that is ok."

"Sure, that is fine," Milton said. "Umm, I'm not sure where we are. I wasn't really expecting a hotel in the mountains. Can I get a brief rundown on what we are doing here?"

"Simple," Michael said, "you are going off grid. You will find this area is a little less tech and a lot less monitored than Atlanta. We have paid cash for the room. Sorry, we are rebuilding the house."

"What happened to the house?" Milton asked.

"Well, it blew up," Abby said.

"Actually, I blew it up," Michael added.

"I should have guessed," Milton replied, "We have had a lot of that lately."

"So I have read," Michael said. "This situation is a little out of control."

"You have read?" Milton said.

"I have access to the latest intel from a variety of sources. I normally don't follow it, but Alan is involved, and I am considering getting involved as well," Michael said.

"I still don't follow," Milton said. "Why would you get involved?"

"I am a problem solver," Michael replied. "I can solve this problem with a degree of efficiency the government agencies will not be able to achieve."

"Well that sounds really good," Jamie said. "Why don't you?"

"I am trying to retire," Michael said. "I also was not involved originally, and there is no contract associated with this situation."

"Contract?" Milton asked.

"Yes, contract," Michael said. "I worked for hire to the highest bidder."

"Like a mercenary?" Jamie asked.

"If you like," Michael said, "but my only open-ended jobs were with the United States Government and one private firm. I took care of the situations no one else was able to solve or that were more easily handled by someone like me."

"This is your solution?" Milton asked Melody. "Bringing us to a freelance assassin?" he looked at Michael. "No offense."

"None taken," Michael replied. "You are seeing this from a very microscopic point of view. This makes you part of one of the non-covert agencies like FBI, or DEA, or perhaps Justice."

"I am a US Marshall," Milton said.

"Makes sense," Michael replied without any emotion. "You are given very limited information to do your job. It is easier that way. The world is much more complex than most people see. It needs to be boiled down to much more simplistic elements so that normal people can do their jobs and go on day to day without being lost in the constant affairs being executed by governments, criminals, and other players. I would love to explain it all to you, but I doubt you would easily believe me or understand. Instead suffice it to say that I did what had to be done so you and a lot of other people could do their jobs without knowing what people like me do."

"You're right," Milton said, "I am not sure if I would believe you. We obviously need your help because nothing we have done has worked at all."

Abby broke in. "For now, why don't you get some sleep?" Abby began handing out keys to each of them.

"Can Maria and Margarite at least be in one room? We can take shifts watching them?" Jamie asked.

"Of course, if that is OK with them," Abby replied.

Maria and Margarite smiled, and Maria said, "Of course."

The keys distributed, the group went to their respective rooms while Michael, Abby, and Melody remained.

Milton turned, and seeing the three remaining, walked back. "Something we should know?"

"Not really," Melody said, "My future husband is down saving someone the Marshall service let get away."

Abby looked at Melody, "Really? That's so sweet."

"Well, he hasn't asked yet, but he will," Melody replied.

Michael laughed. "I am sure he will as well. Melody, I owe Alan. I think I am going to go down and maybe change the game a little."

"It's not a game," Milton said. "This is serious."

"Is to me," Michael said. "Do you think you can help Abby and Melody keep these girls safe?"

"Of course," Milton began.

"Do you want to stay here Mel? Or head to one of our houses? Or yours?" Michael asked.

"I think we can just stay here and keep a low profile," Melody said. "Abby and I do well together."

"Yes," Michael said, "you do. I need to go out to the site and collect a few things Then I will come back before I head out."

"Just like that?" Milton said. "What about your contract?"

"I don't want to write that with myself, the paperwork would be horrible, too much bickering, so I guess I will skip the contract and just go." Michael replied.

"Smartass," Milton said, "Who do you think you are?"

"Nobody special," Michael said as he kissed Abby. "I'll bring back the DB9 and make a call for a ride out of here. Jay is in Guyana, so I will call in a favor."

"Be careful," Abby said as Michael walked to the car. "I want that butt back here in one piece."

Michael looked over his shoulder, "This butt?" danced a few steps, and got in the DB9.

Chapter 33

Alan was once again at the edge of the clearing of the house. He remembered this day like it was yesterday. The clearing was bigger now. The cameras more advanced. The motion sensors far more advanced, and the guards were thick at this hour. It was 4:00 AM and still there was a 3-person roving patrol. Alan considered the situation carefully. He could go in guns blazing and potentially get Magda hurt, he could try to sneak in and fail, or he could try one of a hundred other options, and still likely fail.

The dogs, his biggest asset, were next to Alan, but they too had been rendered useless. There was no easy way to see a path that would not get him caught, unless. Time. Time was his friend perhaps in this case. Alan would use the dogs to draw the guards, then get in and out in an instant. This would only work if he could get Magda out quickly. He motioned to the dogs and they paid close attention. He flashed a laser pointer in the distance and pointed. The dogs ran off through the open area of the yard. Although no guards were there, they would be spotted in an instant.

It was a few seconds later that shots fired. Alan saw the dogs leap into the deep woods. Alan ran to the house door on his side and pulled it open by pure force. The sun was beginning to rise and in a few minutes any element of cover would be gone. He walked through the hallway, opened one door, then the next, the first two were empty, the third was bright white and a young woman was in the room. Alan walked in and said, "Magda."

"You," Magda said, "I remember you."

"We have to leave," Alan said, "Now," He grabbed her hand.

Magda pulled away. "Not without Blanca and her children. They will be killed if I leave."

"We can't help that," Alan grabbed for her again and she backed away. "Get out of here, now, find another way."

Alan reached for her again, "I don't have time to argue."

"He's in here," Magda yelled.

Alan hadn't seen that coming. He backed away to the door as he heard footsteps. Alan waited until the last second and bashed the door down on top of two men about to enter. He bolted for the outside door.

As Alan ran into the grass, he heard commotion behind him. Shots were fired from a pistol. Alan tripped and fell in the yard, got up and continued to run. "Hier!" Alan yelled, running into the woods as fast as he could.

He ran through the woods as fast as his feet would carry him. He was not interested in stealth anymore, instead he crashed through the rainforest like a lumbering elephant, his massive size was as much of a positive as a detriment.

"Don't you get it," Alan heard the yell. "She is mine. She was mine. She always will be mine."

Alan kept running and bounded into a small clearing. As he ran through the tall grass, he looked at his arm. It was bleeding with a piece of a stick lodged under the skin. A giant splinter. He had not felt it but now he reached down and pulled it out even as he sprinted through the open jungle. The pain was unique. Not earthshattering, but enough that he winced and saw stars. He threw the splinter hard to the north of him, hoping someone would track it that way but knowing he was leaving a trail Stevie Wonder could follow in his sleep.

As he reached the edge of the clearing, Shiva and Vishnu joined him. Alan spoke two words, *"geh vouras,"* and the dogs jumped forward with renewed vigor. He pointed behind them, but the dogs heard the crashing noises come to the edge of the clearing. They stopped for only a second, then bounded ahead of Alan.

Alan turned and emptied his rifle across the area. He had no sure point of reference, but he hoped it would slow them at least. He reached in his vest and pulled another magazine as the first one dropped. Slamming the magazine into place, he emptied the second 30 round magazine into the forest behind them.

"Missed us," the voice came, "What in the world were you aiming at, Alan? That was terrible."

Alan ran, wondering how Carlos knew his name. He pushed himself hard, thinking of Melody and their home in the mountains.

"C'mon, Alan. I know you are out there. A deaf man could hear you," the voice boomed. "I am going to get you, and your little dogs too. I know who you are. I have been looking for you for years."

Alan continued to run hard. He heard quads coming fast, but the forest was so thick they would be near useless. His advantage now was in front of him. The dogs knew the area from hunting it when he had arrived. They bounded with no effort in front of him but paced to allow him to keep up. They would find the path out.

"Alan," the voice yelled again, "C'mon out, I will make it quick. Painless for you and the dogs. Better than the pain you left me in, an empty house. So sad."

Alan thought of turning his weapon again but knew it would only give away his position. He kept running hard and the sling of his rifle caught on a branch. He tried to free it but left it and continued to run.

"Spray the area," he heard the yell.

Alan knew the sound. It was AK-47 fire. He remembered a movie with Clint Eastwood where a character had said, "This is the AK-47 Assault Rifle, the preferred weapon of our enemy. It makes a distinctive sound when fired". He would have laughed to himself if he was not being chased by several of them.

Alan ducked and stayed to the ground, then got up again. The dogs were staying in sight, so he started running again. He was gaining distance, heading west, where Alex would be. Where there would be some sanity in the world.

AK-47s blared again. The leaves next to him fell to the ground as bullets saturated the area. Alan dove to the ground, rolling. His arm and shoulder felt wet. He looked down to see a neat pattern of holes through his arm, his shoulder, and his side. He felt the spots and gritted his teeth hard as the pain shot through him. He tried to get his mind off the pain for just a moment as he felt the wounds. All 3 were straight through, all 3 left no bullet inside.

The dogs had doubled back, Alan rolled on the ground. He was losing blood. He ripped his shirt and wrapped the arm and shoulder the best he could. The wound in his side was not bleeding as bad. It was a flesh wound but in this jungle it could be fatal. Alan felt hot and cold at the same time. He was reeling with the pain and his vision started to get fuzzy. He saw Shiva "woof" at Vishnu. Vishnu lay down next to Alan as Shiva ran away from them, disappearing in the woods in only seconds. Shiva barked over and over as he ran. The barks got more and more silent as the distance increased. Alan could hear the pop of gunfire over and over, there were hundreds of shots, maybe thousands. His mind drifted. He felt Vishnu lick his arm and face.

The shots were getting harder to hear. Shiva barked over and over. The distance was growing each second. It was silent for a moment. Then Alan heard another sound. The scream of a dog followed by silence. He saw Vishnu's ears fall back. Alan tried to rise but Vishnu laid on top of him, holding him down. The dog laid its head upon Alan's chest with careful tender precision. Alan's eyes filled with tears. He bit his hand until mercifully, he passed out.

Chapter 34

The MD500Es landed in perfect formation. Three solid black helicopters on the tarmac. Alex told Ronnie to get the fuel trucks there. Ronnie picked up a phone on the wall of the hanger.

Jay walked out to meet a large heavyset man carrying a bottle. Jay picked up a bottle from the table as well.

"Jay," the man boomed. "It was so good to hear from you."

"Maximillian," Jay returned, "You are looking good!"

"I brought you a gift," Maximillian handed Jay the bottle. "From my personal reserves. Highland Park, 50, it is as unique as the bottle. This one is opened but I am sure you will enjoy it. I have two more in my cellars."

"Remind me to visit more often," Jay said. "We should meet and drink this together at a later time. Along with this, I have for you a fine Macallan in crystal. I am sure you have one, but this was given to me in a bar in Scotland after I saved the woman of the house from, well? From some bad times."

"You, dog, you," Maximillian said. "You will bring me my copters back?"

"If I do not, I will make sure you are paid double for them," Jay said.

"I see," Maximillian said with a knowing tone, "Then I would say you should be careful, and make sure the wind is at your back and a clean shirt w'll do ya."

Jay nodded as the man walked back to a single copter with his pilots and took off.

As the copter took off, a plane landed in the darkness. The G650 taxi'd to the hanger and turned around flawlessly in the small space, blowing a few papers as it did.

"What was that all about? Jay," Alex asked.

"He was wishing me a good funeral if I don't succeed."

"I missed something then," Jim said.

"Me too," Alex stated.

"This is a fine scotch he gave me," Jay said. "Worth ten thousand if a penny. I hope we get to drink it."

"We will," Jim said as he ran to the G650 and helped unload the weapons. The three miniguns were unloaded in a hurry and taken to the copters. It was already light outside and they needed to get moving.

"I thought there were two," Jim asked Rachel.

"When we got there, they had four, but one was missing parts, so we took three. I figured we could double mount one copter and single the other." Rachel laughed. "This will be the fun part."

"Mounting hardware?" Jim asked.

"A simple mount. It is in the black nylon bags. We have a bunch of ammo too," Rachel replied. "We are pretty much set. Probably need to get weights from Jay and Terry but this will be a quick install and setup."

"Ronnie!" Jim yelled, "Give us a hand."

Ronnie joined them and walked into the plane. He returned, carrying ammo cans, four at a time. It was only a matter of a few minutes before both choppers had stacks of ammo and weapons at their sides.

Jay and Terry actually began the job of mounting the weapons on the MD500Es. They decided someone would man the guns instead of setting them in a fixed position, even though the brackets and controls allowed for either. Within 45 minutes, the two MD500Es were battle ready.

"Test?" Jay asked Terry.

Terry squeezed the trigger on the mini-gun and it whirred in response. "No ammo. Works fine."

"We'll need to test fire once we get out over the jungle." Jay said. "If we mucked it up, it would be nice to know."

Alex walked to Terry. "How are you holding up?" Alex asked, "You haven't slept."

"Barbara flew on the way back," Terry said, "Rachel and I napped. I will be fine."

"Ready for a run?" Alex said as Jay walked up.

"It will take us about an hour to get there," Terry said. "We will come in fast and drop low the last few miles."

"We have a few surprises," Jay added, "Maximillian set us up. We have extra tanks for range that we won't need but it will be nice to have. And we have active radar if we need it on both choppers. These two are loaded with tech. I haven't gone through it all, but we are flying state-of-the-art machinery."

"We need to get the teams loaded and move," Alex said as he slapped Terry on the back.

Alex cleared his throat, "Listen up, time to gear up. We have two choppers. Jay, Jim and Rachel will take the first. Ronnie, Terry and I the second. Ronnie will be on guns for the second. Jim and Rachel for the two guns on the first. Barbara, you will coordinate from here. We are probably walking into a shitstorm, so be ready for anything. Our target is the 12-mile clearing. We will stop there and wait for feedback. Second target is the 5-mile clearing. We have been loaned these two helicopters and each will seat seven people. We don't know what we will run into, but our expectation is to return with two people and two dogs. Anything else, we are not prepared for at this time. Gear up, we leave in ten minutes."

The group began getting ready. Each changed into flak vests then mounted weapons and necessary gear. All of them were dressed in black, no insignia on anything they carried, and each had a slightly different weapon. Alex changed and mounted his weapons where he could get to them easily. He considered the discussion he had with Michael. He still thought he was a pompous overbearing jerk, but he did have a few points. He would push this set of orders to the limit.

Jay and Terry were both in the pilot's seats of the two helicopters and began to spin the rotors. The slow "whoop, whoop, whoop", of the propellers became a deafening whir as the blades gained speed. Jay rotated the surfaces a little to get the feel of the aircraft while Terry did similar. Jay and Terry both made a sign, and everyone began to load into the big craft. The 7-passenger version was a little longer than the normal 5 passenger version. It allowed the passengers a little more freedom to move around. Jay looked over at Terry, they nodded. As Rachel got on last, the rotors began spinning much faster and the helicopter lifted from the ground. Both tilted forward as they took off and moved with ease through the morning sky, heading for an easy pickup. Or something a lot worse.

Chapter 35

Michael's drive to Pikeville had been easy. He had taken the DB9 and would leave it at the airport where Abby and Melody could pick it up the following day. It was a quick drive from Ivel. A few calls had led him to a new Cessna Citation X owner who would fly him out if Michael would cover fuel costs. He and his wife had agreed to fly him to San Juan first to refuel, then fly over a map area and head back to San Juan.

Michael had explained he would like to jump from the plane over the rainforest. The man, Angus Wheeler, a retired coal mine owner and horse race enthusiast, had laughed. "Fine, as long as the check clears."

When Michael handed over cash that was far beyond the agreed upon price, Angus was ecstatic. Michael was a little concerned about the jump simply because of the wing configuration. He believed if he could get the pilot to lower their airspeed enough, he could push down from the front door and be more than fine. When he found out the Citation X had a Bagade door behind the wings, it became a pretty easy. Then he found it opened outward, which made it harder. Still, he was pretty sure he could use the front door and that Angus could get it back up.

The San Juan layover was short, only about 30 minutes while they refueled. The airport was not extremely busy, so they were back in the air and on their way within 45 minutes.

Michael spent some time with Angus as they flew the last leg while his wife slept in the comfortable back area of the plane.

"What do you do for a living again?" the man asked.

"Extreme adventurer, I am working on a new podcast that will be the bomb," Michael replied. "Listen to many podcasts?"

"No," Angus said, "I saw you had some weapons, what for?"

"Ever been in these jungles?" Michael said, "The Jaguars will eat you and the rest of the forest will strip you down to nothing within a few hours. Gotta even the odds somehow."

"I get it," Angus replied. "What are you really doing down here?"

"What do you mean?" Michael said in an innocent voice, "I told you."

"I'm not an idiot so I made a few calls. Seems a few buddies of mine asked me some questions about you and called me back. You may or may not have done some work for them in the past. Not that I care, but what in the world would bring you to this third-world hole right now."

Michael laughed, "You wouldn't believe me if I told you." In a less accented voice.

"Try me," Angus said.

"Well, I am saving a friend from a pedophile drug lord who lives in a fortress in the middle of the jungle. No one thinks it possible. My friend went in to save a young girl from her father. I am pretty sure he is in over his head, so I am just coming in to back him up and make sure he gets back to his girlfriend who is with my girlfriend right now. Along with the little girl's mother and sister, staying in a cheap hotel in Ivel."

Angus thought about it for a few minutes, "Lot of cheap hotels in Ivel, not much of a city is it?"

"Nope," Michael said snickering to himself. "It's just the right size. The people, well, the people are great."

"Listen, umm, what's your real name?" Angus asked. "My guys said you were probably Michael."

"Yep," Michael said.

"Well, Michael," Angus said, "As you can see, we are really bookin'. I am liking this plane and damn it is fast. We will be to your GPS coordinates in about 20 minutes. How do you want me to do this?"

"Ever done a jump before?" Michael said.

"Never," Angus replied.

"Well, it should be pretty easy. We will slow down to stall speed. I am not entirely sure on this plane, never flown one. But you have serious engines and don't have to worry about stalling much. Max flaps, and as slow as we can go. Then we will open the front door, and I will dive out. You close the door back up and get on your way," Michael said.

"Sounds easy enough," Angus said. "What's the worst that could happen?"

"Well, I could inspect your wing close up and personal, which may not bother you, but it won't do me any good. We could have issues with the door, but it is unlikely. You could just run it to Guyana, which wouldn't be a rough flight. I would cover cost. Other than that, everything else bad is on me."

"Hate to say it, but that sounds ok with me," Angus chuckled as they moved to the back and let the autopilot fly.

"Hate to say it, but I prefer it that way and appreciate the fact you got me here. Wife know how to fly?" Michael asked.

"Enough, but she is no expert," Angus said.

"No issue. She can hold it straight so you can close the door," Michael replied. "I am expecting you can pull it in pretty easily."

"Sure. Still sounds fun," Angus said. "What if you splat?"

"I won't," Michael said, "but I will wear a camera so you can put it on YouTube if I do."

"How can I get the camera?" Angus asked.

"I am sure you can find a way. With the avionics on this, you will know right where I splat." Michael laughed.

Michael grabbed his bag and began putting on equipment. Bullet Proof vest, knives, two FN5.7s mounted on the hips. P90 on his side clipped to a belt. And finally, the parachute package over much of the equipment.

"We should be getting close," Michael said as Angus sat back down in the pilot's seat.

"Yep. Wake Suzette up. I will slow us down. Let's see how slow we can go," Angus said.

Michael went to the back, "Suzette," he said, "Sorry to wake you…"

"I'm awake. I was listening," Suzette said. She as a little younger than Angus, but not much. Her deep brown eyes twinkled with a light all their own. Her skin was like that of a porcelain doll, and her long brown hair was cut with bangs that accentuated her face. "Is this guy really as bad as you summarized?"

"You heard all that," Michael asked.

"It's not that big of a plane," Suzette replied in a whisper. "I also had a say on whether you came. I am a member of a rather exclusive corporation that Angus is not aware of, but you are."

Michael was amazed that it could well be this woman was part of his old part time employer. "Maybe, but if I was, you know I could not reply." Michael whispered back.

"Just know it might be better that this man does not get taken by an organization that might make a deal," Suzette said with a smile, her ruby red lipstick seemed to glow as she smiled at him. "Do you understand me?"

"Of course," Michael said. "If you know who I am, well, you know it will be my choice."

The engine pitch was quite different now. The sound from the wings led Michael to believe the flaps were out, maybe as far as they could go.

"I understand," Suzette said, "Better not keep Angus waiting."

Michael checked all the items on his body. All were secured either by locks or closures. He was ready.

Angus was in the back by the door. "You ready for this?"

"Yep," Michael replied.

"We are teetering at about 80 knots," Angus said, "It will be windy, but not horrible. You should be able to use the rail to hold on for a moment. You know better than me, but I would jump from the bottom."

"It's what I will do," Michael said, "Thanks for this, not exactly a plane that should be used for skydiving, but it got me here quicker."

"Hey, it will be a cool new story. We dropped an extreme adventurer in the middle of nowhere." Angus laughed. "Hold on."

Angus pressed the release and heard the seal of the door break. It was instantly windy, and the plane rocked just a little. Using the arm, he lowered the stairs. The wind whipped through the cabin and the plane shuttered more than a little. A napkin flew around in the passenger area. Michael caught it in the air and put it in his pocket.

Angus yelled, "Good luck, and hope this was worth it."

"Thanks," Michael said, "Hope it doesn't hurt your plane."

"Get out of here," Angus laughed as he yelled, "You are over your area now."

Michael pulled the goggles on his head tight over his eyes. He held on with both hands and worked his way down the stairs. The wind was whipping like an out of control hurricane. The roar of the airflow and the engines was heavy. Michael slipped and grabbed himself, wondering if someone slipped in a hurricane would they just take off? It was a slow progression, but Michael made it to the bottom step. He looked back and he was situated just beneath the wing. This would work fine. He looked up to Angus and nodded. Angus nodded back. Michael pushed off and down and was away from the plane. He rolled as he fell and put out his arms to watch the Citation. He saw the door go back up. He was already far away enough he could not tell if the door sealed. But he did see the plane rocket off and go up at nearly a 45-degree angle. Michael assumed the hatch and lock system sealed.

Michael rolled and saw the ground coming up fast. He checked his altimeter and saw he was coming to five thousand feet and as he did, he pulled his chute. His target was the 5-mile clearing, but he was a little off.

It was fortunate he was using a square parachute. As he caught the air, he maneuvered to a small clearing in his line of sight and nearly floated to the ground.

Michael dropped the chute and staked it to the ground. He wrapped the edges of it and weighed it down then covered it with foliage. Normally he would take the time to bury it but not now. Checking his pack and weapons, he looked at the jungle and pushed inside.

Chapter 36

Alan woke. It was bright around him, everything hurt, and everything seemed to hurt a lot. His eyes were blurry, and he was covered with leaves. He tried to sit up and Vishnu bounded to him. The dog must have been close, just watching. Alan was not successful with his sitting as the pain was more than intense. He remembered the shots, then he remembered Shiva. His eyes welled up and he choked them back. The sadness was replaced by anger, and the anger with determination.

Alan looked down and checked the wounds. They were not good, but not as bad as they could be. The jungle was not the best place to get shot. Alan laughed to himself. He would rather avoid getting shot at all. Alan laughed to himself again. If only he had been a smaller target. He pushed and managed to get to a sitting position.

Alan listened for a few minutes. There were no crashing sounds, quads or gunfire, just the sounds of the jungle. He checked his watch; he had passed out for 2 hours. It felt like two weeks and two minutes at the same time.

Vishnu stayed with him and he looked around the small area. He had been covered with branches. This was Vishnu's doing. He moved the branches and verified he was only shot three times. He also verified it hurt. It actually hurt really bad. His hand slipped and he looked down. He laughed as he counted eight snakes piled next to him. Vishnu had been busy. He had slipped on a boa, it was about four feet long, a baby. Alan's pack was intact, and he had his pistol. He had lost his rifle somewhere during his run. He was careful as he peeled off the makeshift bandages that he had put on his wounds before he passed out. As he took them off, he saw he was still oozing blood.

Alan reached into his pack and took out a first-aid bag. Alan's pack was actually a series of small, compartmentalized bags. The first-aid bag was one of the meatier in the large backpack. Vishnu stared at him. "This is going to hurt, don't laugh at me."

The German Shepherd cocked its head as Alan spoke, not understanding all of the words, but some of them.

Alan took out several alcohol swabs. He ripped them open and first cleaned his hands. "It would be easier if I was on painkillers, right?" Alan asked Vishnu. Alan set the first aside and then took out the second. He breathed deeply and then started to clean the wounds. The pain was intense beyond belief and he saw stars. Vishnu moved to him and licked his face as the grimace became a nightmarish fight as every instinct inside of him was to scream. He had to resist.

His vision started to go dark and he realized he was holding his breath. He breathed. Vishnu kept licking him, somehow knowing he was having a difficult time. It took several minutes but Alan cleaned the general area of all three wounds. The edges were inflamed and puffy. Alan took time and was breathing through the pain now. It hurt, but he was dealing with it. Once the wound was clean, he pulled out a series of wound seal bandages. The outside edges and actually the whole bandage were see through plastic and sealed the area from outside influence. The inside was softer gauze that helped stop the bleeding, keeping the area clean. The bandages were flexible so you could move and didn't come off easily. Alan had tried them out when he first heard of them It had taken over an hour, and a lot of arm hair, to get one off.

"A little better, huh?" Alan said to Vishnu.

Vishnu whined almost imperceptibly.

"I know, I miss him too. Shiva was a good dog," Alan said.

Alan took an autoinjector from his med pack and injected himself with an antibiotic cocktail. He cleaned up all the items he used and put them in a small bag. That bag went into a small belt pouch. Alan tried to stand but was dizzy from blood loss. He sat back down. Alan pulled out a canteen and had a large drink of water. He pulled out the silicon bowl and Vishnu refused to drink. Alan was worried until he remembered the leaves in the forest. Vishnu was likely getting all the water necessary. Alan pulled the pack and his jerky. He gave several pieces to Vishnu and ate the rest.

Alan had not planned for a long stay and he knew he may need more food. He looked down, saw the stack of snakes, and laughed.

"Were you trying to feed me?" Alan reached down and rubbed his chin. Vishnu sat watching Alan, wagging his tail.

Alan patted the dog then rubbed the dog's chin gently. Vishnu moved forward and Alan rubbed the dog all over the face. He was slow and easy, rubbing away the sleep in the dog's eyes, and moving his hands all over. The giant dog seemed to melt and lay down partially across Alan's legs. Alan held the dog for a moment and then tried to move.

"Damn," Alan said to Vishnu as the dog stood and backed away. "Melody is going to be pissed, isn't she?"

Vishnu wagged their tail and watched Alan try to get up. A tree was nearby. Alan leaned out and grabbed the edge of the tree, holding on as he tried to walk up the side. The dizziness was gone, but the pain was still there. "I kinda wish I had packed the morphine," Alan said. "Never thought I would need it. You know you have packed wrong when you are trying to find your morphine, huh? I bet we can make a joke out of that."

Alan took a step and started to move. "Not exactly as easy as when we came in." Vishnu just watched and looked around the jungle. Alan noticed Vishnu's ears almost rotating like radar to the near infinite number of sounds in the jungle. Alan got his footing.

Alan looked down at his shirt and all the blood that stained it. His vest was still open. He latched it up, then tried to tighten it to put more pressure on the wounds. "We have to move. I best start finding a way."

Vishnu turned and ran to Alan's side. "Hey," Alan said, "Where are you going?" Alan started walking in that direction.

"Hands up," a voice said from behind.

Alan raised his hands.

"Turn around."

Alan turned and faced a single gunman. He was maybe 25. A young man. Unlike many in the area, he was pale white with red hair. He wore black tactical pants and a black shirt with black tactical vest.

"Nice outfit," Alan said. "You the angel of death?"

"I am today," the man replied.

"The angel of death is truly a figure in black," Alan said.

"You nuts?" the man said as he edged closer, "Don't move. Give me that pistol."

"Do you want me to give you the pistol? Or not move?" Alan asked.

The man bent to pull Alan's pistol out of the holster and 100 pounds of black Shepherd grabbed him by the face. The man began to scream but the dog held fast. With nearly herculean effort the man pulled away hard, pushing on Vishnu as portions of his mouth and nose tore away in the dog's immovable grip.

The man grabbed at his face as he stepped back. His weapon fell to the ground. Blood was leaking from the entire area that used to be his face. He was trying to scream but the blood made it more of a gurgle. Alan pulled his knife and put it straight through the man's skull at the top of his head. The man crumpled before him.

Vishnu was pushing skin and hair from her mouth, obviously trying to get the bad taste out.

"Never thought about that," Alan said as he staggered a bit, "but bad guys leave a bad taste in my mouth too. At least figuratively."

Alan considered his surroundings. He realized he was still in mild shock and it was throwing him off. Without Vishnu, he may not last. His memory seemed to be impaired and he need to get help. It was an "aha" moment and he reached into his vest pocket and pulled out the sat phone. He looked at the indicator, jammed. He would work his way to a place he could call for help, and then, well? Then, it was time for Carlos to pay for Shiva, and all the other things he had done.

Chapter 37

The two white helicopters sat in the middle of the clearing. The team had been waiting for 25 minutes for a signal, a call, or anything. The outside clearing was not jammed but as they approached the groups could see the towers from the air. Small outcroppings that covered a wide area. Alex paced the area.

Terry sat in one of the helicopters, asleep, while Jay, Jim, and Rachel walked the perimeter. Alex paced between them. Ronnie walked along the back side.

"We should have heard from him by now," Alex said as he walked.

"How do you want to handle it?" Jim asked, "Wait or move?"

Rachel walked over to them and was far less patient. "I say we move."

Jim laughed. "Of course, you do. Maybe we should move up to the five-mile clearing."

Alex looked at his watch, it was nearly 11. "We are moving up."

They all turned at once as they heard the high-pitched whine of engines heading their way. Jim crouched. "Four-wheeler," he said, "Big one."

Ronnie walked up, "Alex, it's a Honda Fourtrax coming in. Two of them. One from the west, and one from the south. You think they are friendlies or not?"

"Most likely not," Alex said. "Jim, they are the Honda Fourtrax quads."

"Ya don't say," Jim said as he locked down his weapon and aimed at the edge of the rainforest. "Is that a special kind?"

"It must be. You know Ronnie and his knowledge of items," Alex said as he locked his weapon.

"I'm on this," Jay said and got in the back of the helicopter and swung the minigun around towards the thick rainforest. Terry did the same on the other side of the second helicopter. They effectively had almost complete coverage of the front and sides of the clearing with the two outside miniguns. "Stay out of the way of these things if we fire." Jay laughed.

There was a buzzing again, this time they heard the Quads rapidly changing speed and direction, then AK47 fire. Then more whining from the engines.

"What the hell?" Jim asked as he and Alan stayed at ready.

Moments later, a black dog broke from the woods running on three legs and stumbling. One leg was pulled up and soaked with what the group assumed was blood. The big dog was panting heavily. Seeing Jim, Alex, Rachel and the group, he stopped dead.

"Call it," Alex asked.

"Shiva, Vishnu," Jim yelled.

The dog's ears went back, and his tail wagged just a little. Shiva limped forward towards Jim, pressing forward slower and slower. The whines of the engines got louder and in one sudden instant one quad broke into the clearing. It was 60 feet in front of Jay heading towards them and focused on the black dog. There was a look of surprise as the rider saw the two helicopters and he slammed forward as he jumped hard on the brakes. Within seconds on the front side of the clearing a second ATV whizzed into the clearing and the reaction was similar. The ATVs sat at idle. The men looked at the spread-out team, then the first ATV swung around his AK-47.

"Bad move," Jay whispered to himself as he squeezed the trigger on the M134 Minigun. The result was a rain of fire, running on a preset of 33 rounds per second. The small pull of the trigger for less than 10 seconds had several effects. The rider was thrown off the back of the ATV and fell with a sick thud. The bike was shredded in multiple places and fell sideways as the left tires popped. And the jungle behind the ATV bounced like a poodle looking for a treat. Terry let loose a salvo on the other side before the man could move with similar efficiency except the jungle behind the man fell forward as multiple lengths of bamboo were cut down.

Smoke began to emanate from the ATV Jay had shot. The team looked at each other. Jim let his rifle fall to the sling and began to slow clap. Shiva lay in the middle of the clearing and Jim moved to his side. Ronnie ran to the dog, pulling out a first aid kit.

"He's been shot," Ronnie said as he raised his paw. The dog looked up at Jim. The chocolate brown eyes pleading something, something known only to Shiva.

"Where's Alan and the other one?" Rachel asked as she looked down on Ronnie checking the dog. Shiva looked over at her when she said Alan's name. "Well, that got a reaction."

"Something went wrong," Alex said, "We are 11 miles out. Whatever happened went down somewhere between here and the mansion. We can bet they heard those guns go off. It's time to get in the air."

"What about the dog?" Ronnie said. "We can't just leave it here to die."

Alex looked at the dog. Shiva's eyes were matted and worn. The dog was wet with the rainforest and its own blood. The once majestic animal had run a long distance in thick rainforest, for some reason, and now was slowly drifting.

"We made room for the dogs, anyway," Jim said, leaning down and picked up Shiva. "Let's take him, and you can tend to him in the air." The dog was dead weight. The only way to tell it was still alive was the slowly blinking eyes. Jim was gentle and laid the dog in the back of the helicopter with one M134. "Ronnie, get in here."

With Ronnie trying to bandage the dog, Jim took the gun as the rotors spun up and lifted them off the ground. They were less than 6 miles away from the second clearing. Ronnie knew it would not take long at all to get there and he wanted to be sure he could help his team as well. He cleaned the gunshot to the shoulder area of the dog and wrapped the shoulder the best he could. He tried to give the dog water, but Shiva would not take it.

Terry looked back at Ronnie. "How is he?"

"Not good," Ronnie said, "I don't know enough to save him. If we could find Alan maybe he knows, but I have the bleeding mostly stopped."

Jim looked over, "Good job, Ronnie. Now gear up."

As Terry swung around, a bright green helicopter was almost upon them and was firing. Tracers spun and missed. Terry swung the helicopter to starboard so far that Ronnie and Shiva were weightless. Jim grabbed Ronnie's arm as he held on to the secure mounted minigun while Terry righted them. Ronnie wrapped his hand in the seatbelt, holding tight to it and to the massive black dog that panted at his side.

"Get us some room," Jim yelled into his headset.

"Working on it," Terry said as the white streaks of tracers shot by them. "Trying not to get us shot." Terry barked.

Jim looked out the window and was facing the tops of trees. Holding on, he checked Ronnie, but he had already wedged himself so that he would not move. Ronnie was holding Shiva tight in his lap. "Where is Jay?" Jim yelled in the headset. "Tell him to get this guy off of us."

"Jay has two more," Terry said. "We are both 100% defensive right now."

Jim looked to the east and saw the other white copter, swinging from side to side while the others tried to pin it in the middle. "How far are we from the second clearing?" Jim asked.

"We passed over it and are now heading back out," Terry said. "We took a few hits on the last pass, but they are superficial. We might lose our deposit."

"Can you get me a shot?" Jim asked.

"I am trying," Terry yelled as he spun the tail around and began flying sideways.

Jim squeezed the trigger as the other helicopter passed but missed by at least 20 yards.

"Damnit," Jim said.

Jay was fairing no better. The MD500E was faster than the smaller Robinson helicopters but not by much. They were being outgunned by the numbers.

"Swing us around again or take us over to Jay. Let's see if we can take out one of his!" Jim yelled. Jim looked at Ronnie cradling the dog but holding his pistol waiting for a shot on his side of the helicopter.

"We are overheating," Terry said, "I am pushing this thing a little too hard."

Jim saw the warning lights but focused back on the helicopter coming at them from the side. It was lining up and he felt the copter stalling a little as the engines whined. Then the helicopter dropped and sputtered a little. They were close. Jim could see the pilot grabbing the controls and struggling to keep his chopper in the air. As Jim watched, the front window splattered with blood. The other helicopter dropped into a steep dive, barely missing their skids as the plunged into the jungle below.

"What the fuck?" Terry asked.

"Language, young man," Jim said. "Head to Jay. Keep me facing them."

Terry flew their helicopter almost sideways, moving straight at the three dancing helicopters to the west of them. Jim had no idea what had just happened, but he wasn't going to look a gift horse in the mouth.

"Holy shit," Terry said as he pointed at the three. Jay's helicopter was upside down, supposedly an impossibility, but he had flipped behind one of the others and was trying to get a shot. Tracers from all three lit up the sky,

Jim keyed his mic. "We're incoming."

One of the two green helicopters flew right in front of Terry's and Jim opened up as they passed. The green paint flaked away from the helicopter. A moment later, it headed down to the jungle at a high rate of speed. Jay's helicopter was smoking bad, and the last green helicopter was upon him. It would only be a moment now.

Jim yelled, "Terry, get us in there."

The MD500E was stressed hard. They had their own warning lights going off, but Terry swung around and lined up Jim's door with the pursuing craft. Jim aimed like a Texas lawman, with precision and finality. When he squeezed the trigger, the back rotor was shaved from the unsuspecting chopper. Without the counter fan, it suddenly went into a hard spin, lost control, and crashed below.

"Where are we?" Jim asked.

"I'm trying to figure that out," Terry said.

"You guys ok?" Jim said as he keyed the radio.

"We need to touch down. We may have lost an oil line." Jay replied.

"Our clearing is at 2:00, about 400 meters out. We are in bad shape too," Terry said. Both helicopters headed for the small clearing. Terry was clicking switches trying to keep the aircraft up. As they reached the clearing, he pushed down on the power and worked his way down. They landed with a thump, and Terry immediately turned off the engines.

Jay landed about 100 feet from them. His landing was much harder. The engines spun down, and the wind blew. Smoke billowed from Jay's copter. Jay got out and kissed the ground.

Ronnie held on to Shiva. The dog slept.

Chapter 38

Michael slung the Nemesis arms ANSR around his back. He had seen the helicopter battle break out and assembled the weapon from his pack. He was happy with his two shots and was impressed he had hit the helicopter pilot square. He was unsure of the glass and was concerned he would not get enough penetration, he was wrong. He was happy he was wrong, but it was unlike him not to be confident of penetration. The 338 was a good bullet but it was a long distance shot and There were a lot of factors at work. It would have been easier if Michael had brought the big 50 caliber Barret. But he didn't know he would be hunting helicopters, so he didn't want to risk the extra weight. The 338 had done fine, if not better.

He saw the second white helicopter even the odds then clear the playing field. But from the look of it, they had pressed the aircraft too far and would have to land. It was fine, Michael would deal with the issues at hand. Michael was impressed. When he had seen that the helicopters were up, he wasn't sure who was who at first. Then he had seen Jim leaning out the back of one of the white MD500Es. That allowed him to choose his targets.

Michael continued on the path towards the house that was within four miles now. He began at a slow jog and sped it up as he moved between branches and trees. The path before him was fairly clear he saw the cuts in the leaves that had all been done recently. Michael stopped. Before him was a viper laying prone on the ground. Michael picked it up and examined it for a moment. The snake had only minor tooth marks in it, but its neck was broken. Michael guessed one of the dogs had killed it for getting too close. There were many snakes in the rainforest. Since quite a few were pit vipers it would be necessary to always be on guard. Michael dropped the snake, checked the path and kept running.

As Michael ran, he thought about Abby and how much fun they had running. He thought for a moment, *she would have loved to be in a jungle such as this*. Michael had been in this jungle before, though not in Venezuela. Instead, he had been in Brazil many years ago. He was contracted by the United States Government to track a small band of elite fighters that were causing problems in the area. The government could not officially help but there had been enough frustrations caused that it ran up the chain to General Samuel Tarkington. Tarkington had contracted Michael to eliminate the issue.

"These little shits are causing me no end of red ass," Tarkington had said. "I want their leader gone and a message sent that there are some people in the world you should not fuck with."

"You really should choose better toilet paper," Michel had said. "All that potty talk."

"You are a smart-ass little screwball, you know that?" Tarkington barked. "Just get the job done."

Michael had left without a retort and flown to the jungle. He was given the items he needed to survive and had spent five days roaming the Brazilian rainforest with his GPS and solar rechargers. On the fifth day, he found the small group training in the jungle with several prisoners tied to stakes. Apparently one of the prisoners was the son of a US senator, but Michael didn't know them at the time. He waited until dark, went into the camp and used six different Philips screwdrivers to kill each man by pressing the tip through their temples as they slept. There was no sound except the faint crunch as the screwdriver pierced the skull and entered the brain. Michael woke no one, not even the prisoners. He arranged the bodies and made sure no trace of him was left. Once in the jungle again, he called the General and let him know the men were dead but that he had left the prisoners for a rescue team. He relayed the coordinates and waited until the helicopters landed. Sitting in a tree from a significant distance, he was slowly eating jerky as he watched. When the marines had arrived, they found the prisoners tied up but in good health and they found six men in a large circle, each holding a screwdriver in the next man's head. In the center of the group was a Soccer ball with a Philips screw partially turned in it, not enough to pop it, but enough that it was visible. As Michael had sat watching from a distance, the Marines took pictures, shook their heads and watched the jungle. Michael enjoyed the macabre humor of the scene and headed back in the jungle.

It had taken only three days for Michael to make it back to the small city he had arrived in and to get on a plane back to the states. Upon arriving, he received a phone call.

"Very funny. They are calling it a group suicide. Of course, they know someone did it, but they just can't explain how. The prisoners keep telling that no one came in or out." Tarkington had told him. "What would you have done if I would have called you a dumbass?"

"You wouldn't have done that. But if you had I would have had to be creative." Michael had laughed. "I am assuming you called to tell me funds have transferred."

"That they have," Tarkington had replied.

"Thank you," Michael had said and hung up the phone.

As Michael ran through the Venezuelan jungle, he scanned side to side to make sure he was not being tracked and that there was nothing native to the jungle tracking him. He knew there were several predators here, but usually they wouldn't pursue a larger animal.

Michael stopped and read the tracks beneath him. He could see Alan's boots and one of the dogs' tracks crossing back and forth. Alan was walking like a drunk man, so Michael wondered if he had been hurt. He looked both coming and going. Looking further ahead, the erratic pattern continued. The dog seemed fine, but Michael was unsure why there was only one dog. He considered the possibility the second dog was traveling wide. Michael had never worked with Alan and did not know how closely the dogs followed or led him.

He checked his GPS. He was less than a mile from the house. Where before the path was clear, now this new trail towards the house was less than clear. Michael stopped multiple times to check the tracks and work his way to his objective. Then he saw a second set of tracks, and a mix of faded only and new. It was hard to read how things had happened, but something had happened here. ATV tracks crossed the area and at least a dozen men had smashed the jungle, leaving muddy prints everywhere. There was no longer an easy way to track Alan. Michael squatted and considered his options.

"This is a mess," he whispered to himself. If Alan was alive, it would be a miracle.

Michael tried the sat phone again and found it was still jammed. He wanted to check on Abby though he knew she could handle anything.

Michael heard voices in front and from behind him. He doubled back upon himself and found a thicket of bamboo. Slipping into the bamboo, he took out his FN 5.7 and waited. The discussion was in Spanish, so Michael listened. Apparently, one of the men was hoping he would be able to now have a woman named Blanca since the master of the house now had a new wife. The other man was arguing that Carlos would keep both and none of them would get any more. The first man was frustrated by this and was hopeful they would find the mad gringo with the dog soon. Michael was sure there were only two now. He needed answers more than he did bodies, so he put his FN 5.7 away and pulled out two Kunai throwing knives.

The blades of these knives were nearly 10 inches long, larger than the two he usually carried in his belt. Michael felt the weight and instead of throwing, held them one in each hand. The men passed the Bamboo thicket with hardly a glance and Michael stepped out behind them. It was not a quiet move, but it was noise in the jungle so only the back man turned. Michael put the knife blade to the man's neck. The man grimaced but was quiet.

The other man was waking forward still talking about women and when he would be able to have his next woman. Michael didn't want him getting far but might need him alive to get answers, so he threw the second Kunai. It wedged into the back of the man's calf, making him stumble, fall, and yell.

Michael drew his FN5.7. As the man turned, Michael simply said, "shhhhhh." The man struggled to get up and Michael lifted the silenced FN5.7 a little higher. As the man began to grab for his weapon, Michael rolled his eyes and shot. The click was quite loud, but most would not think it was a gunshot. The man fell forward with a bullet dead between his eyes.

"You saw that?" Michael said. "I gave him a chance."

The man with the Kunai to his throat nodded over and over like a broken bobblehead.

"What's your name?" Michael asked, "Do you know English, or should we do this in Spanish."

"I know good English, senor. I am Paco."

"Paco," Michael said, "My friend is here somewhere with his two dogs. Where is he?"

"We cannot find him, senor," Paco said. "We hit one of the dogs, but he continues to run. We cannot find the big man or the other dog."

"Sorry, Paco," Michael said, "My name is Michael. Where is the girl?"

"The new girl?" Paco asked. "She is at the big house. Carlos will marry her tomorrow."

"Marry his own daughter?" Michael asked. "Is that normal here?"

"No mister, Michael," Paco said. "I have seen many strange things though since I began working here. Carlos takes women as he wants and is not a good man."

"You work for him?" Michael asked.

"Jobs are scarce. I was in the army, and needed money for my wife and new daughter," Paco said.

"Would you marry your daughter?"

Paco shook his head, blade still at his neck. "No, it would not be right."

"Where is Carlos, Paco?" Michael asked.

"He is in the big house. His anger is huge today," Paco said, "He was tossing dishes and hurting tables and that stuff."

"Why is his anger huge?" Michael asked, "The big man?"

"Yes," Paco said, "The big man got inside and almost took the girl again, except she yelled. Carlos was furious he got past us again. He killed the head of us, the head of security for his bad work."

"How many more of you are there?" Michael asked.

"Senor," Paco said, "there are many of us. At least," he paused for a moment counting, "forty?"

"How many were in the helicopters?" Michael asked.

"This is true. At least four in the helicopters. So perhaps 35 left. Two men chase the dog that is free. Carlos was angry at that too. We think the dog lured us away, so we are now searching for the big man closer to the house. Carlos says he will keep coming until he gets the girl."

"Paco," Michael said, "What am I to do with you? I don't think you are a bad guy, but I can't have you running around interfering with me. If I thought you were going to be a problem, I would just kill you. On the other hand, you have been quite cooperative without me having to push my knife into your neck or shoot you in various painful places."

"Yes, Michael," Paco stammered. "I do not want trouble. If you let me go, I will leave and not come back. I have seen you are serious."

"Ok, that's settled," Michael said. "You head home, and I will go save my friend."

"Si, Senor," Paco replied and turned to walk away.

Michael began walking the other way, his pistol still in his hand. Hearing Paco twist, Michael swung in the blink of an eye, and watched Paco bring his rifle up. Michael shot him in the right arm and walked forward.

"Please, senor," Paco cried. "It would have been more money for my family."

"Did you lie to me?" Michael asked.

"No, no," Paco said, "I would not lie. I would not lie to you."

"Are you sure?" Michael asked.

"Yes," Paco whimpered holding his arm, "I tell the truth, please, my daughter."

"OK," Michael said, "Your daughter is better off without a father who is a liar." Paco cringed as Michael raised the FN 5.7 and shot him between the eyes. His body slumped. Then Michael turned and moved down the path towards the estate.

Chapter 39

Alan was still moving forward. He pulled the GPS out of his pocket as he panted. Looking down, Vishnu looked up at him. "I know," Alan said, "We need some more food. Maybe we should have eaten more snake before we took up this windmill."

Vishnu moved his head back and forth, tilting it from side to side.

"I know," Alan said as he swayed. "The old Man of La Mancha thing is beyond you."

Alan laughed and sat down. "It's really hot, isn't it?" Alan said, "I think I am pushing too hard." Alan looked at his side to check the gunshot wounds. The seals were holding on the bandages, but they were puffy, and blood filled. He was not doing himself any favors by trying to save the girl. He thought for a moment about Shiva and the tears began to well up in his eyes. He choked them back then thought of Melody. They had only just begun their relationship and Alan could see years of excitement and passion in front of him, if only. If only he survived.

Vishnu looked out to the jungle, "Maybe you should go, there is no sense in both of us ending up dead."

The dog looked sad for a moment and stared into Alan's eyes.

"You would do anything for me, wouldn't you?" Alan asked the dog. "I would for you too. I'm sorry about Shiva," Alan sniffed, "I would have saved him if I could."

The dog again shifted his head back and forth as if trying to understand more than just the words, but perhaps the man behind the words. Alan looked at the dog and rubbed his head with slow soothing strokes. "I guess I screwed up this time."

"Do you know where we are?" Alan asked the dog. Alan leaned against a tree, "I need to rest for a second. Just a second. And then we will go get this girl." Alan closed his eyes as he leaned against the tree and slid down to the jungle floor.

Vishnu watched Alan and curled up next to him as he slept on the side of the tree. Vishnu listened intently to the sounds of jungle and the people all around. People were closer now. All over the area it there were people talking, walking and making sounds. Vishnu's ears rotated and he listened to it all. The dog seemed concerned as it looked back and forth across the forest area.

Alan stirred. He opened his eyes and looked at Vishnu, "I was out again, wasn't I?"

Vishnu looked at Alan and cocked his head to the side.

"I know," Alan said, his eyes glazed, "You don't understand, but I appreciate you taking care of me."

Alan reached over and rubbed the dog on the head. The dog closed its eyes as Alan rubbed with deliberate softness. Alan sat back against the tree. "What do you think, Vishnu, are we going to make it out alive? Maybe we should just head out, you and me. We can go home, skip saving the girl. Be home with Melody. We can pick up Shiva along the way. He will want some water. I think I have some water here."

Alan pulled out his canteen and took a drink. He took out the small bowl and poured some for Vishnu. Vishnu took a drink and watched Alan. Vishnu's ears rotated back and forth paying attention to everything.

Alan stood. "We have to save the girl," Alan said, "Sorry, my friend. We will come out ahead." Alan reached in his holster and pulled out his pistol. He checked the magazine. "Full. Let's go."

Alan walked with more determination now. Vishnu stayed close. Alan was making progress like a windup tin soldier cross the floor. He was trying to make sure he made no noise and was doing a good job. Vishnu ran in front of him and made a small woof.

"Yeah, I hear them," he said. Alan made a hand gesture and Vishnu crouched on the ground with him.

Two men crashed through a big group of fronds right into Alan and Vishnu. Alan shot twice, dead center of each man and they fell back. Alan walked forward; the men were not hurt bad. Their bulletproof vests took the brunt of the shot, but it still had to hurt like hell. Alan looked at Vishnu, then shot the first man in the head. The second man was reaching for his weapon. Alan shot for his head and missed. As the man pulled his pistol from the holster, Alan fired again, and the man went limp.

"That was close," he said to Vishnu. "We need to move. I bet they heard that."

Vishnu ran to the front and Alan followed on the way back to the house. He felt like Mike Tyson had pounded his head for an hour, but he had a job to do. He would not let everyone down. Alan pressed forward. Vishnu did not move far ahead but scouted along the way. Another man ran in front of them and saw them too late. Alan shot the man in the chest. Then knelt to him as the man groaned in pain. The bullet proof vest had saved him but again, it was painful.

"How many?" Alan asked with the tip of his weapon in the man's face.

"Go to hell," the man said.

Alan put the gun next to the man's ear and fired. The man screamed, and blood began running from his popped eardrum. Alan whispered in the man's other ear. "How many?"

"Forget it," the man screamed as he cradled his ear with one hand, while reaching for his weapon with his other.

Alan pulled the trigger with the weapon under the man's chin. The man's skull broke, and blood sprayed. He looked at Vishnu again. "I gave him a chance, right?"

Vishnu ran ahead and came right back, waiting for Alan to move forward. Alan stood with determination but obvious effort. "It would be nice to have my rifle," Alan said as he moved further.

Alan saw Vishnu stop and drink the water from a leaf. He remembered Shiva and Vishnu doing that earlier, so he reached down and drank from a leaf too. The water was cool and fresh. It felt good.

Alan stood and began walking again. He actually was starting to feel better. He pulled out the GPS and looked at his position. He was less than one quarter mile from the house. This time she had to come with him.

Vishnu sniffed the air and listened. Alan crouched, waiting. Vishnu crouched as two more men rushed into the area. Alan fired his weapon and hit the man dead center in the chest. The second man whipped his AK47 towards Alan. He pulled the trigger and realized the slide had locked back. Vishnu grabbed the man's arm that held the AK47 and the weapon fired into the air. Alan dropped the magazine from the pistol, reached into his vest, grabbed another magazine, slapped it in the pistol then chambered the round. He fired and hit the man being held by Vishnu in the head. The second man, who was on the ground, was reaching for his weapon only to have Alan shoot him in the head before he could move another inch.

"I am such an idiot," Alan said to Vishnu.

Alan picked up the AK47 and pulled two magazines from each man. The magazines were taped so they could be rotated easily. Alan holstered his pistol and held the AK47 at waist level. Then he began walking forward again.

"Ever feel like you are in a bad video game, Vishnu?" Alan asked. "Like Alan Spears' over the top unknown bad guys." Alan used a semi game show voice like one of the old Price is Right shows.

The dog woofed softly.

"Yeah, me too," Alan said. "It would be a good name though."

The dog once again ran towards the front and moved forward with deliberate steadiness. Alan was less woozy, but he still was nowhere near stable. Alan stopped for a moment and checked his wounds. The strong seals still held but Alan had no idea how. He knew he was pushing too hard. He held the AK47 forward and let the sling take most of the weight.

"Like that's helping," Alan said. "I am still carrying it. And this big pack? Why am I carrying this pack?" He reached back and realized he did not have his pack. "Who took my pack, Vishnu?"

The dog looked at him with his knowing chocolate eyes and woofed softly.

"Oh, that's right," Alan replied to the dog, "I left it, huh? I know. I am in shock I am sure, but we will be ok, Vishnu. We will make it."

Vishnu knelt and looked at the thick leaves. Alan turned and waited with the animal. Moments later, two men broke through the leaves with guns forward. Alan sprayed the area with AK-47 fire and the men fell.

"Whew, that was close huh?" Alan said. "I wonder where this guy gets all the henchmen. Is there a toll-free number somewhere? Henchmen are us?" Alan giggled to himself and tried to shake off the increasing feeling of numbness in his head.

A small breeze blew in the deep jungle. The sounds were deafening now. Rain dripped down from the canopy and the moisture was cooling even though the heat was sweltering. Monkeys screeched in the background.

Then came a moment of silence.

Vishnu jumped and lurched forward as a snare line caught his head. Alan swung his rifle around to fire and was hit broadside by the butt of another rifle. He looked up and saw Vishnu snared by a second line as he twisted and sprung trying to get away.

"Should we kill them?" a voice asked.

"No. He wants them alive at the house," another voice replied.

"This damn dog is like the devil," the first voice replied.

"It'll calm down, or suffocate," the other voice replied.

Alan tried to stand to get to Vishnu. He began crawling to him. Darkness came as he was hit again with the butt of a rifle.

Chapter 40

Jay had the aircraft access doors open and was working on the engine with a great deal of vigor. His hands went back and forth, working on lines as Terry looked behind him.

"How long until we get in the air?" Alex asked.

"As long as it takes," Jay said, "and longer if you keep distracting me. Go through the copters and find me some extra hydraulic fluid."

Alex went off to the second helicopter.

"We don't need any hydraulic fluid," Terry whispered.

"It will get him out of our hair," Jay said as he worked on the engine. "I think we are ok right now. There really wasn't much wrong. I was worried about this rotor connection. It felt like it was sticking but it seems fine. Maybe it was just too much running around in the air like we did."

"Who do you think took out that first bird?" Terry asked.

"Not sure. But it sure saved our asses when we needed it," Jay replied.

"More helicopters?" Terry asked, "They had radios, you know."

"Maybe, but we are in the middle of nowhere. I would say we have at least an hour before there is any chance of more coming. It may be the jammers that are out here were affecting them as well. Hard to say. We won't be here much longer, but if we are, we'll have to deal." Jay started cleaning up. "It's like when you go into a new bar. You never know who is just drinking for fun, and who is drinking to start a fight."

Gunfire erupted again in the direction of the house. Terry looked over. "Someone's pretty pissed."

"Yeah," Jay said, "We can only hope they don't find Alan."

Jay finished, closing up the MD500E, "Start it up." The engine whined, and the rotors began turning. There was no sputter. The rotors were turning as they should. "Shut it down!" Jay yelled. "Let's double check the other one."

Jay and Terry walked to the other helicopter. Ronnie was still in the back with the big black German Shepherd. Jay looked at the dog, "How is he?" Alex was rummaging through the baggage compartment and looked around the edge.

"Sleeping," Ronnie said, "But I'll be damned if I know how he was moving so easily." Ronnie showed Jay and Terry a bullet. "I took this out of his leg. It must have hurt a lot."

"A lot?" Jay echoed. "Ronnie, I am betting it hurt like shoving a leprechaun up his ass."

"Like I said, it hurt a lot," Ronnie said. "The dog is exhausted."

Terry laughed, "He is big on understatement."

"I suppose," Jay said as he opened an access panel.

Jim walked up to them, "How much longer?"

"As long as it takes," Jay said, "You guys should check the guns on these things, so we don't have to reload when we take off."

"Got it," Jim said.

Rachel was walking the clearing and ran back to them.

"There are a few ATVs out there, heading this way," Rachel said. "We got maybe a minute or two before they break clearing, unless they turn."

"I'll check the guns on the other helicopter. Jim, you and Rachel cover us just in case." Alex turned. "Ronnie, get on that gun. Secure the dog and be ready for a fight. Jay, Terry, get us ready to get in the air."

"On it," Terry said.

"I could be sitting in the Scotsman, drinking thousand-dollar scotch, but no, fly a helicopter, sounds fun." He checked all the fittings. "We are looking pretty good here. Try it."

Terry started the helicopter, and it spun up with smooth precision.

"Cut it," Jay called out, closing up all the access hatches as Terry walked back. "These things can take a beating. I am betting we just strained a little too hard with all the twists and turns. We won't be taken by surprise again and may be a little better."

"Got it," Terry said.

"I'll fly Jim and the kid. You take the other two. We need to get moving in a few and get to the house. Get the girl, and get our asses out of here," Jay said.

"You don't have to tell me," Terry said.

"I feel like I am in a bar full of jazz lovers and I want to play classic rock. There's gonna be another fight," Jay said.

"That's a crappy analogy. I like Jazz and Rock," Terry said.

"You would," Jay laughed.

Gunfire erupted as four ATVs came out of the jungle into the tall grass.

Jay pulled out his 1911, and Terry grabbed a rifle.

Shiva looked up but did not move. Ronnie got on the minigun but could not see the shooters.

Jim and Rachel were running. They could see them coming back as the ATVs followed. Rachel was in a hard run. Jim, a little heavier, was running but not quite as fast.

"C'mon, fat boy," Rachel shouted.

"I am not fat," Jim yelled back as he pushed towards the helicopters.

In the helicopter, Alex spun the minigun around to aim behind Jim and Rachel. Rachel spun on her heels and laid down fire with her M16. When Jim passed her, Rachel turned and continued to run. A single ATV came into view well enough to aim at and Ronnie opened up the minigun. The 7.62 shells hit the driver throwing them off the seat, but the ATV kept running towards them, driverless. Jim turned and ran to the ATV that was slowing down as it lost momentum. Rachel turned and ran with him. "I'll drive. You shoot," Jim said.

Jim unslung his M16 and handed it to Rachel. He mounted the ATV and slid behind the handlebars. Rachel jumped on behind him and stood. Her feet were on the footpegs with her shins touching a second set of pegs. "Well, this works," she said, getting a feel for how she could stand. "I hope you have earplugs in."

"I'd be deaf if I didn't," Jim said as he gunned the engine and headed back towards the other ATVs, forcing Rachel to sit down.

"Damn! Warn a gal why don't ya," Rachel shouted.

The other ATVs were leaving the area, not wanting to face the minigun, but Jim and Rachel were on their tails.

Back at the helicopters, Alex was cursing. "Damnit, we should not split up."

"Jay, stay with the dog," Alex barked. "Ronnie, Terry and I will get that double gunned bird in the air," Alex looked over at the edge of the clearing where the ATVs were heading into the thick jungle. The entire area seemed to be filled with shooting, near and far. Alex wondered when their luck would run out, if ever.

Chapter 41

Michael heard voices far ahead. He worked his way through the dense jungle one step at a time, making sure to make no noise and being careful to leave minimal tracks. As he walked, he turned often and checked both in front and behind. He was almost like a modern-day Tarzan, at one with the jungle that surrounded him. There were a number of sounds around him. He had heard the M134s fire somewhere behind him. It was a few miles back. Michael guessed it was from around the clearing. In front, he heard weapons firing, and numerous sounds that he wasn't entirely sure of at the moment. Michael heard the ATVs in the distance, and he heard more gunfire.

Michael picked up the pace as he headed towards the mansion. He was aware time was short. He was not sure of all of the pieces in play on the board, but he knew he had to resolve everything with speed and vigor. Michael felt like a chess player on a giant board. A player that was a piece in play as well. Alan's tracks were now mingled with others. There were people following him, several people. Michael was not sure if that was good or bad, but he supposed it was not good.

It was only a few minutes later that Michael came upon a rear guard. Dressed in dark camo, he was probably over 6 feet tall and very muscular, wearing a tank top instead of a full shirt. A bandolero of ammo was wrapped around his chest and he carried a belt fed M60. The man was watching behind and trying to scan the area. Michael remained in a thicket until the man looked away. Michael took advantage of his distraction and stepped out behind him. The man swung the M60 around. Michael caught the barrel of the weapon and pointed it into the forest as the man pulled the trigger.

"Impressive," Michael said as the man tried to pull away and get a bead on Michael. In his haste to get control of the weapon, Michael pushed down with one arm while he drew an FN5.7 with the other and pointed it at the man's head. "Who's trigger action will make a mark?"

The man dropped his weapon and stared at the pistol pointed at him.

"Who are you?" he asked.

"No one in particular. At least, no one you know," Michael replied. "Who are you?"

"Name's Peter. Peter Castle," the man said in a British or Australian accent.

"I am tempted to tell a joke," Michael replied.

"Don't bother," Peter said, "I've heard them all."

"You're not from around here," Michael said.

"Naw," Peter watched the FN5.7 as it pointed at his head. "I was brought in recently to clean up security a little. The guy here, Carlos, he expected some trouble. You were not on the list."

"I never am," Michael said.

"Ya think you could shoot me before I grabbed you," Peter smiled with a look of an indignant child crossing his face.

The FN5.7, pointed at Peter's face, never moved. Michael's eyes were locked on Peter's as he pulled the second FN5.7 from his left holster and shot Peter in his right foot.

"Aww fuck!" Peter said as he fell to the ground and grabbed his foot. "What did ya do that fer?" Peter's eyes were again looking into Michael's. Michael's crystal blue eyes pierced his very soul.

"You asked me a question. I wanted you to understand the answer before I ask you the next question," Michael said.

"I git ya, I git ya," Peter replied. "Damn, that hurt like hell."

"I put it in the meat of your foot. You will limp, but I didn't cause real damage," Michael recited. "We can pick other places if you like. How many men are still here?"

"I have no fuckin' idea," Peter said.

Michael fired again, and Peter yelped. "That went through the meat of your calf. It is gonna hurt like hell for a while, but the bullet went through. You will be fine."

"What are ya?" Peter said, "some sort of trick shooter? Fuck! Why'd ya shoot me?"

"My time is precious right now," Michael said. "How many men? And do they have the big man? Before you answer," Michael stared in the man's eyes, a pistol in each hand, "my next shot will kill you."

"Fuck," Peter said. "I got paid. Who gives a damn? Yeah, they have the big man. They are takin' him and a dog to the house now. Carlos wants to kill him to show his new girl he has the power."

"...and the number of men?" Michael asked.

"Maybe 20 or 25 left. Some are out trying to find the other dog. Some are trying to deal with the other folks comin' in," Peter said, "You're with them, aren't you?"

Michael squatted as Peter tried to stop the bleeding in his leg. "No," Michael said, "I know them, but I am not with them. I owe a debt to the big man. I will pay it shortly. Do I need to worry about you?"

"Naw," Peter said, "I'm done. Ya can take care of your business with no worries from me. My life isn't worth the money he's payin."

"If you cross me, I will surely kill you," Michael said as his eyes stared at Peter's, never wavering.

"Yeah, yeah, I believe you." Peter said. "Just don't kill me."

Michael holstered one weapon and kept one pointed directly at Peter's nose. He reached with his free a hand and pulled out a zip tie. "Hands," Michael said.

Peter put the zip tie on his hands, pulling it as tight as he could. Michael pulled hard to finish.

"Now how do I keep you from moving," Michael took another zip tie and pushed it through the hole in Peter's calf as Peter screamed. He then tied his hands through the loop, effectively tying Peter to his own leg. "I am sure you could rip your calf apart and come after me, but you won't come very fast."

"I told ya..." Peter began.

"What people say, and what they do, are very different sometimes," Michael said. "I just prevented you from becoming a corpse. You should thank me."

"I will find you and kill you someday," Peter spat.

"I've heard that joke before," Michael laughed, his eyes never leaving Peter's. "You will not see me again unless it is to free you." Michael rummaged through Peter's vest and found a knife. "I will give you a chance." Michael threw the knife into a tree a few feet away. "It will hurt like hell, but you can make it to that tree and cut yourself loose. You can also wait for me to come back through. If I see you and you are untied, I will eliminate you, if you decide to go, better get some distance. If you try to come after me, well? I am being generous today with you because you answered my questions."

To the right of them, a man burst through the undergrowth, perhaps having heard the click of the silenced 5.7. Without his eyes leaving Peter's, Michael drew and shot once.

Peter turned and looked at the man who had just come through. A single bullet hole in his forehead. He twitched only a little before he fell forward.

Peter turned back to Michael, still looking straight at him. "Who are you?"

"No one in particular," Michael said. "Do I have to worry about you calling for help or can I leave the gag off?"

"I won't call," Peter looked at the man who just fell and the blood slowly oozing from a hole between his eyes, "and I will be gone when you come back."

"Good," Michael replied. "Thanks for your help."

"Yer gonna kill this guy?" Peter asked.

"Why?" Michael replied with some amusement.

"Well," Peter said, "I would rather not have to explain this as a reference. Rather just bury the whole thing."

"You won't have to worry about him, one way or another."

"Thanks," Peter said.

Michael stood from his squatting position and began to jog in the direction of the house.

Chapter 42

"I am worried," Melody said. "I don't want to be worried, but I am."

Melody and Abby stood on the hill where the house would be completed eventually. The framing was progressing very well. Abby was a good project manager, keeping everyone on task and moving and in good spirits, as well.

The ride over had been uneventful. Melody was obviously agitated. She had talked about everything and nothing until they had arrived on site. It was not until the crew had arrived and began working on the framing of the house with a new truckload of lumber that she began talking about Alan.

"I am sure he will be ok," Abby said. "He is a big boy. He can take good care of himself."

"I know," Melody said, "this is a bit much for anyone. Have you heard from Michael?"

"No, but that isn't unusual unless he is concerned," Abby replied. "What brought this on?"

"We are sitting here," Melody said, "building your house. It is a foundation for you and Michael, and well? I want that foundation too. We have a house, but we are just starting out. I am not sure what I would do if this suddenly ended."

"Ended," Abby said. "That can be a scary word."

"I know," Melody said. "My whole life has been full of ends. I was hoping to have a longer beginning, this time."

"You will," Abby said as she reviewed the blueprints. "There is nothing better than growing together. When Michael and I were in school, he was dating another girl at first. She and I were best friends and roommates. I never thought they were a good match. Michael was strong and determined, and she was more of a girly girl. You know, not really a fit. They did have good times together, but her parents were very liberal.

They did not like Michael at all, and they were very vocal about it." Abby turned and walked to the trucker that had delivered the load of lumber.

"Your load doesn't seem to match what I have listed here. You need to call someone to figure out where the rest of it is," Abby said to the truck driver.

"Not my problem," the driver said to Abby and turned to walk away.

"Make it your problem," Abby said.

"Why should I?" the driver turned back to her. "I drive from point A to point B. I don't care what I haul. I don't work for the company. I work for me."

David saw Abby talking with the driver and shut down the crane. Climbing down, he ran up to the two. Tom joined them from the top of the framed first floor as they were working up.

"What's the problem?" David asked.

"The load is short. Not a bunch, but enough," Abby explained. "I was just asking this gentleman to call and have it fixed."

"I was just telling this woman, it is not my problem," the driver said.

David looked back at Abby and saw the look in her eyes. Tom looked at David, then Abby and chuckled.

"Let me take care of this," David said.

David put his arm around the driver and walked him towards the truck. Tom followed behind and looked back at Abby, trying to contain a laugh, and finally making a serious face. The driver turned and looked at Abby. David said something, and the driver's head snapped back. The driver started to look again but David held his face. The driver looked him in the eye as David was saying something. Tom put his hands out and added something to the conversation. David and Tom walked back to Abby as the driver pulled out his cell phone and began scanning through numbers.

"What was that all about?" Abby asked, "You do know I can take care of this."

"Oh yeah, I know," David said.

Tom laughed a little. "That was funny."

"What?" Abby said, showing some frustration.

"Well," Tom began, "David told him the first two men from his crew were in the hospital in Pikeville now after mouthing off to you. Driver said he would sue. David said to him, 'You gonna get up in front of all your friends and tell them a five-foot nothing woman beat the hell out of you?' and he said, 'Hell yeah.' Then David asked if anyone would believe it. The driver was trying to figure it out when David said, 'I still can't find JR if that helps ya. He was my third guy.' He is calling to find out where the rest of the load is."

Abby laughed a little, "Not exactly the truth."

"He ain't from around here, so who cares?" David said.

"Truth," Tom replied.

The driver walked up to the small group. David put his hands on Abby's shoulder as though he was straightening the fabric.

"Ma'am," the driver said, "There will be a second truck tomorrow with the rest of the lumber. They apologized for the inconvenience. I will drive it out personally."

"Thank you," Abby said with a grimace. Spinning around, she walked back to the plans with Melody close behind.

When they reached the makeshift table, Abby looked out of the corner of her eye. The driver was looking towards her, shaking his head. As she did, she turned to Melody and laughed, "Why not?" Abby's leather purse was next to her. The brown clutch had two loops on the bottom. Abby slapped the table for a second, acted angry and pulled one of the loops, revealing an 8-inch Kunai throwing knife. She spun around and threw the knife 10 feet into a tree. Shaking her head, she put both hands on the table.

"What's he doing?" Abby asked.

"He got in the truck in a big hurry. He is watching you in the mirror." Melody giggled as she turned back to Abby.

"Well, that was fun," Abby said. "I really need to practice more."

The crane started up again, and Abby watched the boom come down to pick up another load of the lumber.

"You need to stop right now," Melody said, "What happened with Michael that got you together?"

"She left him when he needed her," Abby said, "I thought I told you that before. We were in college, she left him, and we became better friends. We like a lot of the same things. We enjoy each other. And one day, we switched from friends to more. It just made sense. We have been building a relationship since then."

Abby heard the big truck start up. As she turned, she saw it rumble down the hill of the driveway and off.

"I guess he had to go. Anyway," Abby turned back to Melody, "If you think about the danger and all the other things that Michael faces, I just know he will be back. Anything else is not an option. You need to be the same way. We haven't known Alan for long, but Michael was aware of him by reputation. He is not a pushover."

Melody walked to the tree where Abby's knife was still sticking out. She was quiet and looked at the blade embedded in the trunk. She studied the fine edges then reached up and yanked the knife out.

"I know you're right," Melody said. "I need to get a grip. Thanks, Abby."

Tom and David walked over as Abby was reinserting her knife into her purse. "I guess you scared him good enough to go get the load today."

"What?" Abby replied.

"He saw you throw that knife and said he would be back," Tom laughed. "Big ole guy scared of a little knife."

David laughed, "Yeah, yeah."

Tom laughed back. "I got respect. He was plain scared."

David laughed. "Abby, we were gonna break for lunch. You wanna go with us?"

"Mel and I will stay here, if that's ok," Abby said. "We are going to make some phone calls."

"You want some food?" Tom asked.

"Sure," Abby said, "Bring back anything."

"Got it," Tom said. "We will surprise ya."

"You do that," Abby said.

The men loaded into a big Chevy truck and headed out.

"Mel," Abby said, "Let's call Alex and see what he says."

"Good idea," Melody replied.

Abby pulled her phone out of her back pocket and scrolled to "Alex Brown". She pressed call and waited. The phone rang, and within a moment, went to voicemail.

"Voicemail," Abby said. "I am sure they are fine. We will call again in a while if we don't hear from them first."

Melody paced for a moment. "He's a big boy. He can take care of himself."

Chapter 43

"Wake up," Alan heard as the water sprayed over his face. Alan gasped a little as he woke up. The pain was overwhelming in his head and his side. Someone held him by his arms. He became aware of his surroundings a little at a time. It was like the shades of his mind were opening in phases. He was in the yard of the house. Two men were holding him. There were three other men, holding Vishnu to his left. Vishnu rolled and tried to get away. The three ropes held him only slightly. Alan was on his knees in the thick bluegrass of the yard.

Details began to fill in. There were three other guards he could see. His focus went in and out. He was dimly aware that Carlos was not there yet, but Alan was sure he was close. The rest of the yard was open, but no one else was in view. Alan listened. He heard the sounds of the jungle, occasional ATV sounds, and maybe gunfire. Alex must be close. *Had he heard helicopters before?*

Alan still felt out of sorts, but it was not as bad as it had been. Was it the short nap given by the butt of a weapon? Or was it the adrenaline coursing through his veins.

"Let the dog go," Alan said.

"Hell no," one of the men said.

Alan flexed and lifted one of the men holding him off the ground. Both men tackled him and held him down hard. He tried to move, tried to stand but they had leverage. Vishnu struggled more as Alan tried to get to him.

"Damnit," Alan said and pressed hard, throwing one man into the air. As he stood, Carlos walked out of the balcony above him, holding Magda by her arm. He was dressed all in white and holding a stainless-steel revolver. Magda was dressed in a white dress with a near see-through top with her bra showing underneath.

"That is enough," Carlos yelled. "Move again and I will kill you, her, or the dog."

Alan stood still and did not move. One man still holding onto his arm.

"Let him go," Carlos said. "I hold the cards now. He will not try anything as he knows I will act where he will not. Yes, Alan, I know you are weak. I know your name now and I will find those people who are dear to you. You should not have meddled in my affairs. You know you are too weak to do what is necessary. You will instead follow orders. If you had gotten me, tell me Alan, would you have killed me or given me to the DEA?"

"I was not interested in you," Alan said. "Only saving the girl."

"This girl?" Carlos said. "As I said, she is mine. She was mine. She will always be mine. I made her so she could be mine as I did her mother." Carlos licked the side or Magda's face and Magda grimaced. "Do not worry, my daughter. You will come to like being my wife."

"Kiss my ass," Magda said, slamming her foot down.

Carlos laughed. "You missed. It will be good to break you as I broke your mother."

Magda struggled, but Carlos held her tight.

"You are sick," Alan said. "She is your daughter."

"She is a woman for me to do with as I please," Carlos said. "You are so civilized. You just don't understand how life should be."

"Really," Alan replied. "How should life be?" Alan scanned the area, trying to find a solution that would get him free. The second man he had thrown was now next to him on the other side. There were eight men he could see. Three guards, three on the dog, and the two with him. Then there was Carlos and Magda. He saw no easy way at the moment.

"What do you want?" Alan said stalling.

"From you? Nothing unless you can tell me where Maria and Margarite are right now. Tell me, Alan. Can you tell me where they are?" Carlos asked. "Do you think you can tell me where my daughters are?"

"I don't know," Alan said, "and I would not tell you if I did know." Alan stood in defiance, looking straight into Carlos's eyes.

"Are you sure?" Carlos asked.

"Of course, I am sure," Alan replied.

The two shots rang out. The yelp next to him was like a sword being pushed through his soul. Vishnu fell to the ground and struggled for a moment then stopped moving.

Alan swung his arms backwards and smashed both men in the face with his massive fists. They fell backwards as though they had been hit with two sledgehammers. The men holding the dog let loose their ropes, and Alan ran to Vishnu. The dog's brown eyes were open, but there was no life left in them. None. There was a moment that lasted forever as Alan felt that life and remembered from puppy to dog, from dog to friend and all that was in between. Alan felt the times they had together and remembered Shiva's scream only a day ago. The sorrow became pain, the pain became anger, and the anger became something more.

Alan screamed and jumped up. The five men jumped on him and pushed him to his knees. Alan stared at Carlos. "I will watch you die, and you will beg me for it."

"Ohh you Americans," Carlos laughed as he held Magda. "Too much television. Too many action heroes that talk tough and don't say much. Too many things that take you away from reality. I am inevitable. Think about it, Alan. I waited ten years for one of the girls to make a mistake, and then Magda actually reached out to me. You will not see that in your movies."

"You watch too many movies," Alan said, "Too many bad speeches by bad guys."

"I will ask you again," Carlos said, "Where are the girls?"

"I was not lying," Alan said. "I don't know."

"That's too bad," Carlos said, "Who is in the helicopters?"

Alan looked around again. There were five men on him and two guards. *Where was the third?*

"I am not sure, but I could guess," Alan said.

"Then guess for me, Alan. Tell me who has come to help you," Carlos said.

"My friends," Alan said, "they would come for me. They are here to pick me up."

"It will not matter," Carlos replied. "The Army has sent four more helicopters to destroy them. They will soon be no more. You are of no more use to me."

"What if I can get you started in finding the girls?" Alan asked.

"No," Magda said, "Don't tell him."

Carlos slapped her and threw her to the ground. "Learn your place, girl. You will soon be my woman, and you will know your place." Carlos turned to Alan as Magda held her face and began to get up.

"You would not lie to me," Carlos asked, then turned and knocked Magda to the ground again. "Stay down, girl."

"Why would I lie?" Alan said. "I have told you the truth the whole time."

"You said you did not know," Carlos replied.

Alan looked and did not see the missing guard. But a moment later, he saw one of the other guards fall to the ground. A solid black blur, protruding from his eye as he fell. The jungle was so loud there was no sound except the sounds of the bush.

The third guard fell to the ground in the distance. They were well within sight, but the men holding Alan were focused on him. He needed to be a distraction.

"I can show you on a map. Do you have a map of the United States?" Alan asked.

"Let him up," Carlos said to the men and then yelled, "Blanca, tráeme un mapa de los estados unidos."

Carlos waited, and a beautiful young lady brought out a map. She was dressed in a floral gown off the shoulders and had a red flower in her hair. She handed Carlos a map.

"Tell me where to find them," Carlos said.

"I can show you," Alan said. "Throw me the map or come down."

Carlos looked at Alan warily. "What are you planning? It will not work, you know."

"I am planning nothing," Alan said. "You have killed my dogs. What do I have left?"

"It is true," Carlos said, "Without the dogs you are less a man. You threatened to kill me..."

"Stop boring me with your speeches," Alan broke in. "Either kill me or throw me the map. Stop giving me your twisted view of life. It will make me throw up."

Blanca smiled behind Carlos. Magda was still on the ground.

Carlos waved his gun at the men, "Let him go." Carlos threw the map. "Show them."

There was a sound rising in the jungle. It was the sound of several ATVs at high RPM. Alan hoped he still had some luck, or a guardian angel, or Alex, or something that was out there. He pointed to the map and one of the men moved close. Carlos was leaning against the balcony like some sadistic waiting vulture. His gun was dangling loosely in his hands.

Alex showed the man next to him and glanced around, there were four men a few feet away, and one man looking over his shoulder. As he pointed, the man leaned in, and Alan grabbed his head, snapping it down. With a twist, he snapped the man's neck and wobbled towards the house.

Carlos took two seconds to see what was happening and tried to pull his gun up, but Alan was already under the balcony. Carlos had no shot. The remaining four men were pulling out their weapons and suddenly fell to the ground, one by one, each with a single shot in the head. It was as though the hand of death was upon them.

Carlos grabbed Blanca and pulled her in front of him, ducking as he walked backwards toward the house. He peeked forward as he retreated and saw nothing. Once inside, he grabbed Blanca by the neck and pulled her along with him. Carlos yelled loudly and men came through smashed out windows in the front of the house. Gunfire erupted from the house into all areas of the jungle. The sound was deafening. Leaves and trees bounced under the constant onslaught.

Alan bashed in the window next to him and cleared the glass away. He peeked in. The room was small, and the door closed. He knew he should stop. His side hurt bad, so he knew had torn something. Glancing at the yard, he saw the body of Vishnu. Turning like a man renewed, Alan ignored the pain, and jumped into the house.

Chapter 44

Jim gunned the engine on the ATV, and they rocketed through the wood in pursuit of the escaping pair. A branch in front of them blocked the path, and Jim pulled up on the handlebars "Hold on."

They hit hard but there was enough momentum that the ATV launched forward over the log, momentarily airborne. Rachel gripped Jim hard with one arm and held her M16 in the other. As they passed another tree, she could see another ATV in front of them. The path was tight, and the constant twists and turns made aiming hard.

"Don't say anything stupid," Rachel yelled as she stood up and straddled Jim's shoulder. Jim looked over and was face to face with her zipper.

"Well, hello there," Jim yelled. "Fancy meeting you here."

"Damnit, Jim," Rachel said as the increased leverage allowed her to aim. "You are such a pig."

Rachel fired several times at the ATV in front of them. She could see the driver and a rider holding on for dear life at high speed through the dense jungle. Rachel fired one shot at a time while her thighs gripped Jim's shoulder. On the fifth shot, the rider fell off the back. The trees were getting denser, so Rachel slid back behind Jim. "One down," she yelled.

"We have got to be getting close to the house," Jim yelled. "It can't be far now."

The path started to widen and was more well-worn. "Get me closer," Rachel yelled as she stood again to straddle Jim's shoulder.

Jim turned to face her zipper. "We have got to stop meeting like this, people will talk," he yelled.

"Damnit, Jim," Rachel said. "Stop talking to my hoohaa."

"Shut up," Jim yelled, "I am trying to get lucky here."

"In your dreams," Rachel yelled as they gained on the rear ATV. "Tires or transmission?"

"Transmission," Jim said, "Might hit the driver too. Double possibilities."

"On it," Rachel said and began firing. Every third shot was a tracer, and on the sixth shot, the ATV in front of them exploded.

"Gas tank works too," Jim yelled as he avoided the wreckage. "There is another one up there." Jim turned. "Duck!"

Rachel bent over and was now straddling Jim's shoulder with her breasts pushed into his head as they passed under a tree branch. "I am gonna pound you," she yelled as she stood and fired again at the ATV.

"Umm," Jim laughed, "Fluffy pillows."

"Asshole," Rachel yelled as they got a little closer. "Get me closer."

The ATV banked hard right and Jim did the same. Rachel clung to Jim as she tried to aim.

"Damnit," Rachel yelled, "Push it."

Jim twisted the throttle nearly all the way and they started gaining. The whine of the engines blocking the sounds of the jungle and preparing them to stop this last ATV. Or at least the last one they had found. As they rounded another turn in the path, the ATV was suddenly coming at them. With speed and deliberation, it barreled at them. The driver was wide-eyed behind the goggles. The man behind him pulling his gun to bear on them both.

Jim couldn't dodge in time. They would get shot as the MP5 lowered and the spray of 9mm bullets would be next.

The gunman on the back fell off backwards, then the driver slumped over the ATV handlebars. It slowed until it ran into a tree. Jim slowed down, and Rachel jumped off the back to investigate. She walked to the idling vehicle and poked the driver with her M16. She poked him again, but he did not move. Grabbing his shirt, she pulled him back and found the reason. One side of his head had a small hole. The other side of his head had a larger hole. He was dead. Shot in the head by a small caliber weapon.

Jim scanned the area. The jungle looked empty. There were birds everywhere, but no people that he could see. "Would be a hell of a shot," Jim said. "You hear anything?"

"Not a damn thing except you yelling," Rachel replied as she walked to the gunner's body. "This one's dead too. One shot to the head."

"We have a guardian angel?" Jim asked.

Rachel swung her weapon around, looking in the trees. "Reminds me of that movie, you know."

Jim laughed. "Which one?"

"You know. The one where the alien kills everyone," Rachel replied.

"Predator?" Jim asked.

"Yeah," Rachel said, "That's it. They had guns; we have guns. Are we next?"

"It doesn't look like it. Get on," Jim said. "We are almost to the house."

"Alex is going to be pissed," Rachel laughed.

"We are being adaptable little soldiers," Jim laughed. "Why will he be pissed?"

"We are so far off mission, it's not even funny," Rachel said. "We need to get out of here as soon as we can."

"Wow," Jim laughed as he started the ATV. "Rational direction from you. Is the world coming to an end?"

"Not used to people dropping dead with no one in the area," Rachel said. "Next there could be aliens and anal probes."

"You are a mess," Jim laughed as he gunned the engine and headed toward the house.

The path was well worn as they got closer and animals darted out of the way. Rachel rode on the back with her M16 hanging to her side, waiting impatiently for anything to get in their way. Without fanfare or any real warning, they popped out into the cleared lawn of the house. Bodies littered the lawn. They passed three as Jim idled towards the house. Five more men lie dead, and in the middle a black German Shepherd.

"Oh shit," Rachel said.

"Someone made a statement," Jim noted as he cleared the mist from his eyes. "Alan's not here. Something is happening."

Two men ran out of the house towards them. Rachel swung her weapon up as the first man began to fire his M16 at them. Rachel was more accurate, and the first man fell. She spun the weapon towards the second man and fired again. With just a few shots, he fell as well.

"Seems like there are more here," Rachel said. "Wonder what the count is?"

"Well," Jim replied, "So far, we are alive. We get points for that, right?"

"I suppose," Rachel said as they got off the ATV and headed towards the house. They were both on guard, wondering what would come next. They walked crouched, each holding their weapon aimed at the door. Rachel swung behind them often. "Listen."

"What?"

"Helicopters," Rachel replied.

The two white MD500Es came over the forest and seemed to stop in the air as they nosed up. They hovered. One stayed in the air, rotating, while the other landed. Alex got out of the helicopter, crouching, and ran to Rachel and Jim. "You two have fun breaking every rule there is?"

Rachel and Jim looked at each other. It was Jim who spoke first. "I did, how about you?

"Yeah, me too," Rachel replied with a smirk.

"Did you at least find Alan?" Alex asked.

"No," Jim replied, "but we did have a mystery shooter save us. Not sure if it is Alan. Kind of doubt it."

"What?" Alex said.

"People just started dying in front of us," Rachel replied. "I think it is that predator thing. Jim wasn't sure, but there was nothing out there. People just fell with single shots to their heads."

"We need to get out of here," Alex said, "Barbara says there are more helicopters heading this way. Four of them this time. They are maybe 20 minutes out."

"Not a lot of time. We need to find Alan," Jim said. "You saw the other dog?"

"Yeah, I saw," Alex said, "We need to be gone in 10 minutes, or we will have to fight."

"I'm up for the fight," Rachel said. "We know they are coming this time."

"Yeah, and they know we are here," Jim reminded Rachel. "We need to go in and find Alan and the girl."

"OK," Jim checked his watch, clicked a button. "Set for nine minutes. Jay and Ronnie look comfortable in the air. How's the other dog?"

"Worry about it later. Get Alan. Get the girl. And let's get out of here," Alex motioned Jay to land. The wind picked up as Jay came down and the sound was deafening. Jim shrugged and Rachel and Jim ran to the house. Each was on one side of the door. A moment later, they went in as Alex grabbed his weapon and followed.

Chapter 45

Carlos pushed Magda and Blanca down the hall. He yelled for men as he worked his way further into the massive house.

"This is such a mess. We could have been a family," Carlos said.

"You're my father," Magda said, "and you are a total scumbag."

Carlos backhanded her, knocking her on the ground, "You will learn respect."

Blanca grabbed his hands, and the pistol he held clattered to the ground.

Carlos turned and hit her with a fist.

She sprawled onto the floor but got back up right away. "I will not take this anymore." Blanca declared.

"You will take what I give you, or I will give you death," Carlos laughed as he reached for the pistol.

Magda kicked the gun hard, and it slid down the hallway. A foot stepped on it. Carlos looked up to see Alan limping in. Alan spun the weapon behind him as Carlos swung at Magda and missed.

Alan's eyes were ablaze with righteous anger. He limped forward.

"It doesn't matter, Alan," Carlos said. "You have lost. Your dogs are dead, and you will be soon as well. Can you hear that? It is my men running here to kill you. No more speeches. No more explanations. No more torture. I will release you from your pain, Alan."

Alan kept walking towards Carlos. He had no words, just anger. A feeling of rage that he repressed all the time. Carlos ran to him, trying to kick him. Alan caught his foot with his right hand and twisted hard. Carlos flipped over but was loose again.

Carlos stood and swung at Alan, but even though Alan was big and obviously hurt, he ducked. Once, twice, thrice and, on the fourth swing, he blocked Carlos and swung. The punch hit Carlos in the chest. He fell back four feet and rolled on to the floor, coughing.

He got up and swung at Alan again. Once again, Alan proved to be faster than Carlos thought possible. Once again, Alan landed a hard blow on Carlos. Alan stepped forward, grabbed Carlos by the arm, and pulled him to his feet. He lifted him off the ground and over his head, throwing him into the stone wall.

Carlos fell and spit blood on the ground.

"Why did you come back?" Carlos asked.

"You sent people after Margarite. They interrupted my day," Alan said.

Carlos punched Alan in the side multiple times where his gunshots were bandaged. Alan fell to a knee and then swung his massive arm, hitting Carlos in the side. There was a crack, and Carlos fell to the floor again. Alan was sure he had broken ribs.

"You know you were wrong. This was not your affair. You should have let me be. You will die here," Carlos spat blood again. Looking at Alan as he rose again, he ran down the hall alone.

They heard voices and running. Alan turned and pulled his pistol. It was Rachel and Jim. Jim put his weapon up.

"You look like shit," Jim said. "Wow, someone had a field day on your face.

Alan glared, turned, and began walking down the hall, following the path Carlos took.

"Alan, we have to go," Jim said.

"You go," Alan replied, "I have to end this."

"You don't understand," Jim stated as Rachel took Magda away towards the door. "There are helicopters inbound. We have to get out of here, or we're all in a world of hurt."

Jim grabbed Alan's arm. It was like a bridge cable and Alan turned fast. "We have to go, Alan. Melody is waiting for you."

Alan softened, "But Carlos..."

"Yes, Carlos is a butt," Jim said, "He will get his, but not today."

"Blanca, you need to come too," Magda yelled.

"You go, my child," Blanca said, "We will be ok."

Magda ran back to Blanca and hugged her hard, "Don't stay."

"Carlos will not be here. He will run. I will take my family and leave. We will be fine." Blanca said.

"We have to go," Jim said, "We need to get in the air."

Alan limped down the hallway and stumbled. Magda ran to him and helped to steady Alan's massive body. "I'm sorry," she said. "I was trying to protect Blanca. I didn't know."

Alan limped for a few more steps and fell to his knees. Jim came back to him, "Nice blood balloons you got coming out of your side. Looks like they opened up."

"I will be ok," Alan said as he stood again and kept walking. Magda held one of his arms up, and Jim was under the other. Rachel led the way to the door they had entered. It seemed so bright as they reached the door. Alan remembered something about a bright light and death. He stumbled as he moved. He felt dizzy but still he kept going.

For a moment, Alan thought of the dogs, not just Shiva and Vishnu, but all the dogs he had trained. All the dogs that were there for him. His eyes welled up with tears. How could he train another dog? He had trusted them, and they gave their lives for him. Worse, they had trusted him, and died anyway.

Alan thought about Melody. Her long flowing hair. In the short time they had been together, how he had felt finally at ease. Alan kept walking and entered the light of day.

When they got outside, Alan looked for Vishnu, but his body was gone. "C'mon," Alex yelled. "I have the dog. Let's go."

Alan sauntered to the chopper where Alex was standing and climbed in. There Shiva slowly looked up at Alan and whined just a little. Alan got in the plane, sitting on the floor next to the dog, each as battered as the other. Ronnie manned the gun on that side and smiled at the two as Shiva put his head on Alan's legs.

Jim and Rachel got into the second helicopter and manned the guns with Magda between them. The helicopters spun up, and Jay came on the radio. "You know, this reminds me of a bar fight I had in Mexico once. We were all downing Tequila shots and this man walked into the bar. He was a big guy and wanted to dance, but no one wanted to dance with him."

Both helicopters gained altitude quickly, turned, and headed west towards the airfield.

Jay laughed in the microphone. "We lived in Mexico. We lived today. I guess that's something."

Jim came on the microphone. "But we didn't get the Tequila."

The sun was high in the air, and silence fell upon the big house.

Chapter 46

"Barbara, we are inbound. We are going to need an ambulance when we land," she heard talking, "and an emergency veterinarian car or something like that." Jay said on the radio.

"Got it," Barbara replied.

"Let Tarkington know what is going on, and that Carlos is probably going to run. The man is a pedophile. See if they can use that to get his government protection to dissolve. He has four helicopters out here looking for us. Maybe we can get them to dissolve." Alex said on the radio as well.

Barbara was writing everything down as she sat in the cockpit of the G650. She finished, "What else?" she said over her headset.

"Ronnie says he loves you," Jim said on the headset. Barbara heard Ronnie yell, "Hey," in the background.

"Tell him I love him too," Barbara said. "I will get an ambulance and a vet here."

"We are maybe 25 minutes out. You will need to hurry," Alex said.

Barbara got off the plane and looked around the hanger. In one corner was a small golf cart plugged into a charger. She ran over to it and pulled out the plug from the receptacle in the seat area of the cart. The keys were in it, so she got in and turned on the key. She looked at the controls, and there was no stick shift.

"Damnit, I can fly a plane, but I have never driven a golf cart. How do you reverse?" Barbara murmured to herself. She looked around and finally found a switch above where the charging port was below her. She flipped the switch, and a beep started sounding. "Here goes nothing."

Barbara pressed the gas pedal down and went backwards away from the wall. She flipped the switch again, hit the gas, and went forward. She drove out of the hanger and headed for the terminal. It was not a big terminal. In fact, there wasn't much there at all. It was more of a building with a door. A Coke machine, a Pepsi machine, and a few guys playing some game or sleeping next to it.

It took very little time for her to get to them. "English?"

"Yes, we speak English," one man in a uniform said. "We speak English very good."

"I need an ambulance and a veterinarian," Barbara said.

"We speak English very good," the man said. "What do you need? Fill up?"

"Ambulance," Barbara said, "Roo roo roo" she said, making a noise like an ambulance. "Doctor?"

The man stood up, "OK, 911?"

"Do you have a phone?" Barbara asked.

"Yes," the man said, he pointed in the little building. Barbara walked in. "913" he said, and Barbara picked up the phone and dialed.

The number did not ring.

"It's not working," she said. "No work."

The man shrugged.

"Sarah," Barbara said to herself and pulled out her sat phone. She dialed a number.

"Hello," came the voice.

"Sarah," Barbara said in a more frantic voice, "This is Barbara. We are in Guyana, and I need to get an Ambulance."

"Guyana doesn't have a ton," Sarah was calm.

"Sarah, they are inbound and need an ambulance," Barbara said. "Oh, and a veterinarian."

"Hang on," Sarah said. The line went blank and music began to play. Barbara was tapping her foot and went out to sit in the golf cart. She punched the steering wheel. The two men looked at her. She calmed herself and resumed tapping her foot in the cart.

"Barbara," Sarah was back on the line, "There is a contingent of Airforce and army pretty close to you. I have dispatched a helicopter to the airport you are at. It should be there in about 20 minutes. There is a K9 medic with them from an Army ground team in the area. They will stabilize the situation. If they get you stabilized, the best bet will be Puerto Rico. Let me know, and I will have people waiting. Is the plane ok?"

"Yes," Barbara said. "The plane is fine. They are out in helicopters."

"This will be a good story," Sarah said.

"I have to go," Barbara quipped.

"Barbara," Sarah said in a soft tone.

"Yes?" Barbara said as she tapped her foot.

"Slow down. Do a good job. It will be ok," Sarah said.

"Yeah, ok," Barbara hung up the phone.

She floored the little golf cart and headed back to the hangar. It seemed like time was moving differently. Perhaps she was driving through molasses. It was difficult for Barbara to fail. She was the oddball in the group. True, she had all the training, but she was not the super-powered girl like Rachel, nor was she a sniper, or a tactician. She was just a great pilot that loved her job. She wanted to always do a good job.

Barbara ran to the plane. Pulling out the first aid kit, she took it down to the table. She got out several bottled waters and got the area ready for as much as she could. She hoped it would be enough.

Listening, she heard the two helicopters coming in. She waited and wondered how long it would be before the medics made it.

Chapter 47

Carlos ran to the lower level. He heard new voices, voices that were not part of his guards. It was time to regroup. Time to move on for a while and come back stronger. Carlos did not like the idea of leaving his house. He had been here a long time, and the idea of a group of Americans running him out of his house was nauseating at best. Carlos was more than angry as he opened the big garage and turned on the lights.

A dozen cars were in the garage. But he needed power and wanted to be certain he would not be attacked or taken. The black Ford Velociraptor 6x6 called to him. The bullet proof windows, self-sealing tires, and powerful engine would get him to the airport. Then his private plane would take him to the capital where he could plead his case with his family friends in power. For that matter, he could drive the truck all the way and not worry about any attacks. It would be perfect.

Carlos opened a cabinet and got out the keys to the big truck. The black windows, black frame, and black painted bumpers made the truck look like an angel of death. Carlos smiled. It would be the angel of death when he came back for Blanca and her children.

He wondered where his guards had all gone. *Were they all dead? Had the Americans killed everyone?* The thought of recruiting more men made him angry. The big truck faced the garage door. He walked around the front, looking at the double black windows that made seeing inside nearly impossible. The truck was a beast. As he walked around to the driver's side, he stopped.

On the ground in front of him were six guards. Each of them was laying in different positions of death in a circle. Each man held what looked like a screwdriver in the next man's head, making a circle of death with a hole in the middle. Strangely, it looked like something was missing.

Carlos was shaken. He ran to the door, opening it. He began to climb in and faced the barrel of a gun. The FN5.7 was intimidating, and Carlos reached for his pistol.

"Ah ah ah," the man said to Carlos.

"You know," Michael smiled, "this is a nice truck. I have looked at these online before but never paid them much attention. You know how customizations are. Always some type of problem, and nowhere to take it to."

"Who are you?" Carlos asked.

"No one in particular," Michael said as he ran his hands across the truck. The FN 5.7 aimed at Carlos. "You know? I was working on my house this week. I was having fun with my girlfriend this week, and suddenly I have to deal with you."

"I am sorry," Carlos said, looking toward the doors. "Why did you have to deal with me?"

"Well," Michael continued, "I really didn't. I learned about you, and it just hit me that I had to."

"I have money, you know," Carlos said. "I can give you money. A lot of money."

"No, you had money," Michael said. "I have these people I helped once. I made a call, and they stripped all your accounts. The fact they can do that is one of the reasons I keep a lot of cash around. Those hackers. They are pretty spry."

"I can get more. I can help you," Carlos begged.

"No, not really," Michael walked around the garage with seemingly no interest in Carlos.

Carlos was quite aware though, that as Michael walked, the FN 5.7 was always pointed directly at his face. "I do not need help from someone like you."

"Then why?" Carlos groveled. "Why bother with me?"

"I think it was more for me," Michael said. He looked directly at Carlos. Michael's crystal blue eyes seemed to glint. "My first job." Michael paused for a moment. "The first assassination I was ever asked to do was a man who had gotten away with hurting some children. You know how that is. He played with things he should not have played with and got off on a technicality. I found the man as he was unloading his car. It was a rug. But I saw the little feet in the rug. I killed the man. A single shot from a good distance. It was an easy shot for me, and I felt nothing. I still feel nothing for taking the man's life. The police were called. They found the dead man and rescued the child." Michael looked at the ceiling for a moment then continued walking, as he did the FN 5.7 did not waver at all. "This week," Michael stopped as he reached in the toolbox and pulled out a mid-sized screwdriver. "This week, I realized someone should have told that man why he was about to die. He deserved more than a quick ending. Of course, in the United States, he would have gone to prison and would have lived far too long and still not been a good person. He did deserve to die, just not so painlessly."

"Is all this just to kill me?" Carlos was sweating, nearly frantic. He pulled his pistol and tried to grab it with both hands. Michael squeezed the trigger once and the pistol flew out of Carlos's hand. Blood ran out of a hole in Carlos' palm.

"I was a little late today," Michael continued as Carlos grabbed his hand, "You killed Alan's dog. He will suffer from that for a long time, but he will live and be ok. You raped so many women and children, probably boys too, I don't know. It's not that you hurt people. You made them suffer. Not for a minute or an hour or a year, but forever."

"Please don't shoot me," Carlos said. "Please let me go. I will change."

Michael spun the screwdriver in his free hand while the FN5.7 pointed directly at Carlos's forehead.

"Change," Michael echoed. "I know change is possible. By the way, I appreciate whoever stocked your toolbox. Every size and type of screwdriver known, all in one place. It is hard to find a Home Depot open around here."

Carlos was unsure of the screwdriver comment but spoke immediately. "Yes, yes," Carlos saw his opening, "I will change. I will honor the law and be a good person. I only need the chance."

"Thanks for showing me your truck," Michael said. "I had to kill all your guards. Well, most of them. A few ran. A few were mercenaries that really didn't care about you. A few didn't know how to hold a weapon. You need a better recruiter."

"Yes, I will change. I will get a better recruiter," Carlos said. He looked down at the circle of guards laying on the garage floor. "I can be a good man."

"Maybe," Michael turned towards the door and holstered his pistol. "Naw." Michael spun so fast it could barely be seen. The screwdriver flew across the room and embedded between Carlos's eyes. There was a moment of recognition as Carlos realized what happened before he fell. His eyes rolled back, and his body landed in the center of the circle of dead men. Michael walked to the wall and picked up a soccer ball. He smiled at the ball and bounced it around on his leg. Walking over to the makeshift circle with Carlos in the center, he put the ball on Carlos's lap and then turned back to the door of the garage. He looked back at the big truck. "Nice truck," he said as he turned off the light and closed the door.

Chapter 48

Melody walked towards the Emory hospital in Atlanta. It was a college hospital and well respected for its work in just about every area. The drive from Ivel had been frantic. She had gotten the call from Alex that Alan had been hurt and every question she had asked was met with a, "They will take care of him," and "He has already seen the doctors."

At one point, she yelled at Alex as she drove from Ivel. "Why didn't you call me sooner? Who is with the dog?"

Alex was not the wealth of information she had hoped for. He did explain that Vishnu had been killed in Venezuela, and that Shiva was being taken care of by Emory as well. "They are both being taken care of by the best doctors anywhere."

Melody was even more furious. "I will make that determination. If you cross me, Alex, I will rain hell upon you until the end of time."

"Wow," Alex said, "that is pretty intense. We did try to call you from Puerto Rico you know. All the major stuff happened there."

Alex was not exaggerating. The major stuff included Jay taking the team to a bar in old San Juan and introducing them to Pitorro and the exciting ways of Rum. The subsequent arm-wrestling challenge was watched by everyone in the bar as Jim and Jay went at it on an arm-wrestling podium for nearly 10 minutes. Alex had watched and guessed a lot of people lost money when Jay finally slammed Jim's arm to the table.

"What about Michael?" Melody asked as she walked to the door. "Is he OK?"

"Michael wasn't with us," Alex told her. "We never saw him."

"He is just down there alone, dead, and you did nothing about it?" Melody asked.

"We didn't see or hear from Michael," Alex said. "Are you sure he went down to Venezuela?"

"I think so," Melody replied doubting herself. "I will call Abby."

Melody dialed Abby as she walked towards the hospital door. It rang only once.

"Mel," Abby asked, "Are you ok? How is Alan?"

"I don't know," Melody said and began to cry. "One of the dogs is dead, and I am at the door getting ready to walk in. The sun is rising, and Alex said he never saw Michael in Venezuela."

"Michael's here," Abby said. "He got back right after you left."

"I don't understand," Melody said, "Did he go? What happened?"

Abby giggled, "Yeah, he took care of some things and said he balanced the scales the right way. Do you want to talk to him?"

"No," Melody said, "I have to go, Abby. Is he OK?"

"He's fine, Melody," Abby replied, "We were just going to take a nap. We will see you soon. We will head down to the hospital tomorrow."

"Thanks, Abby," Melody said, "I am sorry I drug you two into this."

Melody hung up the phone. She wiped a tear from her eye. Trying to compose herself, she then walked to the door and the smooth gliders opened. As she entered the hospital, Jim walked up to her. The team was there. Alex pacing to the side, Rachel standing against the wall, and Barbara hovering behind Ronnie as he typed on his computer. Magda was there as well, sitting next to Ronnie watching him type as well. Terry was missing.

Jim hugged Melody and she held her hands up shaking a little. "Is he OK?"

"He's fine," Jim said as the other members of the team walked to her.

Rachel grabbed Melody and swung her off the ground in a big hug. "Don't worry," Rachel said, "He is a beast. He actually patched himself up in the jungle and saved himself. The doctors said he would have been fine if he hadn't lost so much blood."

"Blood?" Melody said, "What happened? One of you tell me now."

"Well," Ronnie said, "He was shot 3 times and beaten up a little. Well, maybe more than a little. Doctors say the little kit he had saved his life. The antibiotics worked and he had sealed the wounds and cleaned them as good as a hospital. They opened up his bandages and they were a little full of blood, they say from pushing too hard, but it was clean. They recleaned it and stitched him in San Juan. The doctors said it was pure luck the bullets missed anything important. He will be sore for a while. The doctors here are checking him out right now to let him go home."

"Go home?" Melody said.

"Yeah," Ronnie continued, "they were worried about a concussion from his being hit in the head with a rifle a few times. But the doctors said his head is a rock, and they were surprised it would have knocked him out. We kept him awake on the plane, you know, to be safe."

"He's ok?" Melody asked again. "He's not hurt bad?"

Alan was wheeled out into the waiting room in a wheelchair. The nurse behind him said, "Who is going to sign?"

Alex walked forward and signed some papers, "We have the budget to take care of this." He said as he turned.

"You better," Alan said, "Not exactly a swoop in type rescue. A little late on taking out the bad guys at the house."

"We got there and got in the house as fast as we could." Jim said. "We were stuck in the damn trees with those other ATVs too long. It was good you took care of the guards."

"I thought you took care of the guards," Alan said.

"I am missing something here," Rachel inserted. "We walked in as you were fighting Carlos. We had only been there a few minutes."

Alex looked at the group, "We can figure it out later. I am sure Tarkington will want a complete report to redact."

"I am sure you and Ronnie will have fun writing it," Rachel laughed.

Alan looked back at the nurse and then pushed up on the chair and stood.

"Don't rip those stitches," the nurse said.

He looked down at Melody and smiled. Everyone was watching. Melody slapped Alan across the face. He grabbed his face as it began to glow red.

"You are never doing something like this again without me," Smiling, Melody stood on her tiptoes and kissed Alan, holding his hair as the kiss became more passionate. "It will be fun helping you recuperate."

"I have a block of rooms at a Residence close to here," Alex said as he looked at a text on his phone and glanced at the door.

"A Residence?" Rachel said, "Nice, but why? They are so big."

"They allow animals," Alex said and put his phone away as Terry walked in with a leash and Shiva. Shiva was limping and had a cast on one leg but was getting around fine.

Alan began to tear up and walked to the dog. Shiva wagged his tail and Terry let the dog walk forward in the waiting room. The nurse behind the counter said, "No dogs," and most of the group turned at her with a look that could turn Medusa to stone. The woman went back to her desktop and only peeked over at them from time to time.

Alan rubbed Shiva on the face, forehead and chin. The dog closed his eyes, lost in the moment. In spite of the pain, Alan knelt and held the dog that had saved his life. All the while, Shiva wagged his tail.

Chapter 49

Gertrude Samples had been head of the DEA for only a year but knew all about Sam Tarkington. His feats were legend, and his insubordinate attitude even more so. She knew he was in trouble with the President for his normally foul mouth and she was ready to make him slip.

She slammed into his office like a bull in a china shop. A picture turned on the wall as the door rammed against the doorstop.

"Where is he?" Gertrude yelled. "Where is Tarkington?"

"Umm, Miss Samples," Sarah said. "He is in his office waiting for you. Would you like some coffee, tea, a valium?"

Gertrude glared at her. "How dare you be flippant with me. I will see that you are out of here so fast…"

"Gertrude," Tarkington said as he opened his door, "Let's not say anything we may regret later. Why don't you step in here?"

"I am not done with you," Gertrude said to Sarah as she stormed into Tarkington's office. As she passed him, Tarkington winked at Sarah, then closed the door.

"Sam," Gertrude began, "You really messed up this time. You told me that Carlos had been subdued and that I should send agents to his estate. We would have opened a dozen cases if we could get him to talk. Do you know what we found? Do you?"

"No," Tarkington said, "but I think you will tell me."

She pulled out a folder from her large purse. In it were pictures. A circle of men each holding something in their hands attached to the next man's skull, and Carlos in the center with a screwdriver or ice pick protruding from his head. Sam chuckled at the picture.

"You think this is funny?" Gertrude yelled. "We just lost our key witness in all of this. What did your men think they were doing? He was supposed to be taken alive."

"It's an old joke," Tarkington said, "I believe if you go back a few years to Brazil you will find a similar picture that was unsolved by the marines. A group of men committed suicide. I think it is filed as a "screwball". My team was not around then, this was not by them, nor would it have been.

Tarkington pressed a button. "Sarah, bring me your work please."

Sarah walked in and handed Tarkington a good-sized red folder, smiling at Gertrude before walking out.

"You need to fire that little girl," Gertrude said.

"You will really want me to in a moment," Sam said. "Sarah is not just an assistant. She likes to figure out puzzles. When all this started, the Marshalls' office was frantic about how someone kept finding the girls, and they lost two houses from it. After some very complex fenagling, Sarah found out how."

"Really, I am sure that's interesting, but it has nothing to do with..." Gertrude said in a calmer tone.

"Yes," Sam broke in, "I am sure the Justice Department is going to be interested to know how Carlos Juarez was accidently sent Magda's report card. I am also certain that Justice is going to be really interested about the phone calls from one of your agents before both of their safehouses were destroyed."

"I know you set all this up, Gertrude," Sam continued, "I also think I know why. You were locked in a nowhere struggle with no way to get to Carlos, no leverage at all. New girl on the block, you needed to do something to make a name for yourself. I am betting you thought you could stir the pot if you got Maria, Margarite, and Magda back in the game. That maybe Carlos would make a mistake." Sam waved the folder. "I have enough here to really blow your career."

"What did you expect?" Gertrude said, "You do it all the time."

"No, no," Sam replied, "There are rules I don't break. I don't put 15-year-old girls in a house with a pedophile to try to get some other guy in jail. I don't lie to other agencies. Well, I omit things, but I never lie to them."

Gertrude looked at Sam, "So what?" she said. "He's dead now, and we both lose."

"No, not me," Sam pressed the button. "Sarah, show them in."

A big man and a small woman walked in. "Gertrude, I would like to introduce you to Anton Kolchak, head of the Atlanta sector Marshalls, and Gwen Sei, his section chief. They would love to talk to you about how the witness protection program is supposed to work."

"You, asshole," Gertrude said. "You set me up."

"That I did," Sam said with a smile. He nodded to Gwen. "You can use my office as long as you want. If you need it, I have a few big guards out here if you need to use them."

As Sam walked into the outer area with Sarah, he laughed and handed her the folder. "Blank pages?" he asked.

"No, sir," Sarah said, "Everything you said is in there."

Sam took the folder back for a moment, scanned through it, then handed it back to her, "Good job Sarah, good job. Let's go get coffee."

Chapter 50

The hotel was clean and crisp. The Kennesaw Residence was away from Atlanta but still busy. They had to drive a little, but it made sense to get out of the city. Alan and Melody were wrapped up in the blanket, and Shiva was on the second king size bed snoring.

"I guess he's happy to not be in the jungle," Alan pulled Melody close and kissed her.

As he released her, the covers fell off, revealing her cleavage.

"Nice," he said.

"Yep," Melody replied as she pulled him in for another kiss, "and don't you forget it."

Melody's phone rang. Caller ID showed it was Abby.

"Crap," Melody said, "I didn't call Abby back and tell her we were at the hotel, not the hospital. She was heading here today."

"It's ok," Alan said. "They will understand."

"Abby," Melody said as she answered, "I'm so sorry. We are at a hotel. They let Alan out." She paused. "Oh" she paused again, "Really?" There was a short giggle, "Aww."

"What?" Alan asked. "I feel like a mushroom."

Melody slapped him in the side. Alan winced. Melody made a sad face and mouthed sorry.

"Ok," Melody said.

"Get your clothes on," Melody said, "We are walking over to breakfast. They have an outside lounge. We can bring Shiva."

Alan was sore but got his clothes on. Melody pulled her hair back and they walked to the door.

It was a short walk. The breakfast was inside, but the chairs were outside. Alan sat down on a high-top chair and Shiva laid down next to him with only a little difficulty. Melody put her arms around Alan, holding him with gentle tenderness as Maria, Margarite and Magda walked out. The three women were crying, and all put their arms around Alan. He teared up in only a moment, and they cried together for a few.

"Thank you so much for saving my little one," Maria said. "Thank you for saving her twice."

"You are awesome," Margarite said. "I can't believe how much I owe you."

Magda curled into his arm. "I'm sorry about everything, but now everyone is safe. Blanca too. Thank you for helping me grow up."

"Good job, big guy," Jim said as Alex and the team joined them outside as well.

Abby walked out behind them with Michael behind her.

Abby smiled, "I know it is hard for you, but so many people owe you so much. Michael and I did some work, and well."

Michael stepped out and pulled a German Shepherd puppy from behind his back. The puppy was about 8 weeks old and its ears were still turned down. It wagged its tail constantly as Michael handed the dog to Alan. Shiva sat up and sniffed. Alan held the female out in front of him. It licked his nose and its tail wagged. Alan pulled the puppy and Melody close.

"Thank you," Alan said, "Thank you for everything, Michael."

Michael winked then hugged Abby close to kiss her as he smiled.

The group sat down and began talking. The morning air was crisp. The smell of bacon was in the air, and today was a new day.

Every day was an adventure if you let it be.

About the Author

Andrew Allen Smith was born in Anderson, Indiana. Until the age of fifteen, he moved at least once per year and finally settled in Lexington, Kentucky. Andrew spent a significant amount of his teenage years reading and writing short stories, attempts at novels, and poetry. He published his first book, "A Slice of Passion," in 2005. It was a book of poetry compiled from dozens of years of work.

In 2015, Andrew published "The Theft and Other Short Stories" as a collection of some of his favorite portions of his writings after he was challenged to self-publish a book. Challenged and excited about his success, he published his first novel, "Vengeful Son," in 2016 and began building a franchise with that book. "The Masterson Files" (the series containing "Vengeful Son") now includes six books and has fifteen in outline form. The story follows an ex-assassin that is reluctantly engaged in helping others while trying to retire.

In 2020, after a tragic event, Andrew co-wrote "What NOT to Say to People Who Are Grieving." This book showcased emotions and an approach to helping others be more mindful of their words during grief.

2021 gave us "A Slice of Fear" followed by "Another Slice of Fear" in 2022 with short stories focusing on fears of all types. "Another Slice of Fear" won Andrew a Literary Titan Award and has been reviewed positively for several stories in the genre.

In 2023 Andrew released "Yet Another Slice of Fear" that showcased even more horror and thriller stories followed by a diametric opposite with "Another Slice of Passion", poetry focused on passion.

As Quality Leader and System Architect, Andrew's work gave him credit for a series of instructional manuals for site relationship management systems, various quality documents, and development lifecycles. In Andrew's spare time, he has a passion for many hobbies and his family, which he considers paramount. For more information about Andrew, please visit **andrewallensmith.com**.

Books by Andrew Allen Smith

Fiction

A Slice of Passion
Another Slice of Passion
A Slice of Fear
Another Slice of Fear
Yet Another Slice of Fear
The Theft and Other Short Stories

The Masterson Files Series

Vengeful Son
Sinful Father
Deadly Daughter
Fateful Friend
Silent Sister
Curious Cousin

The Eternal Forever Series

Adam

Non-Fiction

What NOT to say to People Who are Grieving

Books Containing Andrew Allen Smith's prose

Monster Hunter Intern and Other Tales
The Gift and Other Stories
Simple Things: Moments of Isolated Gratitude
The Portrait of Herbert Losh and Other Stories
The Drifter and Other Unusual Tales
Quire

Coming Soon

Burial Ground
Stealth Drive
The Eternal Forever Book 2 – Morgan

www.ingramcontent.com/pod-product-compliance
Lightning Source LLC
Chambersburg PA
CBHW030108260626
47156CB00008B/2575